praise for

LIVEWIRE

"A thrilling superhero adventure that skillfully weaves together themes of identity, belonging, fandom, and love in the face of loneliness and despair. Sarah Raughley's *Livewire* is a delight."

—ELISA A. BONNIN,
author of *Lovely Dark and Deep*

"*Livewire* is full of twists and turns, pop-culture references from around the world, and snappy dialogue...Perfect for fans of Marie Lu, Kekla Magoon, or superhero action with a pop twist."

—BOOKLIST

LIVEWIRE

BOOKS BY SARAH RAUGHLEY

THE QUEEN'S SPADE DUOLOGY

The Queen's Spade

THE BONES OF RUIN TRILOGY

The Bones of Ruin

The Song of Wrath

The Lady of Rapture

THE EFFIGIES SERIES

Fate of Flames

Siege of Shadows

Legacy of Light

STANDALONE NOVELS

Livewire

LIVEWIRE

SARAH RAUGHLEY

BLACK
STONE
PUBLISHING

Published in 2025 by Blackstone Publishing
Cover and book design by Candice Edwards

"A Gullah Song in Mende" translated by Joseph Opala
Excerpt from *The Gullah: Rice, Slavery, and the Sierra Leone-American Connection* by Joseph Opala
Used with kind permission from the author

Printed in the United States of America
Originally published in hardcover by Blackstone Publishing in 2025

First paperback edition: 2025
ISBN 979-8-228-64745-9
Fiction / Science Fiction / Action & Adventure

Version 1

Blackstone Publishing
31 Mistletoe Rd.
Ashland, OR 97520

www.BlackstonePublishing.com

To fans of the following:
Livewire, comic books, manga, anime, K-POP, J-POP, mecha robots, transforming heroes, me, and Utada Hikaru, in that order. The rest of you, we can't hang.
I'm kidding, guys. Enjoy!

1

A storm brewing through the high-arched windows means natural light is out as an option. What the hell? It was literally blue skies just a minute ago.

I'm running through the school halls like an idiot looking for some natural light, braids swinging, ass cheeks out because I tend to take some—ahem—liberties with my private school uniform.

Hey, anything goes when clicks are on the line. And I paid good money for this ass. Courtesy of my own personal Daddy Warbucks.

"Oh, that's a great pose, Amanda!" Lily shouts a couple of feet away from me, filming my stunning hair flips with her latest and greatest mirrorless camera. With her hair done up in *odango* buns, she maneuvers the little black zoom-in lens like it's part of her tiny brown body. Lily Adebayo should be a professional videographer. I'm not sure if she wants to be. But she was the one who offered to be my camerawoman and editor when I first came to the Tokyo International Academy. A successful fangirl, as they call 'em. Bending down to get a better angle of my gorgeously slender and toned body (if I do say so myself), she keeps her camera on me as I strike every pose I've mastered watching YouTube videos of professional '90s models: Naomi, Tyra, Beverly. I stick close to the marble statue of Michelangelo's *David* in the center of the massive rotunda. I think "Daddy" donated this too. Yeah, that's what it says on the plaque underneath David's dick—I mean, his feet. Not that I was looking all that hard. Daddy's name is everywhere and on everything in the school: Toyo Harada. Donations, donations, donations. That's what money buys you when you're a wealthy Japanese man: prestige, a few limos, and your own adopted Black daughter for shits and giggles.

That's me, by the way. Amanda McKee: a wealthy Japanese man's adopted Black daughter. Except I don't go by that name anymore. Here in Tokyo, I'm Andrea Porter now.

"Hello, my lovely followers, this is Andy-P in Tokyo—remember, the *P* stands for Princess—and it is D-Day. Yes, you guessed it. The Valiant Pop Awards are tonight, and as it no doubt says on your calendars, your girl *is* presenting!" I let out a convincing squeal, twiddling my fingers in excitement before a pregnant pause.

Hmm . . .

Nah, that wasn't good. I lower my hands and scrunch my face, rethinking it.

"And remember," I start up again, this time more seductively. "The *P* stands for Princess." I bend over a bit.

Look, some might find this a little off-putting from a sixteen-year-old, but the algorithm says sex will most certainly sell these little ten-minute "don't you wish you had my life" vlogs I do. I haven't gone too far in that direction yet, though, so the cringe rockets up my spine like an electric spark. To be honest, I'm more the cute and perky type of influencer imagewise, but

I'm willing to switch it up if I have to. I mean, I've already got over one million subscribers on YouTube, TikTok, and Instagram. But the numbers could always be higher.

Lily lowers the camera, concerned. "Something wrong, Andrea?"

The "*P* stands for Princess" is in the bio of all my apps. Then a link to Harada Models, even though I'm five foot two and have stubby legs. Yeah, yeah, nepotism, but I'm pretty, and isn't that the whole point of social media?

Lily's never mad. She's always eager to be part of the Mandy Machine. I make sure my literal river of forty-two-inch braids, in high pigtails, are tight in their red ribbons. The red goes with the red and white tie of my navy-blue uniform. "Let's go shoot closer to the school entrance, then get one in class just before lunch period ends. We need some takes in the corner just being chill."

"Chill high school students. Got it!" Lily almost looks cute, nodding resolutely. She was bite-size, like me, completely and devastatingly willing to do whatever I wanted. Shorties sticking together? "This is part of the award show vlog we're making, right?"

"Yep!" My skin buzzed with a little tremor of excitement—that is, if the weather doesn't cancel the whole show. The Valiant Pop Awards has its own problems: too many lip-synching K-POP groups, a bad sound system, stage platform apparatuses that occasionally fall apart and put people's actual lives in danger. Still, Harada got me a great gig presenting the Worldwide Inspiring Favorite Achievement Award. Or is it the Favorite International Dance Artists Global Fan Culture Style Award? Oh well. Either way, I'll be damned if gray skies got in the way of my star skyrocketing.

I could hear the thunder rumbling outside the windows.

When I notice Lily's hand give a nervous tremble, I take her hand in mine. Her shoulders relax, a bright smile widening her V-shaped chin. That's what I like to see.

I make sure my theme song for today, Utada Hikaru's "Michi," is playing from my phone loudly enough for me to hear the sporadic, confident percussion. Then I begin to pull Lily through the halls until we escape the Science Wing. It's not raining yet, but even if it did, the roof on the white corridor would keep us dry while we're out here. Lots of students don't even seem to care. Under the graying, cloudy skies, they're still going about their business in the quad, chatting on the stone fountain in the middle of the garden, even in this prickling cold breeze. Almost every nation from around the world is represented here, students speaking different languages and mingling together in the cacophonic confusion expected of an international school. They're having too much fun gossiping and sneakily passing joints underneath their blazers. They won't run for cover until the rain actually starts pouring. The pink camellias, kiss-red tsubakis, and faded purple azaleas sway across the green field in the ever-worsening wind. Each flower is native to Japan. I'm not. And I feel it every single day.

"Come on inside," I tell Lily once we get to the central annex, and she continues to smile one of her sweet, crooked-toothed grins. Our friendship, power dynamics aside, makes a little more sense when you realize there's not a whole lot of Black girls in Tokyo schools, even an international school meant for the wealthy kids of ambassadors and politicians and whoever else. The Academy is supposed to be somewhat of a safe haven—a Garden of Eden, if you will—for foreign kids like us who live in Japan. We don't quite fit. Like, while my videos are in English, Lily and I only speak Japanese to each other. Harada had me speaking it after he adopted me as a wee babe. I can't even remember the last time I said anything in English since I left America. Lily's mom is Japanese. And yet if the two of us ever entered a regular public "high school here, like one of the ones in that nearby neighborhood"? I wouldn't last a day before someone said something out of pocket and I'd have to throw hands. That's just the truth.

It's tough, but . . . I can't go back to the States. That's just not an option. The very idea of returning in disgrace makes my stomach churn.

Professor Wagner glares at me the moment I walk through the front doors of a smooth, gray-bricked building tall enough to block out the sun if the clouds weren't already doing a decent job of it. Before Wagner's wing-tipped glasses could slide down her nose, I pull down my skirt to where it is supposed to be. I turn off Utada for good measure. Wagner hates fun and immaculate vocals.

"That's better, Miss Porter," Wagner croaks, a voice damaged by excessive cigarette use, as the Tennis Club scurries by, carrying their rackets. Around the corner and up the stairs, in the stairwell, two students are drinking strawberry milk while laughing at a shy girl, her face covered in long black bangs. Miss Shy is giving a letter to some Swedish student; afterward, with her hands quivering, she runs off in terror. Another love confession gone wrong? I wonder what's going on between them . . .

I could find out, easily. And nobody would ever know.

My fingers inch toward my phone.

But with a sigh, I let them relax. The old Amanda McKee who lived in New York wouldn't have hesitated to play gossip girl. She would have used her—*special abilities*—to dig up the dirt. And it would have taken her mere *seconds.*

Andrea "Andy" Porter who now lives a clean life in Japan is more . . . disciplined. I only target who I need to, when I need to.

"Andrea!"

The moment the white class doors of Class 5-C slide open, Nina Weisz, daughter of some wealthy German food mogul, waves me over. The entire class is gathered around the front desks of the spacy but drearily decorated classroom. Like, the entire class. They're all swarming the desks like flies—no, worse—like zombie fangirls stalking their favorite K-POP group at an airport. And when the crowd parts, I am shocked to find out how true that actually is.

The tall girl at the center of everything locks her dark eyes with mine. "Oh wow, this school has gotten so *diverse* since I left! That's so wonderful!"

She boosts herself off the teacher's desk, not giving a single crap that Mrs. Stawski's lesson plans were now spilling on the floor.

I've seen this girl before. She's famous for her incredible height and proportions, her face, small as a bean, and her long flowing black hair, which, since she debuted in BAD CUPID, has never once been dyed or damaged. The straight-cut bangs that frame her forehead are her signature. She can't hold a note to save her life, but that's not why Carmen was chosen to debut in one of Korea's biggest girl groups. Huge round eyes and perfect, filler-filled lips. Sometimes that's all it takes.

"Carmen!"

"Oh my god, Carmen, you came back to visit TIA!"

"Carmen, you're so beautiful!"

And of *course* Carmen, in her black Chelsea boots and slim-fitting blue jeans, looks beautiful. She's the visual of BAD CUPID. Being pretty is her literal job. The other three members at least know how to stay on key.

"Carmen, I can't believe you're here! Isn't the Valiant Pop Awards today?" Our class president, Hiromi Hamaguchi—or

"Prez"—is usually a stone mountain, but as Carmen waves her finger, Hiromi's entranced eyes follow the tip as if it carries the secret of life.

"I'm off-hours." Carmen tilts her head to the side. She has a sharp nose you could skate down. "Call me Ayaka."

The class murmurs in approval. "A-Ayaka . . ." Hiromi looks like she's going to faint.

Ayaka Suzuno is Carmen's real name. She was born in California. You can tell by her accent. Kind of like me whenever I speak Japanese.

Lily's standing on another student's chair in the rightmost corner. I look over and see her camera's been on the entire time, sneakily recording Carmen from the back. My stomach twitches with the faintest curl of jealousy.

"I used to go to this school before I moved to Korea and started my idol training." Carmen leans against the teacher's desk and looks around the class wistfully. "I just *had* to come and see this place again before heading off to the VPAs. I had *so* much fun here."

In other words, she came to be worshipped.

"Oh, we're well aware of what you did while you were here," I say with a very deliberate snort. Boozing, bullying, and partying. She's legendary in these halls all right, but success has a way of burying the past. I'm not impressed.

And this makes me a target.

Nobody appreciates my sass. I suspect nobody ever *really* appreciates my sass.

Carmen sweeps her hair over her broad shoulders. When she approaches me, her slow strides are like a hyena circling its prey.

She smiles. Looks more like she's baring her teeth. "Did you just speak Japanese? You speak it so well for a Black girl!"

Typical. I've heard dumb shit like this so many times; I'm

not even fazed. I fold my arms. "You speak Japanese well, too, for a West Coast bimbo from the Valley."

The class falls silent.

"You know, I think I've seen you around before, but I can't remember from where." She tilts her head and folds her arm.

That's Lily's cue. Before I could twitch my mouth open, she hops off the chair. "That's Andy-P," she says, my videographer and personal PR firm. "She's a huge influencer. She's got over a million followers, like everywhere."

I wonder what *huge* must have sounded like to someone whose fans tried to get her girl group nominated for a Grammy.

Carmen squints. "Andy . . . P?"

"Andrea Porter." No matter how many times I say it, it still sounds foreign on my lips. But I don't waver. I already made the decision to leave the name "Amanda McKee" behind. No turning back.

Carmen thinks. "Nah, never heard of you. Or seen you."

"Didn't you walk with the rest of us girlies at the Tokyo Girls Collection show a couple of months ago?" I slap my forehead. *Wait, your group wasn't invited,* I thought, tapping my chin. "What about Paris Fashion Week later that month? Oh no, wait, that was the other BAD CUPID member: Minju. The popular one."

As the sky grows darker outside the classroom windows, the rest of the class whisper.

"Wow, Andrea's really laying into her."

"Minju is so pretty . . ."

I'm ruthless. How dare this talentless K-POP hack waltz in unannounced and try me in front of *my* classmates—*my* audience. But Carmen isn't done yet. You don't go through the K-POP training system without becoming ruthless too.

"You walked the Tokyo Girls Collection Fashion Show?

Aren't you a little short for that?" As the class ooh-ed, she looked me up and down. "You're like, what, five feet at most?"

I am five foot two, and she should damn well know this. She really went after my height. I'm *seething.* "What about you? Weren't you actually born in the year of our Lord 1999? That's a little old for idols these days."

"Ooh, she's premillennial," someone whispers and giggles behind me.

At some point, Lily sidles up to me and nudges me in the ribs, trying to get me to stop, but my chest, as much as I try to control it, is heaving. Carmen is looking down on me. She walks right up to me just so that she can make a *show* of looking down at me—the shorter, stumpier girl with *melanin*, oh-so dreaded in this entertainment world we both orbited. My mind drifts back to that Tokyo fashion show—the designers furious at me for needing the clothes fitted to my body type. The girls giggling about my skin: "She's so dark. Will anyone in the crowd be able to see her if we don't turn the lights up?" they said.

I see all those jerks in Carmen. The back of my neck hurt from trying to meet her pompous gaze.

"Oh, *now* I know where I've heard of you." Carmen turns her back to me. "My mom told me about you."

I blink, confused. "Your *mom*?"

"My mom was invited to a gala last year in New York. All the big international power brokers were there—including Toyo Harada of Harada Global Conglomerates."

I tense up. Lily bites her lip, but I could barely see her out of the corner of my blurry vision. Carmen picks up a letter opener on the teacher's desk and swivels it around.

"There was all this quiet talk among the wives about this Harada having a little adopted Black girl at home and how, even though he adopted her, he barely acknowledged her. She sat in his mansion. Silent, like a creepy little doll. Unattended. Unwanted."

I can't feel my arms. I don't know when they slid to my sides, weak and limp.

Carmen giggled, shaking her head. "But what a weird rumor! Why would Harada adopt some random kid if he was going to hide her away? Maybe he didn't get the one he wanted."

The class was abuzz now, confused, because my name was Andrea Porter here, and as far as they knew, I had nothing to do with the famous Toyo Harada.

Sprinkles of rain begin to splatter upon the class windows.

"That's enough," Lily says, gently, because in terms of force that was usually all she could ever muster. She waits for me to make some kind of snappy comeback, but my mind is in Harada's Manhattan mansion. I'm thinking of that big, lonely playroom. I'm thinking of myself at five years old, playing with toys while frightening-looking butlers in black suits stay close.

While Harada enjoyed his New York gala, we were playing a game. One of the butlers had a listening device in his ears—a wireless transmitter. None of the butlers spoke to me. There was no noise in the insulated room, not even the buzz of a fly. No sound to the discernible human ear.

But my ears weren't exactly human.

The game was simple: Could I tell which butler had the wireless device in his ears? How much could I hear from what he was listening to through this device? And could I interfere with the transmission with my mind?

I didn't have superhearing. They put noise-silencing headphones on me to make sure. But if I asked nicely without a single word spoken, that listening device would oblige and tell me all its secrets. And that's exactly what it did:

Hi, Amanda. Mr. Harada is currently divulging information to his butler, Mr. Goro, about his dinner menu.

In a friendly voice, the wireless transmitter listed off some menu items: Lacaune lamb. Shallot jam with spring vegetables flown in from Highgrove garden. I didn't know what any of the words meant, but I recited them as they were dictated to me. The butlers wrote down everything they observed about my behavior so they could report it to Harada later.

"Cat got your tongue, Andy-P?" Carmen's taunts bring me out of time and space. I'm back at the Academy. And now students are asking questions.

"What does Andy have to do with Toyo Harada?"

My lips are parched. There's heat behind my eyes as I clench my fingers. Then, mercilessly, my hands reach for my phone.

Carmen made a mistake. She reminded me who I really am.

I go to her public Instagram profile. It's as perfectly curated as you would expect for a celebrity, but behind every highlight reel is a litter of secrets.

And to discover those secrets, I only have to ask.

I shut my eyes. *Terminal. Terminal, you there?*

Within the black space of my mind appears a pure white information booth, like the ones in train stations. A black question mark is painted on the front of the white stall.

No one sits behind the desk, with its silver metal rims. The white stall itself sparks to life.

I give my command. *Let me see into Ayaka Suzuno's Digital Castle.*

You got it, little Amanda!

I always wondered why Terminal's voice sounded like a boring old white man until I did some research. Terminal sounds exactly like Dr. Robert Kahn, one of the fathers of the internet.

A coincidence? Who knows? There are enough oddities in my life that I don't feel particularly like looking under every stone.

Besides, it doesn't matter. Soon I can feel information flipping behind my eyelids. It tickles, like I'm turning pages of a book against my skin. The data flows through me. Becomes part of me. Traces of Ayaka's digital footprint. Files—in audiovisual format.

Perfect.

Terminal, upload it to Livewire.

My eyes snap open. Everyone's looking at me, waiting for me to respond to Carmen because, in real time, this only took a few seconds, but even a few seconds is a little too pregnant a pause when you're in a bitch-fight with one of K-POP's shining stars.

"You bullied Rachel Kim out of BAD CUPID when you were trainees," I say.

Leaving the Digital World always leaves my nerves shot. I feel like I've awoken from a coma. My lips are moving on their own. My emotions are still far away. It's too bad. I would have wanted to relish the shock on Carmen's face.

"Wh-what—" Carmen lets out an incredulous chuckle, her eyes darting everywhere. "What are you talking about?"

"Rachel Kim?" Prez covers her mouth with both hands. "*That* Rachel Kim?"

"Yeah, she was a famous idol trainee before she left the company." Nina Weisz follows this stuff more religiously than anyone. She immediately begins scrolling on her phone.

Carmen bites her overplump lips. "I didn't bully Rachel," she lies, because she knows how seriously bully allegations are taken in her field of work. It's the K-POP kiss of death.

Too late to deny it now. As I lift my phone, the notifications of the entire class go off.

A Livewire update.

I didn't know so many people followed my secret Instagram page, but good thing they do. The CCTV footage of Carmen slapping Rachel after a dance practice is already up, and the views are skyrocketing by the second. The girl swearing is definitely Carmen.

"You ugly bitch, what did you just say to me? My second cousin's sister's aunt is dating the CEO. Did you know that? Did you know I can have him completely *erase* you from the debut lineup? Don't even *think* about trying me."

It's Carmen, without a doubt. Rachel is crying. My classmates are beside themselves with the amount of tea that has just spilled out of the sky like mana.

"Oh my god, is Carmen a *bully*?"

"Oh god, she just keeps hitting that poor girl!"

"It's all here on Livewire."

Lily shakes her head, wide-eyed and in disbelief. "Oh dear. It's high-key over for you, Carmen."

Carmen's phone begins ringing off the hook. Managers, no doubt, trying to confirm the quickly spreading rumors. But the evidence Terminal gave me is ironclad.

Lily's right. It is over for Ms. Carmen. She'll think twice before coming at me again.

The graying skies begin grumbling, and finally the skies open up for a torrent of rain. Ah, sweet pathetic fallacy. How poignant.

But as thunder wails and lightning strikes, as Carmen sinks to her knees in despair, another spark of light flashes outside our window from the distance. This time, unlike a bolt of lightning, it sticks around.

"What is that?" Lily whispers to me.

I can't answer. The lightning bolt—or whatever it is—is clear, bright white. A light beaming down from the heavens to the ground miles away from us. A perfect pillar.

That's not what lightning is supposed to look like.

My phone gives a start as it vibrates in my hand. And vibrates. And vibrates. A cacophony of notification bells, ringing, and other sounds from every students' phone assault the classroom.

"What the heck?" Lily looks at her malfunctioning camera, then at the digital clock at the front of the room, now switching times and numbers as if drawing lottery numbers.

The entire class leaves Carmen on the ground, arguing with her manager, to pin ourselves against the window. The clouds are swirling around the pillar of light, rumbling with flashes and thunder. The hairs on my arms stand on end. I can't breathe. Nobody can.

As I close my eyes, somewhere in the deep recesses of my mind, Terminal muses to me in his old white man voice: *Keep alert, little Amanda. Something's coming.*

And I could feel it. Something hateful.

It smells of blood.

2

After a while, the sky settles and the electrical disturbances end. It must have just been some kind of freak weather thing.

Meanwhile, last period with Mrs. Archambeau passes by in a blur because I know I just triumphed big time. I sent a K-POP princess running back to her hotel crying. But no one would ever know of my victory. No one would ever know the truth about Amanda McKee's extraordinary psychic powers. Harada told me not to tell anyone. If I ever did, my followers would skyrocket for sure, but then I'd probably be kidnapped by the government or something.

Around me, students are hunched over their desks, texting each other about Carmen. When I close my eyes and truly listen, I can hear the letters, see the emojis. I can hear their shock. Their delight. Everyone loves drama.

But now that I'm closing my eyes, I remember the pillar of light. People move on fast, especially when celebrity mess is involved, but I haven't. I can still see that solid white light. The beating heart inside it.

After school ends, Lily and I walk out the front school gates.

And though Lily's scrolling through her phone for updates on Carmen's scandal, I'm still looking up at the sky. Still picturing that celestial beam from above. That's when a long black limo pulls up in front of me.

The back window rolls down.

In the back seat, my adopted father is wearing very big shades. Like, they cover the top half of his face. He must really not want to be recognized, but his triple-breasted black suit and bald head are pretty recognizable, to me at least. So is his thin, chap-lipped scowl.

Toyo Harada says, "Get in." An old voice, too old for someone just north of fifty. His back is so stiff I don't even think it touches the leather seat.

"I'm walking home with one of my friends." I pat Lily on the shoulder, and she looks at me as if to say, "You have other friends?" Of course I don't. Everyone here knows how much of a bitch I am. I force a grin and squeeze Lily's shoulder, so she plays along.

"Get. In." He wasn't going to ask a third time. My heart trembles. These were not asks of an adopted father. They were orders from my benefactor. And he was both.

Harada has never physically come to this school, not even when the board wants to throw galas to celebrate his donations. Lily has never seen Harada up close. She probably doesn't even know who it is.

"Your agent?" she asks me, confirming my suspicions. She must have noticed the tense expression on my face. She slides my hand off her shoulder. "Don't worry. I'll meet you at the Tokyo Dome for the award show, okay?"

"Don't leave," I mouth, but lip-reading is not one of Lily's strengths. She heads off, and with heavy shoulders, I step inside the limo. My butt barely hits the cushioned white leather seats before the engine grumbles to life and takes us down the hill.

An ocean could fit between Harada, sitting in the far-right corner behind the driver's seat, and myself, sitting on the left-most bench. The glass top of the center table reveals Harada's favorite collection of wine—a whole rack of Domaine de la Romanée-Conti Grand Cru—and wineglasses he'll never let my underage hands touch. The plush, ergonomic seats may be white leather, but the soft gray upholstery fits the minimalist interior design. You can stuff an entire boardroom meeting in here. I think he *has* run boardroom meetings in here.

For a while, Harada doesn't speak, so I shut my eyes and let the caverns of my mind shuffle through the limousine's entertainment system. Soon Utada Hikaru's "Automatic" is blaring through the speakers.

"Turn it down," Harada orders me without looking up. Fun makes him break out into hives. The gravel in his voice makes my stomach contract. I obey. It's automatic.

"Hey, did you see that weird pillar of light before?" I hate when I have to make idle conversation just to break the ice with my own father. "Like, the heavens parted and everything. We getting an alien invasion, or what?"

Harada doesn't answer, though his eyes flicker toward the driver and the driver's eyes flicker toward him from the rear-view. They saw it. They have theories. They just won't tell me.

My shoulders slump. Whatever. Aliens existing would be the least weird thing I've encountered in my sixteen years of life.

"I see you've been busy," he says without looking at me as Hikki's voice whispers in the background. Harada is on his silver tablet—the newest generation from the production line of Harada Conglomerates' Electronics Department. So thin and sleek, it looked like half a windowpane. It's not even on the market yet.

"Busy?"

I soon realize what he means. His deft fingers barely need to touch the screen before he brings up my Livewire Instagram page. The post I made just a few hours ago already has tens of thousands of comments.

"Hey," I defend myself with a shrug, "you didn't say I couldn't use my psychic powers for exposing irritating celebrities."

"It's a waste of your gift. Celebrity gossip." He lowers the tablet with a scowl. "The entertainment world is a wasteland of scum and vagabonds. A glittery masquerade of filth."

"And yet you own your own entertainment company." Folding my arms, I tilt my head to the side, my thick braids pooling on the leather. "An interesting venture for someone with such clear disdain for celebrities."

Harada gives me one look. One look is usually all it takes. I am silenced.

"You know what I've always told you: Sometimes artifice is needed to hide what truly lies beneath. You should know that better than anyone."

"That's why you have me lying to everyone at school?" I ask him. "Why you won't let anyone know I'm nothing more than a client under said entertainment company?"

"You're the one who wanted a fresh start after New York."

I bite my lip. He's right. I have no comeback.

As I silently stew, I finally notice someone squirming in the passenger seat. The seats are so big and the lighting so dim I didn't even see him. He's got a tan, a wide face, and an even wider grin. I can count all his teeth.

My whole body is on alert as I turn to Harada. "Who the hell is he?" One of the first lessons Harada taught me was secrecy. *No one must know you're my daughter. No one must know you have powers. Secrecy, secrecy, secrecy.*

But Harada is nonplussed. He looks out the window with a bored expression. "Don't worry. He's part of the Foundation."

"The Harbinger Foundation," the man waves at me, though his seat belt won't let him do much more than that. He looks entangled in it, like a fly in a spiderweb.

The Harbinger Foundation? I grip my plaid skirt, my hands trembling a little.

"Psiot or scientist?" I ask him in barely a whisper.

The man shakes his head quickly. "Psiot? No, no, no, no, not me!" He laughs. "Regular human. A very smart human, if I do say so myself, but, uh, no superpowers. Especially none like yours, Amanda—"

"So scientist." The Harbinger Foundation: Harada's institution funded by Harada Global Conglomerates. A secret institution. A secret organization dedicated to studying freaks like me. Except there are no freaks like me, so I'm the only one in those padded cells. There are buildings all over the world, and I think I've been poked, prodded, and studied in every one of them.

"Let's start again," says the young man in the passenger seat. "I'm Yoshida Sakaguchi, new hire for the Research and Development Department of Harada Global Conglomerates." He untangles his hand from his seat belt and holds it out for me to shake before quickly realizing I'm too far away to grab it. "Call me Yoshi. I'm, uh, helping your father develop some new toys."

"New toys?"

"Comsat International. Bodine Electronics. Even the secret E.R.A. Companies all over the world are on their way to creating the world's first suit of armor," Harada tells me, turning from the window.

I smirk. "Pretty sure they made those back in the Middle Ages."

He ignores me. "Armor that combines nanotech and biological matter on a cellular level. Bio-armor. It'll revolutionize human living. If we lose out on this arms race—"

"You'll lose money?" I shrug. "Does that even matter when you're, like, a gazillionaire?"

"*Amanda*," Harada yells in that deep baritone voice, and my arm muscles twitch.

"*Andrea*," I whisper. "Andrea Porter."

"Amanda McKee. A human miracle. A psiot." His eyes soften as he looks at me. "I never knew until after I adopted you that human beings could exist that are capable of what you're capable of. You represent an evolution in humanity. There's no other like you."

That's why he created that special name for me. I am a "psiot": a human who can use psychic powers. The only one in the world, according to Harada. The Harbinger Foundation wouldn't exist without me. I'm a treasure trove of information his scientists can put to use.

"What I'm trying to do at Harada Global Conglomerates is for the betterment of humankind. You know this."

I do. It's for this reason I've used my powers to spy on his competitors, on his command. It's easy to do when computers give you their secrets oh-so willingly.

"What we're trying to create is called the BioSuit," says Yoshi before he pauses. "I can tell her right?"

Harada clears his throat. "Well, you already have, haven't you?"

Running a finger through his long, shaggy hair, Yoshi lets out a little laugh and continues. "No, but seriously, it's still in the development stages, but when we're done—like, when it's completed." Yoshi, his eyes unfocused, shakes his head. "I mean people wouldn't ever have to worry about being hungry anymore. They won't ever have to worry about finding a place to live. It's all there in this suit, man."

I'm not quite getting what he's saying, but Harada is burning a hole in my skull with his intense glare. The tablet awaits.

"I have a new job for you. You've already memorized a list of our corporate competitors. I want you to delve into their research, schematics, and development schedules," Harada orders.

"Before I do," I say, "I want you to answer a question for me."

Yoshi turns back into his seat. He must have realized this was one of those family moments and he probably shouldn't eavesdrop. Harada seems to have realized the same. With a touch of the button on the door, a blacked-out dividing window separating the back seat from the front of the limo rolls all the way up. We are alone.

His expensive cologne is more pungent with the window up. It's stale because he never gets a new one until he finishes the old one, but it takes him too long to get through one bottle. I twitch my nose, waiting to get the words right on my tongue, but in typical fashion, they come out half-baked.

"You did adopt me before you knew I was a 'human miracle,' right?"

Harada just stares at me. "What?"

"I mean, you didn't adopt me *because* you knew there was something dangerously wrong with me . . ."

"There's nothing wrong with you." He's so good at avoiding a question. "You're perfect the way you are."

"Then why won't you let me use your last name at school?"

I can no longer hear Utada Hikaru's music. The driver must have turned it off without my permission, but my mind is too scared and my emotions too turbulent to access the limo's mainframe again.

"You were the one who wanted a name change when you left New York," he reminds me.

My heart is beating faster than I thought it would, because I remember those nasty kids at Valiant Middle School, their smiles vicious, as if they were demons rather than eighth graders.

"Even in New York, you told me not to use your last name."

"Because I didn't want you to forget that you're your own person." Harada answers without skipping a beat.

"Am I?" I look at him. His stern face. His dark eyes. His complete lack of parental instinct. "Am I my own person?"

"You always have been." To his credit, Harada makes the effort to close the gap between us. A little shuffle to his left. A shuffle closer to me, his daughter, not through genetics or blood. Not even in name. "If you walked around as Amanda Harada, you'd be burdened with a family history and expectations nobody deserves."

For a moment, his eyes dim and his thick brows furrow. I know he's thinking about his past, the one he never tells me about. Like the totality of a solar eclipse, it passes quickly.

"You don't need the Harada name," he says. "Without the Harada name, you can be whoever you want."

Without the Harada name, I have no family. And he still doesn't understand why I need one. He still doesn't get why I need to know the reason a Japanese businessman with all the money in the world would adopt some random Black kid from Jacksonville, Florida. Was it love? Pity? Philanthropy? Utility?

What is a family? What is Harada, if I'm not allowed to call him my father in public?

I bite the inside of my lip, my fingers curling around the fabric of my skirt. "If I can be anything I want, then I can be Livewire without you bitching at me."

"Amanda—"

I reach back and touch the intercom button on the ceiling. "Stop the car." And because the driver doesn't take *my* orders, I shut my eyes and use my mind to stop the car *for* him. The engine fails and rumbles to a halt in the middle of a busy intersection.

"Amanda," Harada says again, just as my hand finds the handle of the limo door. "Your powers are truly extraordinary. More so than you can ever realize. You need to listen to me. You need to learn how to use it before someone takes advantage of your innocence and ignorance."

The cold handle prickles my palm, and yet my hands are hot. My whole body is. "You're already doing that, Dad."

I leap out of the limo and run out into the city.

3

"And here she is, everybody! It's influencer and model Andy-P. Please welcome her!"

I know enough Korean to know it's my cue to walk down the red carpet. The Valiant Pop Awards started out as a Korean show after all, before expanding throughout Asia. I smile and preen just as they expect me to in a pair of yellow palazzo pants and a white crisscross wrap top that exposes pretty much everything but my boobs. The bling around my neck sparkles under the light of the flashing cameras. Everything is so bright; I can't see the photographers behind the lenses or see the screaming fans behind the barricades. There's too much noise—the thumping *untz untz* base of dance music pounding in my ears as the host prattles on, I'm assuming, about my accomplishments as someone who spends a lot of time taking pictures and videos of herself on the internet. I thought looking as gorgeous as I possibly can would make me feel better about Harada's constant gaslighting and rejection. I thought the moment I began posing against the sponsor backdrop with my hair in its high ponytail, sweeping against my thighs, my nerves would calm, and my body would feel less hollowed out.

But when I catch a reflection of myself in someone's lens, I see an Amanda McKee for whom makeup works wonders. An Amanda McKee who nearly starved herself for months to lose weight, who bleached her skin to give herself a lighter, more "palatable" tone, who got a nose job. All so she would be treated more kindly here than she was in New York.

"Andy! Andy!" Lily calls me once I weave through the hallways of rushing staff to my dressing room. She's inside waiting for me. "You look amazing!"

I always thought Lily was prettier. Her pug nose. Her cat-shaped eyes. Everything a blessing from her biological parents who were real to her, not figments of her imagination like mine. She has the staff pass I secured for her. As my manager, she's really my only staff. If I didn't have Harada money, I'd be sharing my dressing room with three other acts. Or they'd just have me wait in a car in the parking lot until it was time to present the award. That's happened before.

We spend half an hour in this white room with tables of refreshments and sandwiches I can't eat or my face will puff on screen. I prattle on in front of Lily's camera for my award show vlog. "What's in my bag" is the quintessential influencer crap you do when you've got nothing else to say, so I go for it. Award show essentials: perfume, lipstick, and a little card to remind me what award I'm supposed to be presenting. Lily has me practice right up until call time.

"Remember, you're presenting in English. Take advantage of that," Lily tells me as we leave the room. "It's got to feel natural, like you're a Hollywood star!"

Hollywood. I laugh, because when I was nine, Harada begrudgingly let me audition for a toy commercial in Los Angeles.

The casting lady told me straight up I was too fat and too dark to be believable as a cute kid. The memory only sinks me deeper into the gaping crater I still find myself in.

"You don't speak a word of English," I remind her.

"But I know what sounds right!"

I'm forcing a smile when someone shoves a whiskey glass into my hand. The man who did it must think I work here. I thrust it into his protruding stomach.

It's Shim Hyun. He used to be in a boy group like, back in the 90s, and now that he's aged out of the idol system, he's stuck doing comedic variety shows to make his bread. He looks murderous at the glass and then me, his flat face screwed up in utter disbelief that some foreign plebian would dare touch him.

"I'm sorry, Hyun," says someone behind me in English. I didn't even hear him slink up behind me. "This is the influencer who's presenting with me."

I have to crane my neck to see his gorgeous face. Chiba Ryoichi is even more perfect in person. His legs are taller than I am, but he fills out that black suit. He looks down at me with a little smile and gives me a wink that makes my insides splat.

Hyun's female assistant takes the whiskey glass and whispers in his ear.

"Oh, I get it," he says in English, before his greedy eye follows a newly debuted girl group walking by. I've heard about them. Their youngest member is thirteen years old and the oldest is sixteen. In their pink dresses, they bow to Hyun with an enthusiastic greeting and carry on their way. He forgets about me and starts to follow them . . .

"That was a close call, right?" Ryoichi says in English. His accent has a bit of Queens in there. Everyone who's ever read his biography knows he spent most of his childhood in New York. Not that I've read it more than a few (dozen) times.

"Yeah, but I can usually handle myself," I say casually in Japanese, and he's a little surprised, but he doesn't make a big deal of it. He just gives me a handsome, sidelong gaze with the slightest hint of mischief.

"We go on next. I'll see you when it's call time." He walks off to his own dressing room down the hall.

And Lily got him on tape. I wonder if her camera picked up my drool too. It suddenly hits me, and I can't believe it. I'm presenting with Ryo . . .

A boy group under Harada's label approaches me, smiling politely before whispering behind their hands.

"You know who she is, right? It's that influencer," one says.

"Yeah, I saw her walk the runway at the Tokyo Girls Show in September. She was terrible."

"Eh, she's a model? She's skinny, I guess, but she's so short!"

"I hate short girls. They're like gremlins."

Lily tugs me by the crook of my elbow. "Don't listen to those idiots. They have the combined IQ of moss on a rock."

But I've had enough. I take off down the hall. I feel like everyone's watching me, and deep breaths just won't stop the murmurs of insecurity. My forehead is starting to sweat, and although Lily chases me down the hall, trying to dab it off with a tissue, she can't enter the waiting venue behind the main stage. I go alone, my heartbeat frenzied with all the lights and the music blaring and the robotic voice listing off nominees to some random, made-up award. Staff members keep looking at me. Like *staring.* And then *whispering.* It's clear what they're saying. I'm different. I'm a virus. I shouldn't be here.

I don't belong here. Maybe I don't belong anywhere. Harada, who won't even acknowledge me as his daughter, has certainly never made me feel any different. I realize it so painfully; it makes my body heavy, but the robotic voice just mentioned

Ryoichi and me—it's our turn to enter the flashy rainbow tube all the presenters travel through to get to the main stage.

"Presenting the Award for Favorite Hot Trend Global Fan Culture Award is Chiba Ryoichi and Andy-P!"

They say it in Korean, Japanese, and English. Ryoichi and I stride through the rainbow tube, cameras capturing our ecstatic faces. I'm smiling brightly as I hold the envelope with the handcrafted winner's card inside, but my hands are shaking. And as I stare out into the seats of the Tokyo Dome, my knees start to shake. The venue is full of fans, and signs, and light sticks, and girls with professional DSLR cameras so big I wonder how security let them into the venue.

Ryoichi speaks his part in Japanese. Then I say mine in English by rote memorization. But I barely hear the words. The fans, the celebrities, the staff, Ryoichi announcing the winners. They all look like puppets made of wood. Strings move them to applause when BAD CUPID comes up on stage to accept their award. Carmen is there. She grins affably, but I can tell she's been crying. She hangs back behind the rest of her members, hiding a little behind Minju whose hair is newly dyed a perfect fire-engine red.

I can hear phones typing across the Tokyo Dome. I can hear what they're typing:

> Carmen is disgusting. I can't believe she showed her ugly face here.

> Nepo-baby bully!

> Ugly! Kick her out of the group!

> BAD CUPID are not a girl group but

a pack of buffalos. Please ban them from public broadcast.

Stupid bitch. Die!

Who's that Black girl? Has anyone ever heard of her? Don't touch Ryoichi!

It doesn't matter what language they type in. With machines, it all becomes one language. A language only I can understand. A language I wish I didn't speak.

That influencer has such a slutty outfit on. This isn't America.

Hey, can you get me a ride share? I'll pay you back.

Farewell Carmen.

There's too many foreigners on this show now.

I think of little Amanda playing with her toys in Harada's New York mansion. The doors locked. Alone.

I don't belong anywhere. Not in Japan or America. Not with Harada. Not with celebrities. Not with humanity. Everywhere I go, I'm different.

Ryoichi is so handsome but why is he surrounded by ugly bitches?

That African girl is so short. She looks like Ursula. But Minju looks like Ariel.

"Enough! Enough!" I drop the envelope and cover my ears, stumbling into Ryoichi, almost knocking him over.

"Andy—" He starts, but I'm shaking my head, trying to block all the puppets out.

"Just shut up! All of you, shut up!" I hate all of them. I hate Harada. I hate myself. I hate my powers. I hate it all.

What's wrong with that girl? Why is she freaking out? So disgusting.

Ugh, she's ruining the vibe and making Ryoichi look bad.

Poor Ryo, my sweet baby. I hope that girl dies!

Just disappear.

Just disappear.

Disappear.

Disappear.

"*You* disappear!" I order all of them, screaming at the top of my lungs.

An explosion from the Tokyo Dome's ceiling answers that wish. My body goes cold and stiff as the screaming starts. In the pandemonium of debris falling and people fleeing the venue, I look through the din of smoke. The jagged hole in the arched white ceiling didn't make itself. Something big crashed through it. *Somethings* . . . two of them . . .

BAD CUPID makes a run for it. Ryoichi grabs my arm and tries to pull me off the stage, but I stand there, transfixed. The sound system folks must have run off, too, because they forgot to turn off BAD CUPID's latest single, "I'm the Drama," still bleating in the dome. The synths and Minju's terrible rapping punctuate the chaos. I squint my eyes to get a better look at the *somethings*, but in a flash, they crash into section D of the arena. A roar rattles the rafters, like some kind of mythological stone gargoyle just shuddered to life.

The smoke clears, and I realize I'm not that far off.

That's when I saw them clearly: the big metal monsters.

Creature from the Black Lagoon; *The Guyver*; *It Came from Outer Space*. I've seen enough campy horror flicks to recognize a monster. These ones are humanoid enough: two arms, two legs, a torso, etcetera. But everything's . . . wrong. You're not supposed to see the crimson, fleshy muscle on the *outside* of the body. And yet there they were, stretching up the neck and across all the joints. Every sinew seems to pulsate before my eyes, connecting the metal gauntlets covering the hands, the cast-iron chest plates, and, oh god, that ant-shaped helmet where the head should be. Or maybe that *was* its head?

There are two beasties: one silver, one red. The silver one's a little slender, and the red one's as big as a tank, with gorilla arms that looked powerful enough to rip the seats off their screws. In fact, it does. It rips several, throwing them at the silver creature, who dodged each one.

This made no sense. In every alien movie, the aliens attack humans. Why were they fighting each other? My mind is empty. I have no time to even consider it before the silver one reaches into his back and pulls out what looks like his spine, but I quickly realize, despite the blood and flesh attached to the bone, it's actually a sword, its edge glowing ghostly white, like the pillar of light that split the clouds this morning. Ghostly white, like their inhuman bug-eyes.

Monsters with swords. And they flew so fast, crashing into each other, I could barely catch each strike.

"Not monsters. They're humans inside machines," I realize, because even though I can't hear their hearts beating or their mouths breathing, my psiot inner ear certainly picks up the silver one's very human mind connecting to the online digital interface of his armor. It's *armor.*

And he's giving it orders:

"Fire up the Totsuka. Let's crack this Eggbreaker in one hit." A brazen male voice. A merciless command loaded with anger and a dangerous, knife-sharp will.

An online digital interface. That's it! It's tiny, but I have a shot to figure out what the hell is going on here.

"Terminal!" I said, plugging my ears with my fingers to block out the noise.

"Miss Andy!" Ryoichi tugs me again, but I shrug him off.

"Terminal, who is that guy? Do you have anything on him? Either of them?"

After I've made the connection, deep within the recesses of my mind comes his answer: *Let me search the web.*

I'm only brave enough to shut my eyes for a second. Pages and texts flip through the back of my eyeballs, sending little shock waves down my nerves.

Now this isn't normal, Terminal tells me after a second. *There's nothing on either of them. No digital footprint. No birth records in hospitals. No trail. But everyone has a trail.*

Humans do, at least. So what the hell are they?

"Come on!" Ryoichi tried one more time before abandoning me, running back through the rainbow tunnel and leaving me on stage alone to witness what came next.

Suddenly, the silver monster's sword bursts with a light so intense, it stings my eyes. I peek through my fingers just long enough to see him aim a blast at his red foe. Quick and deadly, the curved beam slices through the air, tearing up the seats and the floor of the Tokyo Dome until it hits its target with a collision so fierce the entire stadium trembles.

I fall to my knees as the beam slices the red monster in half, leaving both blood, guts, and metal exploding into the air. I hunch over, holding my turning stomach, screaming so loud I can't feel anything else but my throat, scratched raw, and my heart thumping in my chest.

Thump.

Thump.

Thump.

Clunk.

Metal feet land in front of me.

BAD CUPID's song is coming to an end. How long has it been? My sense of time has been blown to bits, just like that red beast.

Against my better judgment, I swallow the saliva in my throat and look up. Carefully. Stupidly.

The silver beast is the only monster left standing in the ruined Tokyo Dome. And his sword is pointed straight at my face.

"Amanda McKee." He sucks in a breath. "I'm here to kill you."

My mind goes blank. The last few sprightly notes of the song's melodic synths give way to silence. I blink at the biotechnical wonder bearing down on me, promising death.

People say, at the moment of your demise, your life's supposed to flash before your eyes. They're right, but it's not a life I want to see. I don't want to see Harada's uncaring, unfatherly expression. I don't want to see the kids at Valiant Middle School—least of all John, with those red freckles and stupid baseball cap. I don't want to see my past. It's just a highlight reel explaining why I'm going to hell.

Instead, I imagine my parents—my real ones. They used to live in Jacksonville, Florida. That's where Harada adopted me from when they died. I wonder how they'd feel if they knew their daughter would be following them into the grave so soon. I wonder if Harada will even cry at my funeral, or if he'll just stumble upon another wonder kid psiot—one who's a little less mouthy. I wonder if he'll like that kid better than me.

I wonder for so long I don't realize I'm not dead yet. That's when I notice the sword trembling in the alien-like creature's gauntlet gloves. In a show of determination, the silver monster grips the hilt of his sword tightly, ready to strike. But he doesn't. His whole arm—made of flesh, muscle, and metal—shakes.

"You're so young," he whispers in a voice so young and green itself, I might have laughed if I weren't terrified. "No. I can do this. This is my mission. I will kill you, Amanda McKee."

I don't even think about it. My mouth is moving on its own. "Don't kill me."

His sword stops trembling.

"Please don't kill me. I don't want to die."

There are tears in my eyes. I can't even close them. They are wide and bulging and desperate. My life is completely in his monstrous hands, and he knows it.

And it scares him.

He struggles with himself, clenching his alien jaw, lowering his sword.

"It's easy," he whispers to himself. "It's a simple mission. Taking some kid's life."

And he raises it again with a sudden sharp movement. The sword hovers above his head as he takes in several deep breaths, his chest heaving. That's before he drops the weapon entirely. As it clatters to the ground, he stumbles back and reaches for the back of his head with a panicked hand. It is a grotesque, squishy sound, like flesh being torn off the bone, as he pries apart his helmet. Ah, so that buglike fusion of meat and machine *was* a helmet. He takes it off, letting it drop to the floor, revealing a very beautiful, very confused-looking boy.

A *boy*. A *kid*.

He's staring at me, wide-eyed, biting his slender lips. The moonlight from the broken ceiling catches his high cheekbones. He scrunches his slim nose, looks at his own shaking hands, and curses at himself.

"I can't do it." He sounds completely gobsmacked. Ashamed, even. He searches every inch of my face with his brown eyes, his thin eyebrows furrowed. "You're Amanda McKee. I have to do it—" He stops and shakes his head, panicking. "Why can't I do it . . . ?"

I can't feel my body, and my sanity is hanging on by a thread, but smiling is an influencer's job. My muscles twitch without much effort, just like I trained them to. And I lift my hand for him to shake.

"Actually, I'm Andrea Porter, aka Andy-P," I say. "The *P* stands for Princess . . ."

And then I passed out.

4

Muffled Yoruba wakes me from my slumber. I'm in the corner of a tiny child's room on a stiff blue cot. Little cartoon characters and flashy stars splash the walls in bright paint.

Wait, I've been here before. This will be Blessing's room: Lily's baby cousin—at least, once her aunt gives birth. Flower curtains only half cover the little window next to me. Rubbing my eyes, I try to decipher the furious debate happening outside the wooden door to my left, but I don't speak Yoruba. Lily does.

Lily's paternal aunt and uncle run a small, out-of-the-way restaurant in Roppongi: West African Snack Hut. They hail from Ibadan, Nigeria. Here in Japan, they serve amazing home-cooked food. It's pretty popular with locals and foreigners alike.

Great, I can use some food. I love their jollof rice.

But, uh, how did I get here?

Suddenly, I remember that boy's face, his flesh-and-tin body armor, his gigantic, bloodthirsty sword, and I jump off the cot. I practically kick the door open.

"Did you see the monsters too?" In the narrow hallway on the top floor of the restaurant, I yell in Lily's shocked face, her aunt and uncle flanking her. "What happened to the Tokyo Dome? The explosion! They were fighting . . . !"

When I'm panicked, I start speaking in English. Lily doesn't understand me as I babble. I don't even see her, or her pregnant aunt in a floral dress, or her lanky uncle and his fuzzy blue sweater. I see that sword, the tip of it, ready to put a hole in my face as if I didn't have enough.

"Uncle Seun? Auntie Bisi?" Lily pleadingly tugs on their arms.

Auntie Bisi's heart-shaped lips spread into an understanding grin. She claps my shoulder a few times. I feel like I'm a child being humored. "Okay, okay, calm down, now. Let's get you something to relax, okay, Andrea?" She says it in Japanese. They know more than enough having lived here longer than I've been alive.

Andrea. I sometimes forget that's my new name. Uncle Seun stays upstairs while I let the women lead me down from the top floor where the Adebayos sleep to the restaurant, now closed. The lights are dimmed. There's a digital clock above the TV screen screwed into the wall on the other side of the bar, but it must be wrong. It's almost two o'clock in the morning?

"Let's see if I've got something to help calm you down." As Auntie Bisi disappears into the kitchen behind the bar, Lily fills me in.

"I was watching you from the monitor backstage when there was this big bang. The entire Dome shook like it was hit by a bomb. Honestly, I thought it was a terrorist attack. Then everyone just started running." Lily sits on the tall stool next to mine. She's still trembling. "I passed out. I went to look for you as soon as I came to and found you on the stage."

Alive. Which means that kid in the suit who said he'd kill me didn't end up pulling the trigger. Or did I hallucinate the whole thing?

"Was anyone with me when you found me?" I pause, biting my lip, remembering the glare of those monster eyes. "Or *anything*?"

"What? No. No one was left in the stadium. No audience. No staff."

I shake my head and slump over the bar ledge. "So what are they saying caused it?"

"To be honest, I don't think anyone knows yet."

Auntie Bisi brings in a silver tray with three steaming cups of tea and some of those delicious puff-puff thingies Lily introduced me to—basically, Nigerian sugar dough. I worship them. Sugar probably isn't the best choice while in a state of panic, but if the dopamine makes me feel better, then we're good.

While I take some off the plate, Auntie Bisi grabs a remote control off the bar table and turns on the TV behind me. It's already on the news—the wreckage of the Tokyo Dome. The chyron reads: "Valiant Pop Awards Disaster. Cause Unknown. Police at the Scene."

Cause unknown. Was it really? I'm sure by now they've found the blood and guts and metal from that exploding red . . . *thing*. Unless it didn't happen. Unless I'm losing it.

"I'm sure it was just an accident." Auntie Bisi takes some puff-puff with a shrug. "You know how these award shows go. Money laundering and terrible organization leads to dangerous infrastructure problems. I say don't worry about it. Just get on your knees and praise Jesus that you're okay because He definitely covered you tonight." She gives my shoulder a squeeze.

I would literally give anything to be as perpetually unbothered as Lily's aunt. "That's me." I take the handle of my teacup. "God's favorite."

Maybe I can find out. Hack into local police files. It's not like the Foundation hasn't had me do it before.

I take a sip of tea before something occurs to me.

"Hey," I turn to Lily. "You brought me here, right?"

"Yeah." Lily's mouth is filled with sugary dough. "I dragged you out and called a taxi."

"Did anyone call me while I was out of it? Or contact you?"

"No . . ." she answers, swallowing the lump in her throat. "Was anyone supposed to?"

I pull my phone out of my pants pocket. No missed calls. The incident is all over the news. No missed calls. Not even one.

Not even one.

Harada doesn't care. I squeeze the handle of my teacup so hard it bites into my veins.

"I'm staying here tonight," I declare, swiveling my face quickly so nobody can see my eyes getting wet. "You don't mind, right?" I don't wait for an answer before I run back upstairs.

I wouldn't rest too soundly if I were you, little Amanda, whispers Terminal in the black void of my dreams. *A new castle's just starting to pop up in the Digital World.*

So? I answer back. *Why does that matter?*

Don't you know what a Digital Castle really is?

Yep. The bowels of hell, where incels made 4chan.

Annoyed, Terminal gives a cluck of his tongue. *Everyone has their own castle in the Digital World. Even you. Anyone can have one as long as they've been online a few times. But not this boy. This boy didn't exist before yesterday. I couldn't find him. Now, suddenly, the bricks are being laid down one by one. He's building his castle, probably without even knowing it.*

Terminal never makes any sense. Especially Dream-Terminal. I don't know where Terminal came from. He's just always been online. And he's always sounded like Dr. Robert Kahn, and I have no idea why. Maybe the fathers of the internet programmed him. Or maybe when they made the internet, the Digital World just kind of programmed itself. It is what it is.

So, Terminal, you're saying a mysterious teenage boy materialized out of nowhere, and now he's surfing the net?

Well . . . yes. In a word . . .

And by being online, he's creating a digital footprint, which is, in effect, constructing his very own personal Digital Castle in the Digital World?

Brick by brick.

What's he searching up? Porn?

No. You.

I remember Terminal's words, but I don't believe him. I pay him no mind when I get to school the next day.

Everyone's phones are buzzing and chiming with notifications. It makes Mrs. Archambeau drop her chalk and turn around with her hands on her frumpy hips.

"Didn't I tell you to put your phones away during class?" she chides, but the students don't hear her. They're too busy gawking at the Livewire blast.

"Hyun got two white girls pregnant in France!"

"Who's Hyun?"

"That old guy from that one K-POP group ages ago. He does comedy shows now."

"I smell a shotgun wedding on the horizon!"

"But to which girl?"

"Class!" Mrs. Archambeau's shrill shout cuts the chatter. Everyone hides their phones underneath their desks, silently pretending to pay attention as she continues her lesson.

I thought exposing that jerk would give me a sorely needed rush this morning, but it's not doing the trick. Maybe I should expose a politician next.

I lay my head on my desk with a heavy sigh, sitting in the back corner of Mrs. Archambeau's class when a text from Harada pops up on my phone:

> Go to Harbinger Labs immediately after school today. After what happened at the Dome, there are some tests we need to run.

That's it? No, "Are you okay?" or a "Do I need to get you a therapist for your mental well-being?" Not even a "Did you get me Lisa's autograph?"

I want to smash my phone against the window. I don't even hear the slight knocking on the door or Mrs. Archambeau opening it with a friendly, "You're late. Did you miss your way?"

Before I know it, she calls for the class's attention.

"Students," she says in her thick French accent, though speaking Japanese, smiling with straight white teeth, and peering at us through her comically large glasses. "I'm happy to tell you that we've got a new student transferring in from Yokohama."

"A student this late in the school term?" whispers Lily, who's sitting next to me, but my attention is out the window. The quad looks particularly well fertilized today. My phone would look great among the daffodils, smashed into little bits of metal.

Out of the corner of my eye, I see Mrs. Archambeau sweep her blond hair off her shoulder. "Go ahead, son, introduce yourself."

The student clears his throat. "My name is Matsuoka Sho."

And just like that, my phone slips from my hands and clatters upon the tiled floor.

That voice.

Lily leans over. "Andy, you okay?"

But I can't register her voice. I can only hear his.

My palms are cold. This isn't happening.

Then, lowering my arms, I look at the front of the class.

What a fascinating face. It's cream-colored and small, with an elevated nose bridge and straight brows, not too thick, not too thin. His lips are actually quite plump now that I'm looking at them. Flush red. His short black hair, cut close to his skull, has those V-shaped bangs in the middle of his forehead. And his big, dark eyes, as if from the darkest depths of the ocean, give him ice-prince vibes. All his features are so tightly architected, as if they were sculpted to produce maximum beauty. I didn't notice he was this pretty when he threatened to murder me. I don't think I would have actually found him all that alluring if he really went through with decapitating me.

I didn't hallucinate anything.

The monster terrorist behind the Tokyo Dome explosion stands in a Tokyo International Academy schoolboy uniform, pitch black with a high collar. My classmates whisper and coo as he affably waves. But his glinting eyes never quite seem to leave me as his grin promises chaos.

"I hope we'll all get along. Please take good care of me."

5

"He is fine as hell," says Josh Puckett from the second row, straining his neck to watch Matsuoka Sho throughout the rest of class. The girl next to him nods, hiding her phone under her desk to take pictures of him. Illegal and gross, but I have worse matters to ponder.

Sho might have noticed, but if he did, he doesn't seem to care. He's interested in me. Sitting in front of Lily, perfectly straight-backed, he doesn't even pretend to write notes from Archambeau's lecture. He's staring at my reflection in the window. I can see his too. And when our eyes lock, he gives me one of those frighteningly jovial grins that reminds me of the smile a slasher gives before the slashing happens.

"Innocent School Boy but Actually I'm Going to Kill You" is his default expression throughout lunch break. He stays the consummate good guy as the class swarms him and batters him with questions.

"What kind of music do you listen to?" Nandini Chowdhury practically slams her hands on his desk.

"I have what you'd call eclectic tastes," he answers coolly.

"Where from Yokohama are you from?" Emma Keller sweeps her hair from her face.

"Why do I have the feeling that if I told you that, you'd follow me home?"

The class laughs. Of course they do; they're idiots and can't see through his facade. That's pretty privilege in a nutshell.

"What does your dad do? He must be really rich, right?"

"What do you think of school so far?"

"Have you met the principal? Isn't he so miserable?"

Sho sweet talks his way through the questions. He sweet talks his way through gym class too, dunking the basketball because he is tall enough to, drawing fangirl shrieks as if they've never seen a ball go into a net before.

Sho's new fangirls shriek again when I rush down the stairwell trying to get to math class and slip—and he catches me effortlessly. My heart skips. How did he get in front of me so fast?

His arms are slender, but I can feel every honed muscle as he grips me around the waist and squeezes me against his chest.

"Are you all right?" he says in a low, seductive voice that draws out more fawning from his fans. But when I don't answer, he whispers hot in my ear. "Don't take my kindness for weakness."

I push him away and rush down the rest of the stairs. I have to get away. Far, far away.

I skip last period and rush off through the hallways. I'm almost at the East Wing, just outside Harada Library, where seniors are studying. Hiding in a nearby hall, my feet nearly slipping on the sleek white marble floor, I catch my breath. It's unoccupied—and a dead end. I lean against the broom closet and take out my phone.

Matsuoka Sho. Matsuoka must be his family name. If it's even his real name. My phone blinks on and, on my command, begins running through birth certificates, death certificates, social insurance numbers, bank accounts, driver's licenses, passports. The faces I see sliding through the phone at light speed are not his. This boy doesn't exist.

He does, Terminal insists when I psychically connect to him. *He does* now *at least.*

What do you mean? I shake my head, my eyes glued to my phone screen. *What do you* ever *mean?*

If you would let me teach you properly about the Digital World, then maybe—

Matsuoka Sho grabs my wrists and slams me against the wall. Something in the closet, a broom maybe, clatters to the floor.

"So you go by Andrea Porter here, huh?" He pins me to the wall with all his weight. "But I know who you really are, Amanda McKee."

My heart is thrashing against my chest. "Are you stalking me?" I squirm, remembering that horrible alien suit he wore in the Tokyo Dome. Metal and flesh that throbbed as if it were breathing. "Who are you? *What* are you? Some kind of freaky hit man?" I clench my teeth, my heartbeat thrashing against my chest. "Why am I on your hit list?"

My questions were a whole lot more interesting than the rest of the class's, yet he doesn't answer a single one. Instead, pressing his lips together, he slips a gun out of his blazer sleeve. It has a silencer on the tip.

My heart stops. I start to scream, but he covers my mouth.

"Look, I'm not doing this because I want to," he whispers. "But you *have* to die, Amanda." He pauses, his bottom lip trembling just a little. "You have to. I'm sorry."

With wide, bulging eyes, I look at the gun, shaking in his unsteady hand. I have to think fast. It's a machine. I am the

Queen of Machines. With a command, I force the gun to jam, but I didn't even need to. Sho doesn't pull the trigger. His finger freezes as his breaths draw more haggard, his chest pulsing, his brown eyes wet. He's hesitating.

It's that hesitation I use to push him off me. I use all my strength; then, glaring at his gun, I force it to sizzle and malfunction. It gets too hot for him to hold, but it's already shattered to pieces before he can drop it. I wonder who'll explain that one to the janitor.

"If you want to kill me, you're going to have to work for it." I glare at him menacingly. "Like hell I'm going to let some sociopathic monster get me."

I lift my fist. As if that would do anything against the monster boy who tore up an arena. Fight or flight is messing with my brain.

"A monster . . ." Sho lowers his gaze to the floor and stares at his hands before a wry smile emerges on his face. "A monster, huh?"

I don't accept it when he backs off from me. I don't accept that look of self-loathing. I need answers.

"Why are you threatening me?" I hiss, squeezing my hands. "Why did you show up at the Tokyo Dome and try to *kill* me?"

Taking a deep breath, he pulls a crystal wristwatch out of his pocket, fastens it on his arm, and clicks the casing. It projects a hologram above it. And this isn't some tiny, shimmering blue, "You're my only hope," Princess Leia crap. The image in front of me is live and in color.

It's a picture of Amanda McKee. She's fourteen and at Central Park on a sunny day.

Who the hell *is* this guy?

"I was told," Sho says, stiffer than before, "that Amanda McKee would be on stage at the Tokyo Dome stadium yesterday at precisely 8:37 p.m. Japan Standard Time."

What does any of this mean? There are no traces of Amanda McKee on the internet anymore. I got rid of them after I left New York. I sealed records. Harada gave me the okay after . . . after what happened.

My mouth is dry, but I draw up enough courage to touch the image. It ripples like water.

"Who the hell are you?" I push again. "Certainly not some innocent high school boy from Yokohama. How did you turn into that—" I shiver, thinking of yesterday. "That *thing*." How is it even possible?

Sho flinched but kept his cool. "It's confidential."

"Confidential? Are you some kind of terrorist?" I shake my head in disbelief.

My voice is getting a little too shrill for the hallway. Some seniors in the library might hear. But when Sho glowers, I have a feeling I've hit the nail on the head.

"A terrorist with access to some kind of—" I stumble, remembering the sword he pulled out of his back. "Some kind of freaky technology. Or magic. Or maybe you're an alien." Hell, *I* am a psiot that talks to machines. I wouldn't be surprised if any of that other stuff existed.

Just then, a thought occurred to me. Harada had told me in the limo: The Harbinger Foundation isn't the only company working on dangerous, avant-garde technology.

"Who's your boss?" I demand. "You working for Comsat?"

"Comsat?" He searches his memories. "Dr. Silk's Webnet of the twenty-first century," he says as if he's reciting a textbook he studied. "Eventually destroyed by a number of international players, especially with the help of Colin Ki—"

"Hey!" I snap my fingers, forcing his attention back to me. "Answer me! Who the hell are you? What was that cosplay crap you were wearing?"

"BioSuit," Sho corrects me. The word makes me flinch. I've heard it before, but I can't remember where, and my mind is a scrambled egg right now. My eyes keep flitting between Sho and that old picture of me. It makes my legs feel like jelly.

"W-what are you talking about?"

"Don't act like you don't know when you, Amanda McKee, are the reason why BioSuits exist in the first place. You're the cause of *everything*."

And then his dark eyes become soft, unfocused. His whole body relaxes, but the pain is still clearly etched on his face. He looks like he's aging right in front of me.

"You're the reason I'm stuck here. The reason I . . ." He trails off. He looks lost.

The two of us are lost here in this hallway. Confused, scared, and unsure. But I have to be strong. I shove him away from me. "If you were going to kill me, you would have done it already. You didn't. You let me live. Not the badass you pretend to be, are you?"

Bingo. It's just like in the Tokyo Dome: the sudden twitch of his expression, the guilt creeping up in his eyes, his furrowed brows. Where did all that bluster go?

He looks at the photo again. I remember that day crystal clear. It was my fourteenth birthday. Harada had a whole picnic set up for me in Central Park, New York. A couple of my butlers went, but no Harada. Fourteen-year-old me looks a little sad.

Sho looks at the picture. Looks at me. Looks at the picture. His hands fall to his side. He really can't do it. He can transform into some kind of alien soldier at will, but he can't kill me.

The school bell rings. Summoning all my courage, I grab his wrist, covering his watch. The picture shuts off. Just then, someone pokes their head into the hallway. It's Miss Omar, the accounting teacher, probably on her way to the library.

"Everything all right here?" she asks, her purple hijab tucked into her blue suit jacket. Luckily, she doesn't notice the gun in pieces on the floor.

"Just fine!" I wave to her, and the moment she disappears, I sneer at Sho.

"I don't know how much you know about me," I tell him decisively. "But you don't want to make me your enemy. For your sake, you better hope you never do."

I leave him shaken and standing alone in the corridor, the click of my heels echoing off the white ceiling plaster. Students are already beginning to flood the hallways.

"You're not my true enemy. Toyo Harada is," he calls behind me.

The blood freezes in my veins. I can feel Sho's gaze drilling a hole through the back of my head. I make sure to fix my face into a neutral expression before I turn around.

"Toyo Harada? Don't know him. Don't care."

"You're lying."

"I'm not."

Sho's silence is infuriating. He's sussing me out, calling my bluff. I take a few failed calming breaths before quickly losing my temper, clasping my hands into fists.

"I said I'm not lying!"

Sho looks at me very seriously. His anger has simmered, flooded by an even greater wave of desperation.

And fear.

"I know you do, because I've been told," he says. "Because one day Toyo Harada and Amanda McKee will destroy humanity."

6

Students, staff, teachers. There are too many people around to question him further. He disappears into the crowd. I have no choice but to follow the flowing throng moving in the opposite direction when my phone vibrates. A text message from "Unknown":

> This isn't a game. I don't want to have to kill you, but I will.
>
> To save billions.

A video file is attached. With trembling fingers, I click play.

Footage of a dark room plays on my screen. I can only see the metallic-red walls until the camera slowly zooms out and purple pipes zip down the earthen ceiling. Round purple pods grow out of the walls like spores. They litter the room. What is this? Some kind of facility?

And who's inside the spores?

I can see two brown arms wrapped around tucked knees.

It's a girl. She's naked and hugging herself like a baby in amniotic fluid. Each breath disturbs the liquid she's immersed in, little violet bubbles floating from her nose. Her eyes are shut.

All their eyes are shut.

It's the same person in each of the spores.

And when one girl's eyes suddenly snap open, I drop my phone and cover the scream erupting from my mouth.

It's me. It's Amanda McKee.

She's just a child—maybe seven years old, maybe younger. She's inside the spore, staring wide-eyed at the camera, emotionless, as if in a trance. Amanda McKees are in *every* spore, at different stages of development—some are babies, some teens, some adults, but all are in this dark, dingy room mocking humanity.

I can't breathe.

It has to be edited. Anyone could make something this sick if they had the skills, right?

With my heart in my throat, I fly out of the school. Matsuoka Sho is insane. He's *insane.*

But he's real.

What he did inside Tokyo Dome and what he transformed into. I didn't hallucinate it.

All those Amandas trapped inside a bunch of sci-fi monster pods? Are they real too?

I need answers. Maybe Harada can get them for me.

Located in Tokyo's flashy Shinjuku district is Harada Entertainment, one of many tall buildings in the Eastside Square. I'm surrounded by bright lights, LED jumbotrons, and wide, white-striped street intersections leading to shops, convenience stores, and restaurants. I tip my taxi driver and walk inside the building.

The moment I walk through the rotating glass doors, I see models being chased by their managers. I give the two ladies at the concierge desk my ID card, always in my pink wallet.

A world map is painted on the marble floor of the lobby. I always like to think that it was Harada's secret message: "Thanks to my wealth and endless resources, I will one day control the world!" It was funnier before I met Sho.

"Hey, you! Do you work here? Can you get someone to please finally talk to me?"

A young man in khaki jeans strides up to me arrogantly as if I should be carrying his bags. He's probably in his late twenties, with somewhat questionable taste considering the white hair dye washes him out entirely. He's got BAD CUPID's logo tattooed on his hairy, pale skin.

I blink. "Um, waiting for what?"

"Waiting to talk to *someone* about Harada Entertainment's mishandling of BAD CUPID's Japanese promotions. I'm Taylor Ronaldo. I'm an *ARROW*." The group's fandom name. "And I run a very successful website."

He shows me his phone. BC-JAPAN. It looks legit, with news, music reviews, and even exclusives. But this guy annoys me, so I touch the screen and shut my eyes. It only takes a second for the doors of his website to unlock. For Terminal to bring information to me.

Behind my eyelids, I see the driver's license of Ohio-born Taylor Ronaldo. I learn all about him. How he waited outside BAD CUPID's hotel room in Toledo, taking illegal pictures of them. How he stalks them across the world. How he tried to grab and *pinch* one of the members at the Incheon International Airport.

"Security!" I flick my head toward this piece of crap.

"Wait!" he yells as two men drag him out of the building. "I need to know if Carmen is staying in the group! They can't kick her out. She's my bias!"

I roll my eyes. Idols fans are such trash, I swear.

The staff members working in the round lobby under the blue ambient light are always so friendly. On the far wall next to the elevator, a TV screen plays the latest music videos produced by Harada Entertainment.

Nobody here knows about the secret laboratory in the basement. They don't know about Harbinger Labs.

Sometimes artifice is needed to hide what truly lies beneath. One of Harada's favorite sayings.

The scientists in the lower levels of the building give me the creeps. Carrying lab specimens in jars and wheeling around metal trolleys with blood samples, they stare at me, some giving me creepy smiles. "Amanda's here," their expectant expressions seem to whisper. "What do we get to do to her now?"

I've given them so much of my blood and tissue over the years, but it never seems to be enough. It's all for the betterment of humankind, Harada would tell me. Learning about human evolution means planning for the next stages of life on Earth.

The same Earth we allegedly destroy, according to Sho.

What does that *psycho* know? Sucking in a breath, I step inside Room A-0301. I always feel like a medical patient here. A science experiment. The sterile white room is filled with monitors and medical equipment. There's a bed in the center of the room and an imposing monitor at the leftmost wall—the megamonitor, I like to call it.

Harada is there. But so is—

"Amanda! Hey! *Amanda*!" Sitting in front of the megamonitor, Yoshida Sakaguchi waves at me like a grade-school boy. He jumps out of his seat and practically runs toward me, holding his hand out for me to shake, but he stops himself after Harada gives him a warning look.

"Amanda," Harada sits up from the middle chair in front of the megamonitor. "You remember Sakaguchi."

The scientist scratches the back of his head. "From the Research and Development Department. I specialize in nanotech biomechanical engineering. Call me Yoshi."

"He's helping the Foundation figure out yesterday's mystery," said Harada, looking like a king on his throne as he sits in front of the megamonitor.

"The Tokyo Dome attack," Yoshi says, sitting on the white-clothed bed.

"And the pillar of light," Harada finishes, crossing his legs.

Seeing Harada mention it all so coolly unnerves me. I wrap my arms around myself. "So they're connected . . ." The alien-like beam from the sky. The monster bash just hours later. Of course they're connected.

"You may have noticed all your digital stuff going haywire during the storm yesterday," Yoshi says, still running his fingers through his shaggy hair. "I've been studying the electrical disturbance, and I think it was some kind of rip in the space-time continuum, which wouldn't make a lot of sense, because I don't think time travel is possible. Then again, it may be possible in the future, so if we somehow advance our knowledge of temporal mechanics, I don't see why we wouldn't—"

"Take a breath!" I yell, a little louder than I'd meant to because he said "time travel," and this is now officially way above my pay grade. He jumps a bit on the bed but stays silent.

"Just so you know, Mr. Sakaguchi's ramblings are just his own theories," Harada says, giving Yoshi an admonishing look. "*Time travel* is not something we're currently considering. What we do know is that the light may have been caused by the two biomechanical objects that appeared last night. You must have seen them, Amanda. At that award show." He pauses. "Hack the CCTV footage around the area at exactly the time of the explosion and see for yourself."

Harada sounds confident. Pressing my lips together, I walk over to the megamonitor. Harada stands, offering his seat. I plunk down with a heavy sigh.

I never needed to understand mechanics and computers and technology. I don't know why they talk to me. But they give up information willingly like I'm one of them. Part of their species.

I put my hand on the keyboard, and the megamonitor blinks alive. In the CCTV footage, monsters fly out from behind the city skyline, fighting hand to hand as they draw dangerously closer to the stadium.

"Zoom in," Harada orders.

I obey him. And when I command the computer, it obeys *me*. The screen pauses just before the two are about to crash through the roof of the stadium.

"Do you see that?" Yoshi points his pen at the back of the red robot. "Those two glowing slits in the back that look like headlights? I think those are rocket engines. There's some kind of propellant thrusting them forward, allowing them to fly. You see that peculiar emission behind them as they're flying around?"

Now that I squint, I do see them: miniscule white particles, almost invisible. The red one seems to have some kind of furnace in its palms for particle blasts. The silver has a blade mounted inside its back. I can see the sinew of muscle pulsating in both. Man and machine.

"They really do look like comic book characters come to life, don't they?" Yoshi says. "You know, *Guyver*? *Tekkaman Blade*? *Kamen Rider*?"

"I love those shows," I say, deadpan, because I'm telling the truth.

"What they are is the mystery," Harada interrupts. "The police are hiding this footage from the general public because they have no clue what to do with it. But we have a theory." Harada nods to Yoshi, who takes his seat next to mine and begins clacking away at the keyboard.

Blue schematics of two full-body suits appear on the screen. They look less like *Detonator Orgun* and more like crash-test dummies. But the eyes are familiar. They're the same as a transformed Sho's, those alien whites, glinting with the promise of murder.

"The BioSuit: the latest from Harada Conglomerates," Yoshi says. "We told you a bit about it in the limo yesterday, remember? But we're still developing it. As you can see, it's still in its very early stages, not even ready for a patent. Nothing like the masterpieces the CCTV captured. These . . ." He pauses to think. "BioSuit *Soldiers*. Ooh, I like that."

"Masterpieces," I repeat in disbelief. That's one way to put it. "Harada, what exactly have you been trying to make here?"

"Hmm, so *now* you're interested?" Harada's teasing tone, as much as it annoys me, strangely makes me relax. "Sakaguchi."

"Yes, sir," answers Yoshi, and he zooms in on the two suits, letting the camera pan from the top of the helmet to the bottom of the clunky feet.

"Amanda," Harada says, his hand still on my shoulder. "Humans haven't been kind to this world, and we're suffering for it. Poverty. Disease. The BioSuit will solve that. It's a techno-organic device, an exoskeleton that, when completed, will provide all the health and nutrients a human body could ever need."

I shake my head, trying to wrap my mind around it.

"And we're so close." Harada's voice gets huskier the more excited he gets. "Imagine the resources we can free up if people never need food or water. People wouldn't need roofs over their heads. The homeless wouldn't need to waste away on the streets. With access to body-regulating technology, people could survive in the woods during the worst winters. And with built-in telecommunication and virtual reality resources, people could live on their own without community pressures."

"That sounds extremely lonely," I say, imagining some poor soul alone in the snow inside one of those cold suits.

"Some people prefer loneliness. People aren't always so kind, Amanda," Harada retorts, his expression stone.

"Besides, with the built-in LYNK system, suits can actually connect with each other," pipes Yoshi. "Theoretically, you'd be able to psychically communicate with someone you've LYNKed with. It's pretty rad. And useful, you know, if you don't want to be a loner."

Something tells me he's had enough experience. So do I. Game recognizes game.

"No more hunger. No more conflict over land disputes. People may even live hundreds of years beyond normal human capacity." Harada's brown eyes glint with glee as he stares at the schematics rotating on the screen. "Imagine it, Amanda. A perfect world. We could end war . . ."

His voice trails off, his hand stiffening upon my shoulder. Suddenly, he seems lost inside himself.

And I know why.

Harada was born in Japan, and much of his family died in Hiroshima. The story of their deaths and the misery of the survivors was passed on from one generation to the next. Something must have happened to him when he saw just how far humans will go for power.

Harada's country also made other nations suffer. Pain begets more pain. It's not surprising he'd want to put an end to it all. But the road to hell is paved with good intentions. And all I can hear is Sho's solemn warning echoing inside me:

One day Toyo Harada and Amanda McKee will destroy humanity.

"Ending war. That's a big dream," I whisper, a little surprised when Harada laughs.

"I dream big. You know better than anyone, Amanda: I want to help people."

It's what he told me when he first began testing my powers. If there were more people like me—more psiots—I wonder what he would do with them?

Yoshi waves his hand at the screen. "These are our prototypes. But these"—he draws up the CCTV footage and zooms in on the silver BioSuit Soldier—"these are complete. They have the same basic design as our BioSuits. But everything is so much more advanced, from the exoskeleton to the combat system."

"I thought you people wanted to end world hunger, not start a fight club," I say.

"That's the issue. The basic designs are ours, but these suits have been tinkered with big time. It's like someone took our design and said, 'Let's do that but make them really badass warriors instead.'" Yoshi is practically salivating at the thought. "That's why I'm saying the pillar of light was a tear in the space-time continuum. It's *time travel.* Someone, at some point in time, finished our designs and made these—"

Harada sighs. "There's still no proof that time travel exists, Yoshida. But, Amanda, the connection between our technology and these . . . mechanical *surprises* is confirmed. We'll need to do what we can to find out the truth. And we'll need your help."

"My psiot powers, you mean." I stare at my hands.

"Yes. Eventually, I believe your powers will be the key to perfecting the BioSuit design. But we need you right now, here in this building." Harada furrows his thick brows. "If any one of my competitors has stolen my designs and developed them, we'll know soon enough."

"You'll know because of me."

"You've done corporate espionage for me in the past, Amanda."

Yes. For the past several years, before I even entered middle school, Harada has made sure to put my psiot gifts to use. Maybe he's right. Maybe using my power is the only way we can figure out what's going on. But the greed in my adopted father's eyes makes me furious. Since I got here, since he's dumped all this insanity on me, he still hasn't even asked if I'm all right. How can I tell him about Sho, about the Tokyo Dome, or even about that horrible video if I'm not even sure he cares about my well-being?

But that's how it's always been with Harada. Am I his adopted daughter? Or his personal tool?

"No," I whisper. And I know Harada is glaring at me. But I don't care. My blood is boiling. That's all I am to him. A means to an end.

"This isn't a request," Harada says. "It's an order, Amanda."

"And I said *no*." The megamonitor begins to spark. The other monitors start beeping out of sync with each other. "You just love making me jump when you say so, don't you? But I'll figure this out on my own terms, not yours."

Sparks fly from the air vents, but Toyo Harada stands firm. It's a showdown between father and adopted daughter, neither of us willing to back down. But Harada knows. With each ragged breath, I'm getting closer and closer to tearing down this entire lab.

Finally, Harada closes his eyes. "The only psiot in existence.

The next stage in humanity's evolution. You're a wonder, Amanda. You're *my* wonder. Because I cherish your abilities, it may not seem like I cherish *you*. But you're wrong. You are my family, Amanda. And you came to me at a time when I had none. That matters."

But which does he cherish more? Me? Or my abilities?

He turns to the black monitor. Looking at the monitor, I see his eyelids flutter. I can see painful histories reflected in those bottomless pupils.

"There was once a time, Amanda, when I had no faith in humankind." His thin, bony fingers curl upon his lap. "When I was a boy, I thought humans were only made to destroy each other. But I was wrong. We can help each other too. I hope, Amanda, that you'll come to believe the same, in time."

But what if I shouldn't?

One day Toyo Harada and Amanda McKee will destroy humanity.

The future. The future is what Harada dreams of. What he's dedicated to sculpt with his own hands.

I should tell Harada about Sho. But as desperate as I am to dismiss Sho's words as lunacy, the more I hear Harada talk about his biomechanical dream, the more my throat constricts in fear. Nothing in this lab feels like it's for the betterment of humanity.

Without another word, he passes by me and walks out of Room A-0301.

7

I'm already out of the building when I get a call from Lily to meet at the rooftop at Harada Entertainment at exactly eight o'clock—and to wear my best. The rooftop? Well, anything's better than the basement. I want nothing to do with Harada Labs.

I spend hours in Harajuku buying new clothes. Come eight o'clock, I'm glad I did.

"Surprise!"

Shouts ring out from the four corners of the Harada Entertainment building's rooftop. Shinjuku's skyline sparkles under the moonlight: silver buildings and flashing billboards both in kanji and English light up the busy shopping district. There are platters of food on round tables. Waiters carry drinks to the crowd. The twinkling lights on strings stretch out over our heads. This is a party for me, I assume, because everyone is staring at me with wide smiles.

Some of the top actors and singers in the agency are here. It's *their* faces on the bright, flashing billboards. Ryoichi's skin-care ad is playing on loop on one of the LED screens. I look around for him on the rooftop and find so many other celebrities in his place. Damn, is that the cute dude from the recent *Boys Over Flowers* remake? I'm shaking in my very expensive knee-high black pumps.

The DJ is playing Utada Hikaru's "Travelling" at his turntable. With a glass of wine in hand, Harada walks to the center of the rooftop and waves me over to join him. I can't help but hesitate. I've been taught my whole life to keep secret any ties we have to each other. He's not going to announce our father–adopted daughter relationship right now, right here . . . is he?

"Thank you for coming," he tells the crowd. "I hope you'll join me in celebrating Andy-P, one of our shining influencers on the roster, who's just booked her first Hollywood role!"

My body goes numb as someone yells, "Cheers!" And the applause begins.

Lily, in a pink dress and with her camera slung around her shoulder, slides out from the crowd and wraps her arms around my neck. "As your 'manager,' I was explicitly instructed to keep this surprise party from you. But you deserve one! You're going to be in a movie!" She squeezes me so hard, I see cartoon stars. "I didn't even know you auditioned!"

"I didn't know I auditioned either . . ." My head is spinning, and not only because of the lack of oxygen. What's going on? What's Harada playing at?

When people disperse to eat, drink, and mingle, Harada slides up to me. "Do you like my present?"

I love a good party. But. "That depends." I look up at him with a suspicious gaze. "Which character am I playing?"

Harada pauses. "You're . . . an extra."

"Figures."

"But it's a start." Harada claps my shoulder. "As is, I hope, our relationship moving forward." He gives it a squeeze. It feels almost fatherly. It should be. This is supposed to be a *successful* attempt at wooing me back to his side.

He removes his hand from me and straightens his tie. "Make sure you enjoy tonight. Then reconsider my proposal when you're in a good mood."

At the end of the day, he still wants me to do as he says. He gives me a little smile before walking off. Yoshi's here too, enjoying a frosted beer at the ledge of the building. Meanwhile, I look around the bustling rooftop. The star power gathered here. It must have taken Harada just a few minutes to bring them all here to celebrate me. None of them are really talking to me.

"How can anyone be up here celebrating?" I put my hand over Lily's frantically snapping camera lens. "After what happened at the Tokyo Dome . . ."

Lily shrugs. "The news says the police are handling it."

"And you believe that?"

Of course she does. She didn't see what I did. Even if she had, people tend to believe lies to hide from the truth.

Beyond the buzzing, glamorous facade of my party, Sho's frightened eyes haunt me.

"There you are, Andy-P. Hollywood movie, huh? Was it a *blind* audition?"

Carmen meanders up to me, drunk and stumbling on her heels.

"You're still in the country?" I scrunch my nose as smoke wafts from the grill. "I thought you left with the rest of your group."

"I've been put on *hiatus*!" She practically screams it, which makes a few people stare. Her crooked smile bleeds with fury. "Oh, you didn't hear? Well, the news should come out tomorrow morning, and then *everyone's* gonna know." She slaps her chest, caught between anger and complete shock. "I'm on hiatus. *Me*! I'm the *visual*, for goodness' sake."

"Yes, you are very pretty." I shrug because I don't know what else to say to this K-POP idol falling apart in front of me.

Lily is gleefully taking video footage behind us. I move to leave, but Carmen grabs my arm.

"All this started when I met you at that stupid school," she snarls. "You, like, cursed me or something."

She's not wrong. "You cursed yourself by being a bully."

"It's the entertainment industry! Do you know how many bitches tried to *kill* me before I debuted? Yelling at some talentless flop is *nothing*. It's not even half as bad as what some of the people here have done." She waves her hand across the rooftop. "Fake stars celebrating your unearned success."

She pushes me once. And again. I stumble back on my feet. But just before Carmen could get another hit in, Ryoichi slides up from behind her.

"Enough," he tells her. "You're drunk. You should get a ride home."

My heart skips a beat. Ryoichi looks beautiful at night under the stars. He looks better than his ad. That prince image he's got going on is just too delicious. And so is he. I'm a stan.

"Why don't *you* take me home, Chiba?" She grabs his collar rather aggressively, stumbling over her feet as she tries to slink up to him. She begins to lean in when a grating voice shouts at her from behind us.

"Carmen! Carmen!"

We all turn to see Taylor Ronaldo, that BAD CUPID fan, running toward her. How did he slither his way up here?

"Ew, you again!" Carmen slaps the phone Taylor's using to snap photos of her. "I told you to stop stalking me!"

"Don't worry, Carmen. ARROWS are gathering funds as we speak to buy billboards across the world to support you." He gets up in her personal space. "And we're renting protest trucks to send a message to your agency in Korea. We won't let them do this to you!"

"Get *away* from me, you freak!"

Carmen lets out a frustrated groan and stomps off, with her superfan scrambling behind her. Ryoichi approaches me, dapper in his three-piece suit. "Andy . . . you okay?"

I rub the back of my neck. "It's the entertainment industry. Do you know how many bitches have tried to kill me?" I forget that he wasn't there when Carmen said that, so he's not going to get the joke. He smiles anyway.

"I mean . . . the Tokyo Dome incident." The weight suddenly feels heavy between us. Ryoichi lowers his head. "I left you there with those . . . those things, and—"

He stops. Oh, I remember. Kind of cowardly, but I don't blame him. Very few dudes are brave in the face of fighting robot monster-terrorists. But this is the first time someone outside of Harbinger Labs has even acknowledged what really happened.

"What do you think that all was?" He shakes his head. "I can't even begin to wrap my head around it. It's been bothering me . . . but if the police have it under control . . ."

"Best not to talk about it," I finish for him. It's written all over his face. I don't blame him. I begin to walk away, but Ryoichi grabs my hand. His touch is electrifying. Like, I can feel his fingers lightly rubbing the skin of my wrist, and my whole body is flushing with heat.

"We should celebrate your Hollywood role sometime." He draws closer to me. I have to crane my neck just to look into those deep brown eyes. "I know a yakiniku place nearby that's out of the way. I go there all the time. They have a private room for me. The paparazzi wouldn't catch us . . . talking, I mean." His grin is somehow both boyish and seductive at the same time.

My lips flatten into a thin line, and I don't think I realize until it's almost too late that I've stopped breathing for a few seconds.

Is Chiba Ryoichi asking me out? Chiba Ryoichi, the man voted number one on Oricon's annual survey: "Top male celebrity you want to receive chocolate from on Valentine's Day?"

The past two days have scrambled my brain entirely. Maybe this is my consolation. I close my eyes, trying to imagine what a date with Japan's most eligible teen bachelor would be like. The two of us canoodling in a little coffee shop away from prying fans and reporters . . .

I hear it before they do: everyone's phones malfunctioning. The notifications that should have been turned off. The ringing that should have been set to vibrate. The machines are panicking. They're telling me to run. "Hide, young psiot," they say.

They can sense it too. The future is coming.

They're coming.

They're here.

What did Yoshi call them again? Right, BioSuit Soldiers. Seven humanoid beasts sheathed in flesh and metal robot armor rise to the sky from behind Harada Entertainment's rooftop. And at the center of the group: a long, lithe feminine form in red and yellow armor. Her shoulder blades are mounds of muscle, sharpened to a point. Her gold helmet covers her head. The eyeslits flash heaven white. They reek of death. She is the leader. I know she is.

People are so shocked they can't even scream. Glasses of wine drop from hands and shatter on the roof. Laughter dies in throats. Only I can hear the leader speak when she points at my father.

"Eggbreakers! Take Toyo Harada," she says in a voice that sounds like gravel. "Spare Amanda McKee."

A pause.

"Do what you want with the rest."

That's when the screaming starts.

8

The leader doesn't move. It's the BioSuit Soldier next to her who goes straight for Harada. It's fast, a yellow-and-brown blur as it parts the skies, forcing the air aside to get to Harada standing at the back of the rooftop.

A crescent moon of energy hurdles from the skies and slices the BioSuit blur, stopping its hunt for Harada. It curves, changing trajectory as if moved by sheer will, missing the bystanders, slicing off a corner of the roof instead. As rubble tumbles from the building to the Shinjuku streets below, I gaze up. The silver BioSuit Soldier.

"Sh-Sho?" I whisper before a crash sends me ducking for cover along with every other celebrity. Another soldier lands on the rooftop. This one is almost twice as big as any other, its armor gray, with its elbows and knees covered in breathing muscle. Orange tinges its hands and helmet. It grabs the barbecue grill, and the metal disintegrates to dust in its hands.

"Attention, citizens!" I can recognize Sho's voice calling out to us from behind his helmet despite the robotic distortion. "Evacuate the building immediately! I repeat. For your own safety, evacuate the building immediately!"

What is this? Is Sho worrying about our safety? Is he . . . is he trying to save us?

The yellow and brown soldier isn't a blur anymore. I can see a long black ponytail protruding out from behind its helmet. With lightning-fast reflexes, it launches itself at Sho, grabbing his fists, trying to crush them.

My party guests begin to run in such a frenzy that I lose sight of my father.

"Oh my god!" I hear Lily's shriek and feel her arm linking around my elbow. She's holding on tight, trying not to get swept away with the flood of bodies. "What's happening?"

Focus, I tell myself as my heart pounds in my ears. You talk to machines. BioSuits are machines. Talk to them. Figure it out.

I focus on the BioSuit Soldier who just destroyed a rather expensive barbecue grill. But these suits—their technology is unlike any machine I've ever encountered. They're linked together by a system that doesn't yet exist in this world, and their security features are impenetrable.

Almost impenetrable. With a little persistence, I can get names.

Here's the first one: Stronghold. The big beast of a BioSuit Soldier throws away the last remaining piece of grill, digs his hands into the roof, and throws chunks of building at Sho, who kicks his foe away to escape. His foe: Mak. Her black ponytail swings in the air.

Law, the BioSuit Soldier with a gray bodice, raises its hands, its blue gloves sparking with energy. Sho notices, but too late. Law shoots two beams of blue energy at him, one from each glittering hand. He dodges them adeptly in the air, but it doesn't stop the others from coming after him. Panic: a long, lithe soldier in a suit so black it almost blends into the sky. Ion: a soldier whose ice-blue suit calls down electrical currents from the suddenly crackling skies.

They call themselves Eggbreakers. They're communicating with each other without words through a secret network I can't touch. They're perfectly in sync.

As the others battle in the skies, Saturn, cloaked in red and violet, stays close to the big boss, a dragon waiting to bite the moment its master gives the command.

But the master isn't concerned with Sho. Her unfeeling white gaze is on Harada, the only person on this rooftop besides Lily and me foolish enough not to run away. He stares up at the robotic beings in awe, tears in his eyes, and not from fear. This is the expression of a man holding his baby for the first time. The expression of blissful confusion, of hope for the future.

The completed BioSuit. A technological wonder. A desire realized.

"I've seen you," he whispers. "In my dreams . . ."

"I can show you," the soldier says. "The future you envision. The seed from which tomorrow will spring. I can show you how you, Toyo Harada, will one day save humanity."

Harada reaches for her, his fingers twitching, aching for this beast's touch.

"Dad!" I scream, pushing away Lily and running for him as the soldier lunges for him and snatches him off the roof. I stumble and fall to the ground, but not even the pain searing through my scuffed arms stops me. Harada's been kidnapped. The BioSuit squadron's leader—she's taking Harada away . . .

Let him go! I order the master's machine, trying to bend it to my will, but it's impossible. Laughable. The orange and red BioSuit Soldier is laughing at me. *Let my dad go!*

I speak to the machine, and it speaks back.

If you want him, then come get him, Amanda.

She's taunting me. But the greatest taunt of all is her name, which I pry from the cold crevices of her technological armor.

Livewire.

"What?" I whisper, my body numb. "That's not your name. That can't be your name. Why is that your name . . . ?"

Livewire launches into the skies toward a tall building. Cars are honking. Do the people below notice? Do they see this monster with my dad about to crash into Ryoichi's billboard ad?

"Dad!" I scream again, my body leaden, my eyes wide in horror. They're going to crash through the building. She's going to kill him. Livewire is going to kill Harada.

No. She doesn't. She doesn't break through the billboard.

She slips inside it.

The LED screen ripples like water as Livewire and Toyo Harada melt into the digital surface, becoming one with it, disappearing into its blinding lights. How? *How?*

Lily grabs my arm and lifts me up to my feet. "Come on!" She clutches her camera like a security blanket. "We've got to get out of here!"

My brain is scrambled, but I know she's right. The soldiers are still fighting Sho above. Electrical currents and energy blasts crackle toward him, and though he dodges them, he can't dodge Mak, whose martial arts prowess seems unmatched. He's surrounded. There's no way he'll win this fight.

But that's not why I'm shaking.

"Livewire took my dad." The words sound hollow in my throbbing throat. I don't understand them. My limbs are so weak, I can't stop Lily from dragging me down the emergency stairwell. The entire building shakes from a heavy smash. A BioSuit Soldier? Is it Sho? I cover my head from the rubble streaming down from the ceiling.

We run into the empty lobby and out into the streets. The soldiers are so far away, fighting in the night sky. Pedestrians squint as they look up, confused, clouds swirling and gathering around the battle. One BioSuit Soldier is thrown down into a back alley with such force, the impact causes the street to rumble. That's when cars stop and bystanders start running.

"That was Sho," I tell Lily, because I saw the silver streak with my own eyes just as I can now see another soldier going after him. "Stay here!"

"Andy!"

I ignore Lily's cries and rush down the street, past the bright colors and distractions, past the college girls recording the fight on their phones and the schoolboys riding away on rental bikes. I must be absolutely out of my mind. I've seen all the horror movies. The victims are always the ones stupid enough to run *toward* danger. But I need answers. Harada's been kidnapped. BioSuit Soldiers are running wild; meanwhile, Sho's warnings of a dystopian future echo in my brain with each hurried step.

Who took my father? Who are the Eggbreakers? Who is Sho? Who is Livewire? I mean, *I'm* Livewire. I made the password and the username and everything! What's going on?

I slip through the narrow backstreets, the graffiti on the pipes and brick shops rushing past my eyesight while I avoid tripping over store signs and baskets of trash. I find the warriors in an alley between a convenience store and a ramen shop. The smell of pork rising from the vents is as thick as the billowing smoke. There is Sho, struggling on the dirty ground. And another stalks toward him, dragging its sharp fingers against the brick, taking bits of building with it.

Law. The Eggbreaker charges up her armored gloves with that same pulsing blue energy.

"Matsuoka Sho," she says in a stinging, high-pitched voice. "Special agent of the Castaway Active Resistance Division. Resident of Haven. Anti-Harada terrorist. Traitor to humanity. You'll meet your end today. But first—"

Blue energy swirls around Law's arms like clouds. She aims them at Sho. "Return the BioSuit to us. Return the Izanagi."

Even distorted, Sho's laughter sounds boyishly defiant. "Why would I give you back this suit when I went through so much trouble stealing it?" With robotic clinks and whirs, Sho pushes himself onto his unstable armored knees. "You'll have to tear it from my cold, dead body, Eggbreaker."

"That can be arranged." Law's hands begin to flash.

"Andy!"

I turn around. Lily's behind me. She was following me. She can barely speak, her chest heaving as she clutches it. She's holding her phone in her other hand, the video still running.

Law turns around and aims her blast at my friend.

Suddenly, my legs are sprinting toward Law faster than I've ever run before. I grip Law's gray chest armor. It's pristine, smooth, but frigid. Just touching it sends an electrical pulse rocketing to my skull, so powerful, my head might shatter. My heels are planted in the gravel, the lactic acid eating away at my thighs, but I ignore the pain. The suit is alive. A mixture of nanotechnology and biological function, intertwined such that I can barely discern where life ends and machinery begins. The gravitational pull between us is so powerful, I feel like Law's BioSuit is going to suck the life out of me.

I suck the life out of her instead.

I'm not sure how it happens. I'm not sure how I did it, but I did it. The machine untangles itself from the flesh inside the suit, from its DNA, its cells. I pull it toward me, like draining color from a painting, and it seeps into my own body. It can't resist my will, my desire to save my best friend. It can't resist my unconscious commands.

Suitless Law is nothing but a rotted corpse. A naked body. She falls to the ground, twitching on the ground as the BioSuit latches on to my chromosomes. It's infecting me, colonizing me. My frantic heartbeat screams at the technology: *Get out! Get out of me!*

It doesn't. Because there's an even more powerful voice deep inside my soul, unrepentant, filled with rage.

I want power. The power to save my father. The power to stop these freaks once and for all! That's the voice the machine hears. That's the command it obeys.

As the machine connects to me, I access its knowledge. I'm so used to just psychically peeking into the Digital World from the outside, real world with Terminal as my guide. But the Digital World can be accessed. Flesh-and-blood human beings can transform into data through the process of digitization. We can digitize and enter the Digital World through the power of Bio-Suits, leaving the real world behind.

Livewire must have taken Harada into the Digital World. They didn't just go inside Ryoichi's billboard. They digitized into the global network that connects billions of devices: the internet. My adopted father has disappeared from the real world. He's in the Digital World now.

That's where I need to go too.

"Andy!" Lily's shrieking seems so far away as the suit begins to form around my body.

Just before the helmet covers my face, I see Sho in his silver armor, sprinting toward me, but I turn from him. The world looks uncanny from inside this suit. Too sharp, like there's a video setting higher than 4K. But I know I can digitize with the power of this suit. I just need something to digitize into.

Lily's phone. I can digitize into Lily's phone. Just like the billboard, it can act as a simple door, a gateway into the Digital World.

I move one armored leg, then the other, with heavy steps.

It's instinctual, like all the training I've ever done with Harada has unexpectedly prepared me for this technopathic moment. As I touch Lily's phone, my body begins to collapse and fold, becoming one with the telecommunications network that's hiding Toyo Harada and Livewire.

Sho reaches for me from behind.

Don't do it, his mind says. *You idiot! You'll kill yourself!*

Hundreds of thoughts within my disorderly mind respond to him at once. *I thought you wanted me dead already? Livewire stole my dad. I have to go. Livewire stole my dad. Livewire. But* I'm *Livewire. What's happening? What am I doing?*

What is it that Terminal told me once as a child? Ah yes. Trying to access the Digital World within a chaotic mindset can lead to *accidents*. My mind's doing triple duty, trying to access the Digital World, communicate with Sho, and make sense of this situation all at the same time. It can't handle it all.

For a moment, my mind splits in two, and Sho's mind slips through the crevice left in its wake. My BioSuit and Sho's connect, locking together in an impenetrable bond. I stop digitizing. Sho pulls me out of Lily's phone, out of the door to the Digital World.

Armored up like one of those monsters, I can't move, not until Sho moves his left leg forward. When Sho reaches to the right, so do I. And when he de-armors, I do too, my BioSuit disappearing into my body, leaving me standing in the alleyway in my black dress.

Breathing rapidly, I grab my chest, unsure if the warm flesh is really mine. I tear my gaze away from Lily's terrified face to Sho, standing behind me in a pair of jeans and a T-shirt, his beautiful face contorted in horror.

"Oh god," he whispers, his fingers twitching at his sides. "We've LYNKed."

I have no clue what that means, and it doesn't matter. Memories of my father being kidnapped taunt me, my skull about to crack from all the pounding. Everything I do next is by instinct. I suit up again, pulling the blue and gray nanotech BioSuit out of my cells, groaning in pain as it wraps around my skin, sinking its teeth into my flesh like cat claws.

"Wait, stop!" Sho says. I can see through my visor that he's suiting up too, but it doesn't look like he wants to. "If you don't stop—"

But I won't stop. Not until I get to the bottom of this.

I don't waste another moment. I digitize and jump inside Lily's phone.

9

"Why does the inside of Lily's phone look like Shinjuku Station?" I'm in shock. It's the only thing I can think to say.

Oh, the whole Digital World resembles a series of train stations, says Terminal. *None of us knows why. The prevailing theory is that Vint Cerf had a* not-so-mild *train obsession as a child. The internet's all about connection, after all.*

I shouldn't have asked. Maybe it depends on where you access the Digital World too. This is the nearest station to where I was in the real world. Shinjuku is the scariest train station I've ever been in. It's just so busy: a massive hub connecting five different railroads, taking people across the country. I always get lost, despite the millions of flashing overhead signs and the yellow paint on the platforms.

But this isn't the real world. I'm inside the Digital World.

And in this fake Shinjuku Station, nobody's here.

What the hell are these directions? I'm used to the yellow signs pointing me toward the Odakyu Line, the Marunouchi Line, and the Toei Oedo Line, toward different subways and train platforms. This time, internet service providers are written in black across the yellow paint.

Amanda, says Terminal. *We need to talk. Come to the East Gate. Don't get lost now. And bring your mysterious guest, will you?*

Guest?

"Amanda!"

Sho's voice causes a spark inside my skull. I grip my head, and before I know it, the BioSuit leeches back into my skin. I almost forgot I was wearing it. It's scary how quickly this suit starts to feel one with your flesh.

Wincing, I turn around. Sho's here in this empty station with me, standing in front of the silver automatic ticket gates. I see the last bit of silver recede into his skin as he stomps across the marble floor.

"You stole that Eggbreaker's suit right off her body with nothing but your bare hands. Law's BioSuit responded to your *touch*."

So I was right. The BioSuit Soldier who almost killed Lily was named Law. The big white sign over the conventional line gates is distracting. Instead of "JR Lines," it's IP addresses and server locations flashing above the metal ticket machines.

"It was like the suit listened to your command," Sho continued. "That's not possible, not unless you're a *special* kind of human." He doesn't stop striding forward until he's a mere breath away from me. "It's exactly as C.A.S.T told me. Amanda McKee—you're a psiot."

My throat closes. No one should know that word except the people who work for the Harbinger Foundation. Nobody should know I'm a psiot, the only one in existence. But Sho's smoldering brown eyes tear through my carefully constructed facade. I don't need to say yes. My fearful expression does it for me.

I stumble back on my heels and almost slip, only to be caught by Sho. For a moment, his expression softens. He's worried, actually worried, about me. I can feel sweat forming beneath my hairline.

Clenching his jaw, Sho steadies me on my feet and glares at the floor. "I've been taught that Amanda McKee was the first psiot discovered by Toyo Harada in the twenty-first century," he tells me. "She was a psionic technopath—that is to say that she had the power to communicate with machines, to control them, to manipulate microcircuitry with her mind."

Countless times, Harada's told me the extent of my powers—what I might be able to do one day when I quit playing Gossip Girl and start channeling my powers to their limits.

Sho searches my face. "Where I'm from, Amanda, your powers become detrimental to the human race."

My whole body contracts like it's going to combust with fury and fear. I hit his chest with my fists, snarling up at him. "Oh yeah? I'm the villain, am I?" I throw my arms out wide as if I could embrace the whole world. "Then go ahead! I'm Amanda McKee, the psiot. That makes me a monster, right? Drive a stake through my heart! Go on! Do it!"

Tears begin to form in my eyes because, for the first time ever, I'm starting to believe the world would be a less complicated place if Amanda McKee weren't in it.

Sho stares at me quietly. His hands are limp at his sides, his long fingers tugging at the loose strings of his blue jeans. It takes him a while before he speaks again. "Being a psiot doesn't make you a monster. I'm . . . I'm a psiot too."

My heart skips a beat. Sho looks at me earnestly.

I suck in a deep breath. "You're . . . a psiot?" But Harada said I was the only one . . .

Ahem! A very annoyed clearing of the throat followed Terminal's interjection. *I believe I can be of service in helping you untangle this rather unwieldy web of a mystery. Amanda. Sho. Come to the East Gate, please and thank you!*

The yellow paint on the marble floor begins to sparkle beneath our feet. Terminal is showing us the way.

With a sigh, Sho waves his hand down the hall. "Ladies first." He says it like being a gentleman is entirely foreign to him.

"Oh, *now* it's ladies first. Before, you were all, 'I'm going to *kill* you, Amanda.'"

"Will you just *go*?"

With a haughty *humph*, I swing around and begin to follow the bright path. It takes us through the halls and walkways of the empty train station, past the department stores with no shoppers, the bakeries with no yummy cream puffs, and the bus terminal with no passengers waiting to get inside.

I don't know what's more insane: being inside the Digital World, or the Digital World having a staircase that takes us down to a vast square. Nobody leans against the boxy white pillars, the coin lockers, or the green walls. The air is so lonely and chilly.

"Have you been inside the Digital World before?" I ask Sho beside me.

He snorted. "Me? No. I'm a Castaway. I live in the real world on solid ground—earth and soil. Where I'm from, only Harada's docile puppets come here."

Hearing him talk about Harada as if he were some kind of evil mastermind frightens me.

"You need a BioSuit to enter the Digital World," Sho continues. "I never had one until now."

He mutters that last part, causing me to narrow my eyes, confused. Sho suddenly realizes that he's talking too much. He shuts up. But I want him to keep talking. I want to know more.

"I wonder if my body is still in that alley, with Lily." Saying Lily's name makes my muscles seize. I hope she's okay.

Sho is reluctant to answer. But eventually, the fearful glint in my eyes seems to move him. "The BioSuit," he says. "A techno-organic device that supplies food, oxygen, and other resources to the body. But it can do more than that. With it, the wearers can turn themselves into data. Then their entire bodies leave the real world and enter the digital."

Almost instinctively, I grab my arms. They feel fleshy enough.

"The BioSuit is symbiotic, but not everyone can wear one. The haves and the have-nots. That's just how Harada, leader of the Harbinger Foundation, likes it."

"What do you mean by that?"

But he doesn't answer me.

I shake my head, looking at my brown skin. "Harada uses the Harbinger Foundation to conduct research to better the world," I say. The words slip off my tongue through years of rote memorization. It's what Harada always told me.

Sho's laughter is as biting as it is bitter. "What Harada considers a better world is a nightmare for everyone else. He's destroyed society. Community. He's destroyed humanity."

Why does he keep talking as if this has all already happened? I glare at him. "*One day Toyo Harada and Amanda McKee will destroy humanity.*" I imitate his irritatingly stone-cold voice, satisfied when it draws a scowl out of him. "What are you, a fortune teller? Can you see into my future?"

"Like I said, I can help with that."

We'd come directly to an information booth. The compact white cubicle is supposed to help passengers find their way through the labyrinthine station. There should be a worker inside. Instead, the unit itself springs to life, sparking with bright energy. Yep. This is Terminal. The Terminal I used to only see in my mind's eye whenever I contacted him through machines is right here in front of me. The black question mark painted on the front is exactly how I feel.

"Amanda! Welcome! I'm so excited to see you!" Terminal's voice is so sharp and clear now that we're this close.

Sho turns to me and points at him. "Why is this information booth talking to us?"

"Oh, I can take any form inside the Digital World," Terminal says. "I'm the *voice* of the Digital World, after all. Its will. Amanda's the first person in history to ever really communicate with us. When you were a child, you saw inside computers and devices. You peeked inside the Network. Now you've actually come inside the Digital World. Truly a special moment."

"But what *is* the Digital World?" I ask Terminal.

"A hellscape," Sho answers.

"An alternate world created by Earth's electronic telecommunications network," Terminal corrects with the slightest hint of annoyance. "A parallel world made up of data."

Sho steps threateningly toward the information booth. I don't know what he thinks he's going to do to it. "It's nothing more than Harada's soma to control the population. Privileged assholes strap on their BioSuits, digitize, and spend days, months, years in their own little corner of the Digital World, inside their castles, living out their mind-numbing fantasies."

"Not fantasies necessarily," replies Terminal. "Though, what constitutes someone's Digital Castle does depend on each person."

Digital Castle. I've accessed some psychically in the real world, just to get dirt on people and post it on my Livewire site. Really, I'd just contact Terminal and have him do it for me while I sit on my butt in class. Does this mean I can actually travel *inside* someone's castle here in the Digital World?

"Only psiots can use the BioSuits. Norms can't." Sho won't

back down. "Psiots live in the Digital World detached from reality, completely obedient to Harada and the fascist rules he thinks are 'helping' humanity, trapped in their own dream worlds. Meanwhile, norms are left behind in a dead world, a physically scarred planet uncared for because why care about the earth if you can just escape into a world of data?" Sho balls his hands into fists, a vein bulging in his neck that I think might pop any second. "We're Castaways, living in the worst conditions imaginable, having to do hard labor just to keep the Network's hardware functioning for the others. There's barely any food. Barely any resources left . . ."

Years of suffering paint shadows across his face. He bites his lip, unable to go on. His pain is coming from a real place. My shoulders soften as I start to see him trembling.

"Sounds harrowing," says Terminal. "Except: Nothing you've just described exists yet."

I frown, looking between the two. "What do you mean?"

"Nobody has ever actually digitized into the Digital World before today. And you: Matsuoka Sho—"

Sho lifts his head.

"A few days ago, you didn't exist. You had no digital footprint; therefore, no castle. But since you've accessed the internet and left traces of yourself behind, your very own castle has begun building itself. Should be done right about now. And like I said, one's Digital Castle is a reflection of their footprint—a reflection of one's self."

Sho looked away, his slender body shaking like it could barely contain the years' worth of pent-up anger that possessed him.

"One's internet activity can reveal a lot about a person," says Terminal. "But you babbling about a reality that doesn't exist yet just exposed everything I needed to know."

Terminal shakes as if it's laughing. The light sparkles around it like a halo. "Matsuoka Sho, you angry little boy you—you're from the future, aren't you?"

10

Yoshi was right: Time travel is real. If he were here, he'd be screaming with joy.

Sho is from the future. He's not denying it.

"The pillar of light," I say, my heart shuddering as I remember that beam splitting the heavens. "Was that . . ." I pause because I almost can't believe what I'm saying. "Was that you?"

Sho doesn't answer. His back is straight. He bites his lips, angry with himself, perhaps, that he couldn't keep the secret for more than two days.

"The world's telecommunication systems went haywire that very moment," says Terminal. "You punched a hole through space and time right into our world, young man! No technology we have in this century can achieve that. Humanity's probably at least three-hundred years away from creating the symbiotic nanotechnology you both have inside you."

"Three hundred years away?" I stare at Sho, wide-eyed from head to toe.

"Close, but you're off by a few hundred years." Sho folds his arms. "I'm from the twenty-seventh century."

My body stiffens as his voice echoes across the empty station. I have to fight to draw the words up from the pits of my churning stomach. "And you came here for me."

Sho's jaw tightened. "I-I came here to . . . to stop Amanda McKee. Y-you." But he can't even meet my eyes.

"And you brought those *things* with you," I snarl.

"No!" Sho whips around. "I didn't bring those Eggbreakers with me. They're *Harada's* soldiers. His slaves. They *chased* me here. You have to believe me." The way his round eyes flash makes it clear he's dead serious. "I never wanted to get anyone here hurt."

"Nobody but me, that is." My skin crawls at the thought.

Sho is quiet for a while, staring guiltily at the floor like a little boy being scolded. "You have to understand," he starts, almost sheepishly, but with a quiet, steadfast determination. "I was told by my superiors that Amanda McKee is the psiot whose powers inevitably help Harada produce the advanced BioSuit. Amanda McKee is the psiot who unlocks the potential of the Digital World." He looks at me. "Maybe not the 'you' of today. But one day, your powers will be responsible for humanity's future. Whether Harada forces you or you help him willingly: The world you and Harada create . . . by the twenty-seventh century, it's a hellhole." His voice dips, earnestly, sorrowfully. "That makes you humanity's greatest threat."

"Bullshit!" I stumble back, my black dress swaying against my legs as I cover my ears. "Okay, I'm a psiot. I talk to machines. But I'm just a kid! I go to school. I make videos faking an amazing life so people can be jealous enough to like and subscribe." I'm speaking so fast I barely have time to wipe the saliva from the corner of my lips. I look up at him, pleading. "I'm an *influencer*—an internet snake-oil salesman. I tell people how to look pretty on a budget. I'm not some evil mastermind!"

I hastily wipe the tears from my eyes because it makes me look weak. And even if that moment of weakness softens Sho, it still doesn't sit right with me. "You're lying." I shake my head. "You act as if my father's this evil mastermind. You're from the future. How am I supposed to believe any of it?"

"I'm not lying!" Sho stands his ground. Silent memories hollow out his face. "You and your glamorous life. Your rooftop parties. Your award shows. You have no idea what I've been through."

The weight of something I can't see bears down on him, causing his shoulders to hunch. His fingers twitch a little, though he doesn't seem to notice. As much as I want to deny his emotions, I can't. It's clear as day he's been through it.

"Ahem." Terminal clears his throat. Wait, does an information booth have a throat? The Digital World is very weird. "There is a way to clear this up. Remember, everyone with a digital footprint has their very own parallel pocket dimension in the Digital World: a Digital Castle. You didn't have a castle before you got here, Sho, but since you've time-traveled here and accessed our networks, you do. It's not finished, of course. The basement's all built. You start with the foundation when you build anything, don't you? Lucky for you, Matsuoka Sho, the basement—or, as I like to call it, the *dungeon*—is exactly where you need to go if you want to show little Amanda the truth about your life. The dungeon houses people's memories. Their secrets . . ."

Sho and I stare at each other as the keyboard connected to the kiosk's monitor begins clacking on its own behind the giant window. The monitor spits out two pink train tickets that float onto the ledge, ready for us to take.

"A paper ticket?" I tilt my head to the side. "In the *Digital* World?

"Don't judge how we do things here," snarls Terminal. "Humans. Everything has to always makes '*sense.*' Boring bunch."

Well, yeah, things making sense would be comforting right about now, but beggars can't be choosers. I turn my ticket over. It's all in 0101s, but I can understand machine language just fine. We'll be taking Train Number 103.155.232.229 to Matsuoko Sho's Digital Castle. It'll be leaving from the East Gate in ten minutes.

"You! Boy!" Sho jumps at Terminal's sharp call. "You said that, in *your* time, only the lucky few get to live in their own Digital Castles, dreaming endlessly. Castles reflect who you really are. Haven't you ever wondered what *your* castle might look like?"

With narrowed eyes, Sho closes his hand around the ticket. "I'm not interested in losing touch with reality. But if going to my castle will show Amanda how serious this situation is . . ."

We exchange wary glances, neither of us truly trusting the other. That's when a yellow path lights up beneath our feet once more, leading us away from the information kiosk and through the automatic ticket gate behind it.

"Well, then, get a move on," Terminal tells us. "But remember this: I don't know how advanced the Digital World gets in the twenty-seventh century. The fact that people other than Amanda can come inside here? Inside their own Digital Castles? Stranger still—according to you, Sho, in your century, these 'Digital Castles' are wonderful fantasy worlds. That's bizarre."

"What do you mean?" I ask him.

"Like I said, Digital Castles are based on your digital footprint. Therefore, they reflect who you really are. You can't control what's in it. You can only accept it as it is," explains Terminal quite seriously. "Sometimes what you see inside your castle can be distorted. Metaphorical. A little wild and a smidge creepy."

"Sounds fun," I snort.

"If in the twenty-seventh century, someone has figured out how to *manipulate* people's castles . . . if someone ends up being able to change a Digital Castle to reflect whatever they *want* a person to see . . ." Terminal sighs. "I think only a technopath can pull off something like that."

I narrow my eyes. "What are you saying?"

"Maybe you and your father really do warp the Digital World one day."

Sho is staring at me as Terminal trails off. I'm not taking either of their crap anymore. I'm getting to the bottom of this.

"Well, then, come on, rebel from the future." I brush past Sho, my heels clicking against the yellow path, my eyes on the automatic ticket gate. "We've got a train to catch."

A cutesy jingle over the speakers signals the arrival of our train. The doors slide open to a ghost-silent, chilly corridor. Sho and I exchange suspicious glares before stepping inside. Whoever's driving this train does *not* have time for our "petty" hesitation. The train takes off before we can even find a seat.

Outside the windows, violet and blue and yellow streak across a black void, as if the train has jumped off the tracks and launched into space. I take it all in, holding my breath, until a sudden jerk has me reaching for the ceiling straps to keep me steady on my feet.

Sho, on the other hand, stays balanced well enough in the speeding locomotive, like he's gone through some pretty sick training. He's watching the scene outside the windows in awe too, but when he catches me noticing his childlike excitement, his expression goes rigid. Playing it cool, he takes his seat on the red velvet bench, folding his arms like a regular haughty passenger waiting for his stop.

"You sure look comfortable." The leather strap chafes my palm. "Cool as a cucumber."

"Cool as a what?"

His bewildered expression catches me off guard. "What, there aren't any cucumbers in the twenty-seventh century?" I'm actually afraid of his answer.

Sho looks away, silent. Oh, this is going to be a fun ride.

I take the time to really size him up. His legs are long, like model long. Despite his sharp jaw and high cheekbones, the bones in his small face look rather fine. Sho could give Ryoichi a run for his money. Why he chose the life of a sci-fi comic book character, I'll never know.

"Law's BioSuit," he says, glancing at me. "Can you handle it being inside you?"

My hand squeezes the strap. Actually, now that I think of it, when I shut my eyes, I can sense it. The nanotech combined with my DNA. "Can you feel yours inside *you*?"

Sho shakes his head. "It melds with your body seamlessly until it's time to bring it out of you. Then you definitely feel it: the exoskeleton armor. The digital processing sharpening all your senses . . ." And for a moment, he looks almost worried about me. Maybe I hallucinated it. "These aren't regular BioSuits, you know. These are suits especially fitted for battle." And as I silently freak out, he adds underneath his breath, "Now that we're LYNKed, I might have to teach you how to use it."

"What? What did you say?" I look at my arms like there's a nuclear bomb in them. Wait, there basically is. "Can this thing actually hurt me?"

Sho clucks his tongue. "Stop flailing around. The suit is

dormant until you summon it psychically with your will. You're the human. You're in control. Never forget that."

"This whole thing is insane! The *BioSuit* . . . Whose stupid idea was this?"

I stop, my gaze meeting Sho's for one uncomfortable moment. I know the answer. I was *shown* the answer in the labs beneath Harada Entertainment.

Sho stares at the ceiling. "Regular people don't get BioSuits like these—ones fitted for battle. Only Harada's Eggbreakers. The one I have now, I had to steal from the Harbinger Foundation."

I flinched as he said my adopted father's name with such palpable venom. "Harada's . . . Eggbreakers . . ."

"Toyo Harada's vision for humanity is absolute. His fantasy of what the world should be is absolute. He insists that he's helping us live our best lives, and his enforcers make sure we don't dissent. In my world, you play by Toyo Harada's rules. Live like docile dolls, or—"

Sho stopped and shook his head. One thing Harada has always told me is how badly he wants to help humanity. *Help* humanity, not rule them like some dictator!

"How can my dad even be around in the twenty-seventh century?"

"BioSuits expand your lifespan. The same Toyo Harada born in 1933, your adopted father, provides the Earth with the single Network that connects people to the Digital World. Everyone is dependent on the Network, making Harada the most powerful man on the planet. Do you really think he wouldn't have a suit of his own—and the most powerful one at that? He's a king. Why wouldn't he dress like one?"

Helping people is the goal of the Harbinger Foundation. The reason why Harada has treated me more like a lab experiment than a daughter.

Still.

"That can't be." My mouth shuts the moment I realize no good arguments are materializing on my lips. I lower my head. "It can't be my dad."

The train begins to slow to a crawl.

Sho stands. "I guess we'll see, now won't we?"

The darkness outside the windows doesn't change. It only becomes more cold and dead. Both Sho and I are hesitant about getting off the train. But once the doors open—

"No!" I scream because it feels like the air is gripping me, sucking me outside into the night sky blanketing a dead earth. I kick my feet, finding nothing for them to touch, terrified that gravity will have its fun and drop me down onto the dead land covered in wires and the ruins of broken buildings. I can hardly take a breath; the air is so polluted.

Sho wraps his arm around my waist. My breath hitches. It's like he's trying to keep me from being flung around his memories. I feel like I'm trapped in the center of a tornado. It takes every ounce of will not to be swept away.

"I shouldn't have come." Sho stares down at the white brick forming a ring wide enough to contain a small city. But what kind of city is made up of thick black cables spiraling like vines ready to choke whatever life dares to grow? "I didn't want to have to come back . . ."

Static shorts out the world around us. We're in a ruined city at the foot of a long black tower spiraling into the gray sky. The Harbinger Foundation. The letters are written above the door—a secret organization out in the open. I guess because in the twenty-seventh century, there isn't any reason to keep it a secret any longer.

Dad . . . I shiver in the cold. *Is it true?*

I don't have time to think. Another short out and we're back in the sky. A force more merciless than gravity begins to fling us into different scenes, different moments.

The Digital World exists because of humans. I hear Terminal's voice echoing through the moonless, sunless sky. *It responds to human feelings. Sho, these are pieces of your memories. If you don't calm yourself—*

We're flung onto a playground covered in filth. This is the first time I see people, and it's horrible: men, women, and children huddled underneath a broken metal plate that looks like it could fall at any moment. Fenced in like animals. The gravel is warm beneath my feet as I stare, dumbfounded, through the fence. Sho slips his fingers through the fence holes and peers inside.

"This is where Castaways live," Sho whispers. "If you aren't a psiot, you can't physically survive wearing a BioSuit. If you can't wear a suit, you can't escape this broken Earth and live in your digital Eden. Harada couldn't care less."

Nearby the edge of the fence, children search piles of junk for something to play with. A child who looks remarkably like Sho is among them.

"Haven City," he says, though there's nothing city-like about this dumpster and certainly nothing in eyesight that would qualify it as a safe harbor. "It's off the books. Nobody here technically exists. Makes it a useful dumping ground for other cities that have trash—or people—they want to throw away."

Little Sho fights another child for what looks like an old truck shift stick. And before I have time to wonder if they still have trucks in the twenty-seventh century, a man walks up to them. A thick brown cigar burns in his aging, pale hands. He isn't like the locals wearing torn sacks and filthy makeshift tunics. He's in a fine black suit, along with his bodyguards behind him.

Sho presses his forehead against the fence. "It's gonna happen," he whispers.

"What's going to happen?" I grip his shoulder so he doesn't crumble into pieces.

"I'm here," the man says in a grizzled voice, drawing my attention back. His wrinkles deepen as he peers over at the children. "Where's the psiot?"

"Psiot?" The children descend into pandemonium at the mere mention of the word.

"Psiot!"

"Oh my god, there's a psiot!"

"I hate psiots!"

"Freaks!"

That last word is like an arrow piercing through my skull. Bull's-eye. Before I know it, I'm trembling worse than the boy gathered up by the bodyguards. They have some kind of metallic tracker in their hand, round and small. It beeps off the charts when they grab the boy.

"It's Sho! It's Sho!"

"He's been lying to us this whole time! Evil psiot!"

"Throw rocks at the psiot freak!"

Little Sho fights tooth and nail not to go with the men, even as the children start to throw stones at him. The man with the grizzled voice doesn't seem to care. He takes a drag from his cigar and puts it out on Sho's arm.

And while Sho cries, as he begs, his damaged skin begins to repair itself.

Sho's power. He can heal himself.

"Yep, he's the one, Prescott," a bodyguard says.

Prescott throws his cigar onto the ground and stomps it out with his expensive shoes. "Finding a psiot in Haven is like finding clean water," Prescott says with a filthy chuckle. "We'll start training him immediately. The only way to stand against Harada and his Network is to fight fire with fire."

As little Sho screams, the distressed Sho next to me turns his back and leans against the fence. "George Thomas Prescott." He tangles a hand in his hair. "A rich power broker who helps finance the Harbinger Foundation's military activities overseas. He recruited me into C.A.R.D."

Military activities. I clench my teeth, remembering that evil lair that wore its name proudly. The Harbinger Foundation. Scourge of humankind. This can't be real.

"The Castaway Active Resistance Division," Sho continues. "C.A.R.D's goal has always been to democratize access to Eden. Maybe Prescott resented the fact that he couldn't have his own slice of paradise as a norm who can't wear a BioSuit. But then, Prescott and his team of scientists started to think a little bigger."

Static shock. The scene changes. And when I open my eyes again, tiny Sho is in a small room that resembles a jail cell, rocking back and forth on a hard bed attached to the stone wall.

"It's all just energy," he whispers to himself, his trembling hands covering his ears in the darkness. "Fear is just energy." Tears are trickling down his pink, chubby cheeks. "Feel the wave and let it wash over you . . ."

I'm so alone . . .

Sho's voice. His true thoughts . . . blanket us.

Please help me. I don't want to be alone . . . someone help me.

Static shock. In the next second, Sho is a little older, his hair longer and shaggier. He's in a long white shirt, in the center of a sterile lab.

It certainly feels familiar to me: a child in the center of adults in lab coats, holding their tablets, writing down notes. I guess this is how us psiot kids are treated in every century.

The big screen at the far end of the oval room shows schematic plans for the inside of a building.

"Are you sure, Prescott, sir?" One of the men in lab coats

gives Sho a suspicious glare. "Sho's emotions are too easily swayed. He's too softhearted for this mission."

"And yet he's passed every test." Prescott balances the cigar on his lips.

There's a picture of me on the monitor screen. Sho blushes, then scrunches his face, half embarrassed at his reaction, half confused at what it all means.

"Your target, Sho, Amanda McKee. A psiot. The first psiot." Prescott scowls at me as if I'm a demon. "Your mission is to assassinate her."

Sho's arms fall to his side. He stands, limp, staring at my visage on the screen, his eyes wide with fear. "Kill someone?" His lips twitch. Fear hollows out his pale face. "Kill her? But she's just a kid! A kid . . . and a psiot like me . . ."

Prescott punches him in the face so hard he crashes onto the floor.

"What have we been doing for the past several years?" Prescott screams. "What have we been working toward?"

Sho's body begins to shake, but he grips himself, trying to stay strong as Prescott berates him. This isn't the first time this has happened.

"Your psiot power is unique, Sho." Prescott's voice is quieter now, the soothing balm meant to distract from the wound. "You're the only one who can do it: Project Rising Future. You're going to infiltrate the Harbinger Foundation. You'll steal and bind with the silver BioSuit: the Izanagi. Then—"

"You'll go back in time and change everything." It's the Sho next to me who speaks. His eyes are bloodshot. They match those of his younger self, feigning confidence and obedience, but bulging in terror. "You definitely made sure my body was ready, Prescott. Poking and prodding it. 'Don't call it torture. It's training.' Don't call it torture . . ."

He coughs and clutches his mouth. Blood seeps through his lips.

"Sho?" I gape at the red trickling over his fingers before being flung into another memory. The ruined city inside white brick walls. People lay down in the streets as if they're sleeping. At least, I think they're people. They're in slim white suits fitted to their bodies. BioSuits. Their design is closer to what Harada showed me inside his lab. They're smooth and streamlined to perfection. Rows of people lie next to each other, spaced apart evenly, their helmets covering their faces, making them anonymous and legion.

"You can't stay in the Digital World indefinitely," Sho says. "The body needs to recover. They come out after a few months, maybe years. Charge up and go back in."

Those are the only words Sho can speak before we're flung into another memory: Sho has successfully stolen the Izanagi. Inside his silver BioSuit, he's being chased by three Eggbreakers down a metal corridor. Law shoots her blue energy blasts like she doesn't care if the low ceiling collapses upon them. Sho dodges everyone.

I have to go back to the past. I can hear his tearful, frightened thoughts. *I have to kill Amanda McKee. Those are my orders.*

Kill someone. I have to commit murder . . .

Kill a kid like me? Can I do it?

I don't want to do it. I don't want to hurt anyone . . .

Duty and humanity battle each other inside Sho as he tries to survive the Eggbreakers.

Sho, Terminal's omniscient voice chides him, *you have to calm your mind, or this stroll down memory lane is going to get even bumpier.*

Static shock. Castaways in Haven are being rounded up by Eggbreakers. We're inside the fences now, but the sight is no less grim. A crying infant drops to the ground, his fall softened by garbage. As an Eggbreaker drags his mother away, she's still reaching for his little hand.

"Anti-Harada terrorist located," says the Eggbreaker, and I'd know that suit anywhere. It's the leader. The one in red and yellow armor, the one who kidnapped Harada.

The one called Livewire.

Even without the helmet, I can tell how cold she is, how brutal, as she drags the woman away from the crying baby. "Place her inside the camp," she tells the two other Eggbreakers with her. "Go through Haven and root out any other traitors to Harada's regime."

"Mom!" Sho begins to run toward his mother, but when that static buzzes, that intangible, unforgiving force flings us out of this memory and into another.

Standing inside a dark, circular lab, Sho takes a silver chip, as small as a phone's SIM card, from inside the supercomputer in front of him. He swallows it and the BioSuit comes alive, wrapping its armor around his body as he screams.

"The Izanagi," Sho whispers next to me, his voice his hoarse. "The BioSuit even the Eggbreakers fear. A suit with the ability to break the space-time continuum. Harada's crowning glory meant for only the self-professed Father of Humanity himself. I stole it." He laughs. "I did it. They said I couldn't. That I was too soft. Too weak . . ."

A crazed lilt slips into Sho's tone, but I'm not looking at either Sho anymore. I'm looking at the purple pods growing out of the walls like living spores. I'm looking at the fourteen-year-old girl floating inside them like a baby trapped in a womb.

"In a world where data is the key to life, Amanda McKee's psiot powers were too precious to waste," Sho tells me, without daring to look at me. "It was her psiot powers that discovered the Digital World. Her powers that allowed the production of the BioSuits. The Harbinger Foundation's wondrous resource. Harada cloned her and—"

"Stop." I turn from him, but Amanda clones surround me in this horrid lab. The video Sho sent me is nothing compared to the real thing. I can hear the spores pulsating, slurping with greed. I can see them breath, the veins bubbling across their surface rising with each exhale.

"This is disgusting." I shut my eyes. "Stop it, Sho. I want to leave."

We do and go back to the corridor where the Eggbreakers are chasing Sho in the Izanagi. The red Eggbreaker who nearly destroyed the Tokyo Dome grabs the back of Sho's suit and smashes him against the floor, but Sho breaks out of his grasp and smashes through the wall. He escapes into the open air, if you can call it air. The smog is sickening, but I'm breathing it in as I fly along with him, as he flees into the graying clouds crackling with lightning. The winds shift. The clouds part. The Izanagi's speed goes into overdrive.

"I'm the only one with a body that can withstand the jump," Sho whispers next to me, as if he's been told this a million times by Prescott and his scientists. "The target is Tokyo, Japan, in the twenty-first century."

I'm spinning, my body yanked alongside the Izanagi, so fast I'm going to throw up.

"My mission: To change the future. To save humanity." Sho looks at me. "To kill Amanda McKee."

And then Sho's hands are around my neck. His crazed eyes are bulging and wet with tears that drop down his cheeks as he tries to crush my windpipe. "I'm not weak, Prescott. I'm not. I'm not weak . . ."

With shaking hands, unable to breathe, I feebly grab at

his arms, my hands numbing as the pressure inside my throat builds. Sho is trembling. Tears are streaming from both our eyes.

Damn it! I warned that boy he could lose his mind in here. Amanda! Terminal cries as quickly as he can. *This is the Digital World. No matter whose dungeon you're in, this whole place is your domain. Don't forget* your *power!*

I don't want to be here anymore. The pain shoots up to my skull and down to my toes. My entire body buckles. *I don't want to be here!* I'm getting dizzy. The world's growing dark.

Izanagi disappears through a pillar of light with a thunder crack. Sho is crying. He's crying as he's killing me.

Eff this! With an unfathomable force of will bursting within me, I draw out the sleeping BioSuit inside my body. It sheathes me in gray and blue armor. Sho can't react fast enough. Now that this suit has combined with my DNA, I can communicate with it faster than a jump between neurons.

Teach me how to use you, I command, and it obeys. Before Sho knows what's happening, I lift my blue gloves and blast off his arm with an energy beam the color of clear sky.

He loses consciousness immediately. I grab his other arm to keep him from falling through the sky.

"Terminal!" I yell, panting heavily, each breath scratching my throat. "Get us the hell out of here!"

The train flies through the sky right on cue. I waste no time dragging Sho's body inside, and the moment we're in, it takes us away from Sho's accursed memories.

I keep my suit on just in case.

11

"So . . . um . . ." Back at the East Gate, in front of Terminal, I have Sho's left arm slung around my neck. His other one, the one I blasted off, has already started to heal. Blood isn't dripping from it anymore, like it self-cauterized. "Sho's going to be okay, right?"

"When you come inside the Digital World, you leave the real world behind. So if you die in here, that's it," says Terminal. "Though, with Sho's psiot powers, I bet he can handle a severed limb or two."

A golden door with a round top appears against the white plaster.

"You also don't want to stay too long in the Digital World for your own health," Terminal says. "Your body isn't used to it. I'd give you twenty-four hours, tops."

I stare down at Sho, but now that he's drooped over, I can only see the top of his head. I came here to find my father. What I found was a labyrinth of trauma so deep we almost lost ourselves inside it.

"There are two sides to every story, right?" I whisper, staring at my feet before snapping my head up. "Terminal, is my father inside the Digital World?"

"Yes," he answers. "With an Eggbreaker called—"

"Livewire." I press my lips together, my thoughts thrown into turmoil as I remember that yellow-and-red-armored woman tearing a mother away from her child. "Terminal, who is she?"

"No idea. She has no Digital Castle here. No digital footprint."

I have to talk to my father. I have to find out from his mouth what he intends to do to the future. To do that, I'll have to find him. And to find him, I'll have to defeat Livewire.

"You'll see me again," I tell Terminal as I begin to drag Sho toward the glowing door.

"Okay, but just a heads-up, little Amanda," Terminal calls after me. "The next time you go inside someone's digital domain, it'll be different. Memories, as hectic as they may be, tend to be real to life, but those are all stashed inside the castle's dungeon."

I look over my shoulder. "So what does the rest of a Digital Castle like?"

Terminal laughs nervously. "Well, you humans like metaphors, so . . ." He lets out a cough, like he's about to give a speech—or a cancer diagnosis. "It's like if you take someone's deepest, darkest internet secrets that reveal the weirdos they really are deep down and turn them into the strangest, life-size metaphor you can think of."

"You know what?" I turn back around, the golden door flashing in front of me. "I guess I'll just have to see for myself when I come back."

I walk into the blinding light, dragging Sho behind me.

Apparently, time moves differently in the Digital World. By the time I jump out of Lily's phone, Lily's still in the Shinjuku back alley where I left her. I've got no armor on, but Sho's got one arm and Lily's three seconds from fainting.

"Monster robots. Monster robots." Lily grabs her head. "With monster laser slits in their helmets for eyes and crazy superpowers and a real hatred for barbecue! And why is that boy from school here? Why does it look like he's only got one arm? Oh my god . . ."

"Help me get him somewhere safe," I tell her as the melanin in the poor girl's shocked face becomes ashen and gray. "Don't worry. I'll explain everything." Lofty promise to make when I can barely make sense of anything myself.

Limping out into the streets, I hail a taxi. There's only one safe place I can think of going.

I hope Lily doesn't mind.

My sense of time is completely out of whack. In my brain, it's, like, past midnight. In reality, it's only around nine thirty at night, and the African Snack Hut is packed. Lily is in a complete state of shock when we slip in through the back door and go upstairs to where the baby's crib awaits its owner, still marinating inside Auntie Bisi's pregnant body.

I toss Sho rather unceremoniously onto the bed.

"My god," Lily whispers. His arm is growing back. The bones are growing longer, the flesh weaving around the marrow to cover it. Lily turns away quickly, covering her face, and I have to give her the biggest hug to keep her from screaming.

"I will tell you everything," I promise again. "But we can't leave Sho alone. And I can't go home."

I take Lily's hand, and we sit in the corner of the room, the baby's empty crib in front of us. It takes me hours, but I tell her everything I know. I tell her about the Digital World. About Sho and the twenty-seventh century. About the Eggbreakers who attacked us. The BioSuits. Harada and the Harbinger Foundation. I tell her about my powers. My adoption. I tell her everything, and as I do, I feel the tension in my shoulders unraveling, my lungs slowly softening. So this is what it feels like to not keep secrets.

Lily listens quietly, but her expression hardens with each minute that passes. It's not like I don't notice, but I have faith as I confide in my friend.

"You saw me jump inside your phone," I tell her. "You saw the Eggbreakers on the rooftop. I mean, you can't *not* believe me."

Lily fiddles with her camera. "I do believe you," she says quietly as she turns the camera around and begins running back the footage she took on the rooftop. She captured it—the exact moment Livewire took Harada and entered the digital billboard on the other side of the street. "Toyo Harada is your adopted father." She scoffs. "No wonder you got that Hollywood role."

"Oh, I'm not doing that. I've got way too much to worry about right now."

"Like what?" Lily glares at me. "What exactly are you planning to do from here on out?"

That's a very good question. I draw my knees up to my chest. "I have to go back inside the Digital World. I have to save my father."

"God, this is insane!" Lily throws her camera across the room. It narrowly misses Sho's bedframe. "You want to save your father, who apparently ends up destroying humanity—"

"*Allegedly*!" I can't believe what I'm saying. After everything

I've seen, everything I've experienced, I'm still defending him. I'm in denial. I know it, but I can't stop it.

"Allegedly, your name is Amanda McKee, and you've been lying to me from day one!"

"I had to!" I'm losing her. Or maybe I already did the second I jumped inside her phone. "From the minute he adopted me, Harada told me we had to keep our relationship a secret. My powers had to be secret. And after I left New York and moved to Japan—" I press my fingers against my temples because sometimes it's the only way I can repress the memory threatening to bubble to the surface. "I didn't want to be Amanda McKee anymore."

"Why?" Lily demands. "What was so bad in New York that you came here and basically created a new identity for yourself?"

I think, in my heart of hearts, I always knew this time would come. You can only lie to everyone for so long, but eventually the artifice cracks, and you're left with the cold, ugly truth.

I wanted to keep this a secret forever. I used my powers to erase it from the internet. But if I'm going to win Lily back, I have to let every wall fall—including my firewalls. Everything.

I don't even know where my phone is. It must still be on the rooftop. So I ask for Lily's. Hesitantly, she places it into my expectant hands. I slide it on the ground a few centimeters away. I need to show her how this works.

"Okay, Lily's phone. Turn on," I order, and the phone does as I say. I didn't need to touch it. Lily's eyes widen as she watches me psychically flip through her apps.

I turn on her internet browser and go through her history. I guess old habits die hard.

"Wait!" Lily jumps to her feet when I get to her alt social media accounts, which reveal a very naughty fangirl life. And that potty mouth. Phew! She writes like a trucker. Not at all the nervous little mouse that squeaks in real life.

"You ship Sansa and Jon?" I frown. "Aren't they related or something?"

Lily wrings her hands together. "Stop snooping!"

I oblige with a little smirk, waving for her to sit back down, because she isn't the butt of this joke. I am.

I suck in a deep breath and draw out *that* video from the deepest recesses of the internet. Beneath the dark web. Beneath the nebula. I call it out from the depths of despair because Lily is the only friend I have, and she needs to know that I'm serious about keeping this friendship alive. I'm serious about telling her the truth.

Without touching the phone, I download the video I once buried and begin to play it.

It's a music video.

"'Karma' by Amanda McKee? Is that . . ." Lily crawls on her hands and feet to get closer to the phone. She doesn't touch it. Maybe she thinks it'll explode if she does. I sort of wish it would because I haven't seen this in years and thought human eyes never would again. "Is that you?"

It's the old Amanda, yes. The one with a desire to be a famous celebrity and a billionaire father who could make it happen. Harada usually had his assistants give me jewelry or something for my birthday. But for my fourteenth birthday, I wanted something different. Something spectacular. He had this irritated scowl when I told him, but he relented and said he'd make the preparations and get it done—if only I let his scientists take a few more blood samples.

"God, this music video looks so . . ." Lily leans in closer. "Cheap?"

A lot of money was spent; it just wasn't well spent. Wrong director, confused vision for the setting. As if this is penance for my lying to Lily, I force myself to watch as fourteen-year-old

Amanda McKee wears a funeral veil on a stranded island surrounded by shirtless male dancers in body paint.

I'm not the same girl that you used to know
You'd probably crap your pants if you knew just
how much I've grown
I'm a pretty young thing, I swear you'll regret it
I bet when you'll beg and say you didn't mean it
Don't cry now, it's too late
Don't whine now, I won't take your bait
My name is Karma, boy, and I'm coming
Coming for you-uuu*!*

Lily can't help it. She bursts out laughing. It's not a mean laugh—not the cruel, heartless kind that followed me throughout the halls of my old school after I stupidly dropped this video on every social media platform thinking it would launch my career in the spotlight. It's bright, innocent, baffled.

"You look so silly." Lily states the obvious after little Amanda starts awkwardly dancing.

Those Manhattan kids said something similar, but in a much meaner way, for weeks after the music video was out. They followed me around singing the song, doing the choreography in the school hallways. They made their own videos where they performed dramatic readings of the lyrics. It got so bad, I didn't see a way out unless I buried the video and left New York entirely.

"This is actually kind of amazing?" Lily picks up the phone and replays certain parts. "I mean, you look so badass! It's very goth."

I stare at Lily, not sure if this is some kind of trap, but as always, she wears her heart on her sleeve. She's completely serious.

"I never would have had the guts to do this." Then, with a little smile, she looks at me. "You really are kind of a nepo baby, aren't you?"

"I swear I'm never beating those allegations." I twirl one of my braids around my finger. "Though, according to Danger Boy here, I'm a nepo baby who destroys the world."

"Well, we can't have that."

Lily grabs her phone and shuts it off. Thank goodness. Silence pervades the room for what feels like a solid minute.

Then we just start laughing. Loudly. Crazily. I think we're both insane by this point, but if I've gone mad, at least I'm not alone.

I'm not alone.

"You literally talk to machines."

"I mean, I just did; otherwise, I wouldn't have discovered your passion for incest."

Lily's eyebrows raise. "*Fictional* incest."

"Whatever."

"But anyway . . . you're not actually going to doom humanity with your evil dad, are you?"

The room goes silent again. I sit up straight, crossing my legs. "Hours before the party, Harada showed me his plans for some new technology his company's making. It was the BioSuit. But he says it's supposed to solve world hunger and eliminate diseases. For as long as I've known him, Harada has only wanted to use the Harbinger Foundation to help humanity. But I can't deny what I saw with my own eyes."

Not just Sho's memories but my own. Harada willingly took Livewire's hand and let her drag him off the rooftop.

"I don't want to deny what I saw." I bury my head in my hands.

"Do you mean that?"

It wasn't Lily who spoke. I look toward the bed. Sho has

fully recovered. And now conscious, whatever murderous craze had come over him has dissipated into a thoughtful calm.

"Yes," I tell him, standing up. "I won't deny your memories, your past, or your pain. But I won't deny mine either."

I remember how tightly I hugged Harada when he said he'd make that music video. How tightly he hugged me back. And when I told him I wanted to flee to Japan, he filled out the paperwork and made everything happen as fast as he could.

He was a drill sergeant. A billionaire with a dream. A mentor. Sometimes he was a father. Sometimes he truly frightened me. Toyo Harada had more identities than I did. When I find him in the Digital World, that's when I'll know once and for all which Harada he truly wants to be.

"I'll find Harada in the Digital World, and I'll question him myself. He's my father. I owe him a conversation."

I thought Sho would respond with something sassy like, "Yeah, and *I* owe him a sword in his back!" But he said nothing. He opened and shut his mouth twice, thinking and rethinking his words. Then, without turning, he shut his eyes.

"I'm sorry, Amanda," he whispers. "I'm sorry. For everything."

Silence. I think of that lonely, alienated boy stuck in cold metal walls of C.A.R.D, forced to be part of a resistance mission only because of the miracle of his powers. The tears in his eyes when they told him he'd have to kill for the future . . .

"Relationships are complicated," Lily finally says. "And the future isn't set in stone. Now that Amanda knows what's going to happen, the future will already change, right?" She looked at me. "I mean, that's how it works, right? Like *Back to the Future* or something?"

Oh my god, that movie. Alarmed, I look at my hands. "Wait, am I going to disappear? Oh, this sucks!" I clasp my face. "I'm about to be zapped out of the timeline, aren't I?"

Laughter. This time not from me or Lily. *Sho* is laughing. A cheerful, childlike laughter I would have thought he'd be incapable of.

"By the way, you really can't sing," he says, sitting up and shaking his head in disbelief. "That yodeling could wake the dead. I was half dead, and it woke *me* up."

"I tried!" I protest with a flushed face. A couple of singing lessons count, right?

Sho swings his left leg over the bed. "Let's do it."

I narrow my eyes, still burning from humiliation. "Do what?"

"Go into the Digital World, find your father, and confront him. It won't be easy," he adds. "You got a good shot in back there, but it was just on instinct. You need to learn how to use the BioSuit. Wherever Harada is, I doubt the Eggbreakers will let us near him without a fight. They're probably in the Digital World now, guarding him."

I shut my eyes and psychically search for them. The technology of their armored suits lets off a specific frequency that's impossible to miss. I stretch my technopathic mind as far out as it can go. The Eggbreakers are no longer in the real world. They've gone inside the Digital World.

But I can't track their exact location. I can't track Harada either. Despite the fact that he's no longer flesh and blood, despite the fact that his whole body's been digitized into data, I can't pinpoint him. There are only hints of him scattered everywhere. As far as the internet can reach.

I can't figure this out alone. I can't get this done alone.

"So you'll train me?" I give Sho an earnest look. "You'll train me so I can get through the Eggbreakers and find my father?"

Sho's cheeks flush at my vulnerable, almost pleading expression. He shifts on his bed. "Yeah. I . . . I promise I won't kill him if you manage to get through to him as his daughter. If I'm certain he isn't a threat anymore . . ."

"As his daughter," I speak as Sho trails off.

"I'll help too!" Lily jumps up to her feet as well and pumps her fist in the air. "The three of us can do it." For a moment, she looks as if she knows she's gone insane, but hey, what the hell, right? "We can save the future!"

I slap myself to toughen up. "Yeah!" I nod and hold Lily's hand. We squeeze each other tight, a similar kind of fear and madness intermingling across our faces.

"Yeah." Sho whispers underneath his breath. He actually sounds hopeful.

He looks at the two of us, and out of the corner of my eye, I see that lonely little boy who once begged for companionship.

To be a psiot is to be used, feared, hated. To be a psiot is to be alone. I think both Sho and I are realizing at this very moment that it doesn't have to be that way. We exchange knowing glances, our eyes locking meaningfully before we both look away shyly.

Mission Save the Future is a go.

12

Now that he's dropped the whole "you must die, Amanda" thing, Sho at least seems to adjust to school life a little easier. It helps that he's willing to give this friendship thing a try.

Lunchtime typically sees the students of the Tokyo International Academy either running to the state-of-the-art cafeteria in the North Wing or staying in their homerooms to eat food packed from home. Because Lily's rushing up to me with the bags of Auntie Bisi's cooking in hand, I take out my earbuds, currently blaring "Give Me a Reason" by Utada Hikaru.

As Sho pulls up a seat, I give him one of the lunchboxes Lily's aunt packed. It's filled with jollof rice and steamed chicken. There's a little pack of chin-chin (bite-size sugar dough) we can eat too. His face softens when he opens the plastic lid and the heavenly smell of home cooking wafts up into the air. He parts his lips, like a child gazing at a treasure. The way he looks at me for permission makes my heart skip a little beat. When I nod, he tastes it.

And his eyes pop open. It's like Christmas.

"You people eat food like this all the time?" He swivels

excitedly between the two of us. "This food is . . . this is like . . ." He shoves rice into his mouth. "Like nectar from the gods! Thank you." He grabs my hand. "Thank you!" His eyes are wet. He means it.

Lily and I giggle as he practically inhales Auntie Bisi's cooking. I stare at him, amazed. It's like, since I saw his memories, since he shared his trauma with me, a weight has been lifted off his shoulders, if only a little. After everything I witnessed in his Digital Castle, it's . . . nice to see.

"What's this?" Lev, a giant from the volleyball team, looks over at us. "Our very own Matsuoka Sho has a bit of pep in his step. So spill. Which one of you is dating him?"

I throw a chopstick at his face. Dangerous, but warranted. How dare he even suggest it.

"By the way, Andy, Lily—you guys were at Harada Entertainment when the bombing happened, right?" says Hiromi, class president.

"Tell us the details!" someone else in class insists, but I brush them off with the finger.

Yeah, that's right. Harada Entertainment was the sight of a "terrorist attack" yesterday. Police and media are connecting it to the "bombing" at the Tokyo Dome two days ago.

Harada Entertainment's operations have moved to one of the outpost buildings in Shibuya. Meanwhile, the CEO of Harada Entertainment and main shareholder—Toyo Harada himself—is getting flack for choosing now to go on a business trip to Hawaii.

Hey, Harada is gone. His body isn't in the real world anymore. It's in the Digital World. This was the only story I could think of to cover it up. I made sure to use my technopathic abilities to fake the flight logs and business schedules—whatever information's publicly available. Can't have his enemies finding out the real reason for his disappearance.

I can't tell anyone from the Harbinger Foundation what's really going on. I don't trust them. But with Dad kidnapped and a dystopic version of Harada's technology currently mating with my DNA, I'll need someone here as a guide. And I know who would be good to consult.

Indeed, Yoshi was all for coming to TIA when I sent him an SOS text this morning. Still, I didn't expect to walk into the computer lab last period only to find Yoshi Sakaguchi acting as our brand-new interim computer science teacher.

"Hello, class!" He waves awkwardly inside the dim room flooded with computer screen light. At least he's combed his hair; it's in a little ponytail at the base of his neck. "Your regular teacher, Mr. Shooter, called in sick with a bad case of food poisoning, so I'll be filling in for the next few days."

"Food poisoning?" Nina Weisz scrunches up her face in disbelief.

"Yeah!" Yoshi's in a very ugly checkered sweater vest and a pair of khaki pants that don't look washed. "Don't play around with oysters if you don't have the stomach for it," he warns us with a laugh. "They're great, but the diarrhea. Phew!"

While every student makes a grossed-out face, his inappropriate laughter is cut off by the sound of his phone vibrating. Yoshi digs it out of his pocket and sees the text I sent him with my mind:

> Were *you* the one who gave him the oysters?

Yoshi clears his throat. "Um, anyway, I hear you're working on some basic programming. Good for you! I'll give you a few exercises to work through on your own. Just don't think you can sneak onto any naughty sites while I'm not watching!"

I don't think he actually cares what the students do, because as soon as he sits down at his desk, while students are clacking away at their keyboards, he's texting me:

I stopped over this morning and gave Shooter some very strong "tea." He'll be out for a few days.

You poisoned him?

I scrunch my face and look up from my phone.

Out of necessity!

He can't hide that sheepish expression.

Sighing, I send out another text:

Anyway, we've got more important things to worry about. The kid sitting at the computer to my right?

I flick my head in Sho's direction.

He's the silver BioSuit soldier from Tokyo Dome. He's from the future. Turns out you were right all along. Oh yeah, and I got my own armor now too.

"What?" Yoshi jumps out of his seat so fast the chair tips backward and clatters to the ground. The entire class looks up while he flails about. "Uh, sorry, it was, uh—" He pauses. "Um, an unexpected fart?" His cheeks redden.

He's not very good at thinking on his feet. As the students utter their disgust in whispers, Yoshi places his chair back on the floor. The next time he sees his phone, he'll find all our messages deleted except one new one I've just beamed over with my mind.

> I'll explain the rest after school so please stop acting like a weirdo.

Yoshi's shoulders slump over right at the moment another weirdo grabs my attention. I can hear Terminal's voice whispering to me from inside the computer.

Amanda. Little Amanda . . .

"Terminal," I whisper, drawing attention from Lily and Sho on either side of me. Discretely, they scooch closer. My computer goes dark, and suddenly text appears on the screen:

> The truth about last night's attack on Harada Entertainment has leaked. Or at least, some form of truth.

Sho and I exchange wary glances as the text disappears as quickly as it materializes:

> I thought the police and the media were running with that terrorist narrative?

My thoughts appear as text on the screen, responding to Terminal.

A lot of people were at the rooftop that night the Eggbreakers attacked. More people were on the streets below. The Eggbreakers weren't exactly subtle yesterday. That's going to make things more complicated.

"What does he mean by that?" Lily whispers next to me.

I don't know. But we have someone here who might help us figure it out. After the bell rings and the students file out of the classroom, Yoshi bumbles toward us.

"Amanda!" Yoshi can barely contain his excitement. "So I was right! Time travel exists! God, I'm so *good*!"

"This is Yoshida Sakaguchi," I introduce him while Sho and Lily shoot me a confused look. "He works for my dad at the Harbinger Foundation."

This quickly puts Sho on alert. I grab his wrist before he can round on him. "Yoshi is one of Harada's top engineers. You said you wanted to train me, right? He helped build the BioSuit prototype. If we're going to stop the Eggbreakers, we're going to need all the help we can get."

Sho's face darkens. "So you help bring about the fall of humanity, Yoshida."

Yoshi chokes on his next words. "Wh-what?" He looks at me, eyes wide. "Fall of humanity? What?"

"Actually, you're right, Sho." I shrug. "All this time, you had the wrong target. Kill him, not me."

"Excuse me?" Yoshi's nervous smile is frozen on his face. "Kill?"

Before Yoshi can prattle further, I tell him everything. Everything he hypothesized about the BioSuits was correct. He's smart. That's why he'll be helpful if I want to reach Harada.

"You want your boss back too, don't you?" I say, patting him on the back as he mumbles incoherently to himself in shock.

"The Digital World." Tugging his little ponytail, he walks over to a computer and begins clacking away. "You said part of the Digital World looks like the inside of a train station?"

"Yeah." I exchange a knowing glance with Sho at the teacher's desk. "With signs for network providers and IP addresses and stuff, instead of actual train lines and platform hubs."

"Hubs. Millions of devices worldwide are connected through the internet. Hubs act as connecting nodes that transfer data information between servers. You said anyone who's used the internet has their own so-called 'Digital Castle'? The inside of the Digital World is probably just mining data from unique IP addresses. But certain protocols specify how data is transmitted through channels."

Lily and I are lost. Only Sho, who doesn't know what a cucumber is, follows Yoshi's technobabble. I guess it's not so surprising, given how central internet networks are to his doomed world.

"Right now, Toyo Harada is data inside the Digital World." He pauses and considers it. "So how do we find him? Why *wouldn't* we be able to find him?"

He falls silent and starts typing for so long, the three of us gather around his computer. He's searching social media sites—multiple ones on multiple browsers—scanning for any chatter about the rooftop attack.

"You said an Eggbreaker took Harada."

"Livewire," I tell Yoshi, which makes his eyebrows raise.

"Um, isn't that your—"

"I know!" I yell, drawing stares from Lily and Sho.

"Well . . ." Yoshi tugs on his collar. "If Livewire knows about the Digital World and Harada, she probably knows about you and your powers. She told the Eggbreakers to spare you on the rooftop."

Lily nods. "Because she knows Amanda needs to be kept alive if she's going to help Harada complete his evil future plans with the Network and humanity living like zombies in suits inside the internet and—"

She trails off when she sees Sho stiffen.

"She knows Amanda will be searching for her father," Yoshi continues. "She knows Amanda can do it as a technopath. So she's gotta be extra careful about where she keeps Harada. And Harada's been digitized—his physical body has been turned into data—but you said hints of him are scattered along networks . . . Of course!"

He snaps his fingers, like goofy scientists do when they have their "eureka" moment. Lily claps for him politely but looks thoroughly confused.

"Why not hide him among other Harada-centric data? It's like hiding a needle in a stack of needles." Yoshi spreads his hands across the computer screen. There's a lot of talk about the rooftop incident. And, well, it's Harada Entertainment's rooftop, so Harada's name is being flung about on the internet. But there's one social media post Yoshi brings up. A post-and-delete that Yoshi's able to drudge up because nothing can truly be deleted off the internet.

> I saw that thing take Toyo Harada with my own eyes. He's been spirited away and we're all next. It's the end of days.

I lean in over Yoshi's shoulder. "Carmen wrote that?"

Lily reads the retrieved post. "I heard she checked herself into a hospital."

"I don't see how any of this helps us get to Harada," an impatient Sho interjects.

Yoshi swiveled around in his chair. "I don't know where Livewire's final destination is."

Neither do I. Though I remember Livewire promising to show Harada some brave new world: "The seed of tomorrow," she said. "She has a destination in mind for sure."

"And just like when you go on a trip, you plan your route. I mean, if you're going all the way to Toronto, you get your plane ticket, and then maybe you stop along the way to rest, right? And you have to choose the right hotel, because you don't want to choose one with low ratings, or bedbugs, or—"

"Okay, and?" I didn't mean to raise my voice that high. The memory of seeing my dad reach for that armored nutcase's hand has me on edge.

"Livewire is going to hide your father, currently data, where his data is most intense: social media chatter. You want to find your father? You've got to find out who's talking about Harada the most. Those are your hotels—or Digital Castles, to use Digital World speak. You can map out a route from there."

Sho places a finger on his chin. "It might work."

Lily claps her hands. "I didn't understand any of that, but we might as well give it a try!"

"Hiding a needle in a stack of needles . . ." I whisper, trying to shut out the look of elation on Harada's face as he flew off with Livewire into the Digital World.

Does he even want to be saved?

"We'll work on that," says Sho. "But you also need to work on your fighting skills. The Eggbreakers won't be easy to deal with."

Yoshi leaps out of his chair. "You've got to show me this . . . this future BioSuit armor you've conjoined with."

"Ew, don't say conjoined." I shivered. "I haven't *conjoined* with anything." I don't know why I add that, but I suddenly feel like I can't look at Sho in the eyes.

Sho ignores me. "Your body has probably acclimatized to the tech by now. Operating the BioSuit technology takes mind over matter. But now that we're LYNKed, you won't be able to suit up or fire a single blast unless you and I are on the same wavelength. When two suits LYNK, their suits become intimately connected."

My face heats up at the thought of "intimately connecting" with Sho.

"Um . . ." Yoshi lifts a gentle hand. "Can I see it?"

"See what?" I huff. "Us intimately connecting?"

Now it's Sho's turn to blush. "He wants to see us suit up. Why don't you try it?"

Lily readies her camera.

I shut my eyes. This BioSuit once belonged to Law. The police have probably confiscated her decomposed body by now. How did her body get that way in the first place? Is that the consequence of using the armor? I can feel it nestled inside me, a foreign invader. It feels . . . strange.

"I can't . . ." I try to draw out the suit, but the nanotechnology does not so much as budge. "I can't draw it out of me."

"Because I won't draw mine out of me." Sho looks at his palms. "I've adapted to the current situation. The mental training C.A.R.D beat into me so I can control the Izanagi is as strong as it's ever been. If I don't want to suit up, you won't. Whoever has the greater mental strength in a LYNK pairing is the one who calls the shots."

I grit my teeth. Having this armor inside me is bad enough,

knowing someone else is in *charge* of my armor-wielding pisses me off for some reason. I should be in control.

"Yeah, right," I grumble, and I try again. I'm the technopath. I am a psiot, the first known in history, according to Harada. This has been my identity for as long as I can remember. This has structured my entire life from the day Harada adopted me. This is what makes me special. This is why I'm alive. Where would I be if I hadn't been adopted? What kind of life would I have? No one is going to beat me at my own game.

I talk to Law's suit. I scream at it. I plead with it as my mind grows more and more frantic. It's not talking back. It had the nerve to loop itself around my atoms, yet it won't chat with me. I squeeze my eyes so tight my head begins to pound.

"Amanda." As Sho calls my name, he grips my arm. Strangely enough, by now his touch is somewhat familiar. Is that also a byproduct of that LYNK-ing thing? "Don't overdo it."

This is who I am. If I can't talk to machines, if I can't use my powers to find my dad, I'm nothing. I'm no one.

Warm liquid begins dripping from inside my nose, trickling onto my lips. It tastes a little salty.

"Amanda!" Yoshi and Lily scream at the same time.

Oh, it's my blood. I realize it before passing out.

13

This . . . looks like the nurse's office. It's the same coffee-colored walls and white fluttery drapes separating one sick student from the others. And the old-school ceiling fan swishing overhead. It's definitely the nurse's office.

To my right, Lily's sitting on my bed, holding my hand. Since all the curtains are drawn, I can see Sho sitting on the bed behind her, one knee up, the other leg dangling, watching me carefully. Yoshi tinkers with some kind of monitor that looks too technologically developed to be in a high school.

After asking it, the monitor tells me it's from Harbinger Labs. Yoshi had arranged some supplies to be brought over from the basement of Harada Entertainment.

But . . . "Why is there a needle in my arm?" I can feel the slight pinch from the needle that leads to a bag of clear fluid dangling overhead.

"IV drip," Lily tells me. "You really pushed yourself back there."

As Yoshi takes samples from underneath my fingernails, Sho watches, his face scrunched up with disgust.

"You seem far too comfortable poking around inside her body." He gets off the bed and draws closer. "The Harbinger Foundation. From the files I read, you treated Amanda McKee like a series of biological samples until you got what you wanted out of her."

Yoshi looks at me a little guiltily as he watches the monitor at my bedside.

"W-well," he stutters. "I mean, I'm new to Harbinger Labs, but my understanding is that Amanda, as the only known psiot in our century, has always offered herself willingly so we can learn from her powers and figure out how to use them to benefit society."

"And benefit society you did." Though Sho clearly wants to say more, he gives me a wary glance before quieting down. Like he doesn't want to upset me.

Yoshi doesn't seem to have the same emotional intelligence. "Now that I think of it, Amanda being the only psiot in the world in this century doesn't quite make sense considering how many psiots there apparently are in the future. Only psiots can use the BioSuits, correct? And pockets of so-called 'norms' in society are left in pigpen-like ratholes on a damaged Earth—"

Sho gives Yoshi a withering look, which makes him jump and get twitchy.

"I'm just saying," Yoshi continues. "Where did all those psiots suddenly come from? Are there normal people out there with the latent potential to activate their power? Is there a process by which they can be activated? Or are there more known psiots today, in *this* century? Considering Harada's goals, it's rather a tall coincidence that the child he adopted happened to be such a special little girl . . ."

Tall . . . coincidence?

"What do you mean?" Lily asks, instead of me, because my mouth suddenly feels sour and gluey.

"I mean, Toyo Harada, whose stated goal has always been to help people, to create the means by which humanity can evolve beyond its current form, to end war and famine. He just happens to adopt the only psiot in the world who can make that happen? I know he's my boss and everything, but isn't that a bit of a stretch?"

Memories bubble up to the surface without my wanting them to. Yesterday, when I was sitting at the megamonitor with Yoshi and Harada in the basement beneath the glittering facade of Harada Entertainment. Yes, facade, everything is a facade. Everything is a lie. What did Dad always say? You need artifice to cover up the truth. So what's the truth?

And now my head is spinning. I see several things at once: a teenage girl lying in a nurse's room turned Harbinger Lab having my flesh cut off and dissected. A child sitting in the center of a room full of butlers, her powers being tested. A BioSuit warrior using her newfound power to blow off Sho's right arm. I'm data and blood. I'm a baby without parents. A daughter with a kidnapped father. A spy. A girl. An influencer. A freak.

Memories haunting me. Memories rising up, screaming for blood and then falling silent again, hiding back in the recesses of my mind.

Harada is my father. No matter how driven, he's my father. He's the only family I've ever had.

And he took Livewire's hand willingly. He followed her into the Digital World.

Livewire? But *I'm* Livewire. I'm Livewire.

Everyone's calling my name, but all I can hear is the blood rushing past my eardrums. My heart is battering my rib cage, leaping up at irregular rhythms as if trying to escape my body through my throat. The worst is the strange electric tingling in my limbs and stomach. I feel like my whole body's been hooked up to a frayed electrical outlet. Or a Livewire. Ha! Hahaha . . .

"She's having a panic attack!" Lily cries.

"Oh god, I'm so sorry," Yoshi says. He says something more, but I can't bring myself to listen, not while my body is on high alert.

It's strange. I'm lying still in a hospital bed surrounded by people who, I think, only want what's best for me. So why do I feel like I'm being chased by a bear? Why is Harada's euphoric expression as he takes Livewire's hand swirling around so fast it's creating mirage images of itself just to torture me? My right hand begins to twitch.

My whole life.

Is my whole life . . . ?

A pair of large hands envelop my twitching fingers. "You're okay. The wave is coming, but you don't need to fear it. Let it wash over you."

Sho. Sho's voice is gentle and tender. It's wise and knowing. Compassionate. My mouth is open. A little bit of saliva drips from the corners. But I hear Sho. I hear him.

"This is normal. I've felt it too. You don't need to fight it." His voice is the only one that feels close enough to touch. "Because you're actually safe. So that wave that you're in, just let it wash over you. Let it wash over you and feel everything. All that energy. Feel it. Let your body do what it wants. Let the wave wash over until it passes. And it will pass. It will . . ."

It's what he told himself when he was a child locked up in the C.A.R.D facility. I remember. I remember all his sad memories . . . they almost make my heart beat faster, but Sho's compassionate, soothing voice calms me down.

It takes some time, but I'm finally able to close my mouth

and swallow my saliva. I relax my jaw. Whatever horrid energy was rippling through me has indeed passed. It's over.

And next to me, Sho still has my right hand in both of his. He's squeezing it tightly, taking Lily's old spot next to me on the bed, watching me with worried eyes.

"Everything . . ." Pausing, he turns away for a moment, his face flushing at his own kindness. But with a childlike innocence, he glances at me again and gives my hand another squeeze. "Everything's going to be all right," he tells me.

I must be insane because I believe him.

That panic attack was serious. I felt like I was going to die back there. But thanks to Sho, I can breathe again.

Now that I think of it, Sho's memories are a confessional. He never wanted to hurt Amanda McKee. Not really. I can still feel the pain of his contradictory emotions in the C.A.R.D lab as he struggled against his own programming.

I don't want to hurt anyone . . .

Could abuse, hatred, and desperation turn a kind boy into a killer? I guess, not all the time. Sometimes artifice is needed to hide what truly lies beneath. An obediently trained terrorist hiding a good heart, perhaps. I ponder it as I leave Lily and Sho behind to return to my dorm.

The dorm buildings are behind the school—one for girls, one for guys. There's enough space that every student can have their own room. I wouldn't have come here if I had to have a roommate. Hell, Harada wouldn't have let me stay in the dorms if there was a chance I'd have been sleeping in the same room with another person every night. The only psiot in the world needs to keep to herself as much as possible. Secret identities need to remain just that.

But like Yoshi said, what if I'm not the only psiot in the world?

Stop thinking about it, I warn myself. I don't want another panic attack. Sho isn't even here to calm me down. I remember his warm hand on mine and his compassion. And when my cheeks flush, I shake my head quickly, take in a deep breath, and push that fluttering away.

After changing into a pair of loose pink plaid pants and a white tank, I lay back against my fluffy, comfy bed, the pumpkin-colored bedsheets shifting against my back as I fidget around. Colorful flower sticker notes with reminders for homework assignments decorate my cream walls. Piles of textbooks on the desk to my right still need to be memorized. I don't need to bother with the remote control on the night table. I turn on the TV in front of me with a flick of my mind. I flip through channels, but my mind barely registers the images. I think of my father, who gifted me this TV, even though it was against school regulations. I don't want to believe that Harada is the monster everyone says he is. I'm not ready to.

My phone buzzes with notification after notification in my desk drawer. Was it always there? I thought I'd lost it on the rooftop . . .

No, wait, that's my second phone, the one for business inquiries. Maybe it's a reporter trying to get information on the rooftop attack. I walk over to the desk and pull out the drawer. I pick it up and check the texts.

Hello. Is this Andy-P?

I mean Andrea Porter?

This is Andrea Porter, right?

Sorry for bothering you. This is Ryoichi.
I got your number from a friend.

I can't feel my hands. The phone almost slips out of my grip. Chiba Ryoichi, the actor?

I just wanted to see if you were alright
after that incident at the party.

This could be a trap. A prank call. Reporters can do anything to get a celebrity's number and pretend to be anyone. So can stalkers. I can still remember the hatred of all those fans at the Valiant Pop Awards when we dared to stand next to each other.

But what if it's really him? Can I pass up this opportunity?

Tentatively, I dial the number.

"Hello?"

I've watched enough of his dramas to recognize the voice on the other side of the phone. I can't believe it. It's him.

"H-hello." My knees buckle, and I collapse onto the chair at my desk. "I'm Amanda—I mean, Andrea Porter. Andy-P, the influencer?"

Ryoichi goes from suspicious to lively in a flash. "Andy!" He perks up immediately, forcing a quiet sigh out of me. He sounds so young and sweet and innocent. But soon his tone turns serious. "Andy, are you okay? I've been wondering if you were okay ever since the . . ."

Ever since the rooftop attack. He pauses, because how can anyone say it?

"I'm all right," I whisper, but when I shut my eyes, I see my father flying off with Livewire.

"Hey, Andy . . ." He trails off. "That night . . . you saw

them too, right? Those . . ." He searches for the right word. "Monsters?"

What do I do? Would it really work to lie to him? He knows what he saw. If I lie, I become part of a conspiracy. Or I become some evil witch trying to gaslight him into thinking he's gone insane. Plus, it's Ryoichi! I can't lie to *Ryoichi*.

"To be honest, I'm not sure what's going on," I lie anyway. "I'm still processing." That isn't a lie. I lean against the back of my chair. "And I kind of want to forget it ever happened." The biggest truth I've told today.

Ryoichi sighs. "Might be better that way."

"I highly recommend it."

"Then I'll take your advice." He laughs softly. "I mean, the police are handling it. They'll get to the bottom of it."

He falls silent for a long time. I can hear him breathing, and in those breaths is a struggle for peace. Wrestling between what you know to be true in your heart and what you want to believe is the worst kind of pain. I should know.

"Bye, Ryoichi. Try to get some rest," I tell him before almost shutting off the phone.

"Wait!" Ryoichi's voice stops me through the speakers. "The offer I made that night. It still stands. The yakiniku restaurant, I mean."

My stomach flops. With all the mad events I'd been bludgeoned with, I forgot the maddest of all: Ryoichi asking me out on a date.

"I think we can both use it," he insists. "How about it? I'm free next Sunday at eight o'clock."

My mind's gone blank. All the blood rushes from my head as I stutter, "Y-yes."

"Great!" Ryoichi sounds somewhat triumphant, and maybe a little overconfident, but maybe that's just how some guys are.

"Sunday at eight o'clock. Ask for my private room. I'll send you the address."

As soon as the phone goes dead, I shove it back into my drawer with shaky hands and try to relax. I watch TV for a couple of hours—anything from variety shows to dramas to the shopping network. But I can barely get any real rest, not without my heart pounding from excitement, from fear, from confusion, over how bizarre my life has gotten in the past week.

Well, *stranger.*

By the time the sun has gone down, I'm somehow fatigued and wired at the same time. I stare listlessly out the window, watching the trees in the night sky. If my body won't let me sleep, I might as well get work done.

I access the Digital World through the Wi-Fi. Dumping Yoshida's theories onto Terminal doesn't seem to bother him. In fact, Terminal was, apparently, thinking along the same lines.

Right now, social media chatter about Harada is at an all-time *high.* I see a clunky digital cutout of Terminal's kiosk on the black TV screen. *But the Digital World also responds to emotions—as you saw when you entered Sho's dungeon. Poor boy.*

I shivered. His trauma and heartache wouldn't be so easily forgotten.

Those who were on the rooftop that night—who saw Harada get kidnapped by the Eggbreakers—are chatting about it with family and friends in their private group chats. Or they're writing about it on secret social media accounts. That will likely be where Harada's being hidden for the time being. The Eggbreakers will jump from Digital Castle to Digital Castle, hiding him. They'll move through the Network only when necessary. If you're going to catch him, it'll be in those castles, not on the rails. I'll map out a route for your journey ASAP.

"But where are they even taking him?" I lift myself up.

"Livewire told Harada that she'd show him 'the seed from which all life in the Digital World sprouts,' or some crap like that."

The Seed. Terminal sparkles as he says the word with a kind of reverence. *Ah, so that's it.*

"What's it?"

Some beginnings are mysterious, little Amanda, says Terminal. *Some say the Big Bang created the universe. Well, it's the same for my world. The Seed is the beginning. That first energy spark that burst from the Seed created the Digital World. It was the beginning of all life here. 1983. When all networks were combined with a universal language. The humans of the* so-called *"real world" unknowingly gave life to the Digital World when they created the Transfer Control Protocol, or the Internetwork Protocol. They wanted a tool to facilitate connection and information sharing. They wanted to find a way for computers to be able to talk to each other.*

"The internet," I say, with a nod.

When human beings created the internet, they ended up accidentally creating a world parallel to their own, one that exists within these "talking computers." A parallel universe made of data, where information hubs are connected by lines of transit.

Well. Maybe that explains the trains.

Terminal continues. *The Digital World is a parallel universe that spans the globe. If you were to take a map of my world and superimpose it onto yours, all that would change are the names written on the countries.*

I'd probably see a lot more IP addresses on that map. And internet service providers. Just like in those train stations.

The Digital World is a parallel universe, and its living, breathing heart is the Seed. I remember those early days when the Protocol first turned on and the Seed was created, like a flaming star bursting into existence. Like a sun being born. It felt like a switch was turned on.

"And any switch that can be turned on can also be turned off."

Sho's voice from my now open window nearly makes me swallow my own tonsils. I watch in shock as he climbs through and lands silently on the fuzzy red carpet.

"What the hell are you doing here?" I almost scream, then remember that if anyone outside hears and comes inside, I'll be double dead. "Why aren't you in the boys' dorm? When did you even open my window? How did you even get here?"

"I climbed." Sho shuts the windows and draws the curtains.

"My room is four floors up!"

"I know." He checks out my room, taken aback, judging by the look on his face. "This place is, uh, colorful," he muses before clearing his throat. "Terminal." He gets right to business. "What happens if the Seed were ever to be destroyed?"

Destroyed? Now it was Terminal's turn for incredulous yelling. *Perish the thought! The Seed still exists, somewhere in the Inner Sanctum, the very center of the Digital World. If it's destroyed, it'll be the end of us. The end of the internet. The end of human society as we know it.*

"In my time, Harada is well aware of that," Sho says, leaning against the window. "The Blackout. Thanks to his harvesting of a hyperadvanced version of Amanda McKee's powers, he holds the kill switch and uses it as a twisted, authoritarian deterrent to his power. Why do you think it's been so hard for anyone in the world to go against him?"

"Harvesting . . ." Thinking of those Amandas inside the purple pods, I draw my knees up and wrap my arms around them. "You think he's being taken there? To the Inner Sanctum?"

Very likely, yes. Maybe that Eggbreaker wants to show the Harada of today what's possible if he continues on his relentless track toward creating and perfecting the BioSuit.

"But he was going to create them anyway!" I say. "Why kidnap him?"

"Because I changed things." Sho looks down at the floor as he answers, his eyebrows furrowed. "I came back in time to make sure that future never comes to pass. Maybe the Egg-breakers felt that they needed to take drastic measures to keep the future on course."

"Great." I let out a frustrated sigh. "Well, it's good to know that my dad is a bona fide supervillain complete with a kill switch that activates a societal nuclear bomb."

I can't help it. I bury my face in my knees. I can hear Sho calling me softly, hesitantly. But I don't look up. I can't. This isn't happening.

The journey to the Inner Sanctum isn't a quick little trip, says Terminal. *It could take months inside the Digital World. For every one hour in the Digital World, one second passes in the real world. You have time to prepare here before going inside to find your father.*

There's time to save my father. Time to find out if he really should be saved.

You'll be jumping from Digital Castle to Digital Castle to get to him. I'll find shortcuts along the path so you can catch up to your father in time. It'll be a bit tricky, but I'll figure it out. Especially now that I know to look for Harada's data traces.

Terminal must have thought this would make me feel better. It didn't. And when I don't look up, he lets out a nervous chuckle that dies in his digital throat.

Okay, then. Cheers! He waves. The television goes dark.

Eventually, I hear Sho shuffling toward the television screen. "So," he starts in such an awkward tone of voice, I would have laughed if I didn't feel so crappy. "This is your . . . room," he says again, clearly because I can't think of anything else. "Lots of personality."

"Well, don't you have an eye for decor," I mumble into my knees.

"My room in C.A.R.D.'s secret training facility is pretty plain. White walls. Small. Lonely." He trails off.

"Loneliness is the worst, isn't it?" I whisper.

He pauses. "Yes. Yes, it is."

I finally look up. Facing my closet, Sho breathes in, so deeply, I can see his well-toned chest rise and fall from behind the white T-shirt.

"The air's clean in here." He sniffs. "Fruity."

My lips quirk into a smile. "That's the mango air freshener." I flick my head toward the plug-in next to the window.

"So this is Amanda McKee's world," he whispers to himself and stands there, staring at the plush dolls on my shelves, and the books on my desk and the stray dirty clothes on my fuzzy carpet. He looks like he doesn't know what to do with his arms. He suddenly looks a bit panicked.

"Sho," I say and then blurt it out all at once: "You wanna watch some TV?"

"What?" He blinks, eyes wide, like he's caught between two different worlds—mine and his haunting memories.

I turn on the television and begin flipping through channels. "Oh, this is a great drama. It's about a high school delinquent who falls in love with a blind girl. I think it's a rerun."

Sho really looks like a deer about to be shot by a hunter in the midst of all this peaceful girly fluffiness. Since I'm feeling strangely emboldened by this, I slide off my bed, and before I second-guess it, I grab his arm and pull him onto the bed with me. Totally innocent. Both our backs against the red headboard.

Totally innocent.

I shove the apricot pillow between us. It doesn't slow down the suddenly quickened beating of my heart. But I'm not the only nervous one. Sho goes from placing his arms behind his head to stretching his right bicep. Then he clears his throat, leaving his hands on his lap. They're veiny and stiff as stone.

"Do you think this is easy for me?" says the male lead of the television drama, grabbing his much shorter costar by her shoulders, gently but firmly. "You have no idea, do you? How different my life was before I met you. How I was wrong about you! How you changed my life!"

I turn up the volume, but Sho isn't watching. He's staring at me and not so sneakily either. He's sizing me up. Studying my face. Does he not realize I *know* he's staring? Looks like C.A.R.D. didn't teach social skills in that training facility.

"You said if I'm going to use my BioSuit," I say to break the tension, "then I have to be mentally strong. And we have to be on the same psychological page."

"That's right."

Sho's voice is velvety soft. Like back when he talked me down from my panic attack.

"How do we do that?"

"Face me." Sho begins to shift ninety degrees toward me on the bed. After an inconspicuous gulp, I do the same thing. He holds out both hands for me to take. I wipe mine on my plaid pants before taking them.

The touch of my hand actually makes him flinch. The tiniest blush appears underneath his eyes. He swallows and clears his throat before relaxing his body.

"I'd always imagine the sound of rain when I needed to focus," Sho tells me, looking right in my eyes. I try my best not to look away. "Not the smell. Whenever it rained in Haven, it would hit the piles of trash, and the chemicals would release this spicy ammonia that corroded the inside of your nose. But I still remembered the sound. The patter."

"I guess the pattering of rain sounds the same everywhere."

Like the night after one of the students at Valiant Middle School, John T., recreated my music video, "Karma." He went the extra mile: bought a wig, did the terrible choreo, released his own parody video on social media platforms. All to become the jokester king of our class, at my expense. I responded the only way I knew how. I used my psiot powers to uncover that his congressman dad was cheating on his mom. The man was even hiding a secret love child in the Bronx. I released all of it on social media. I sent it to news outlets. John went from jokester to joke in under a weekend. And he never went to school again.

He overdosed a week after that.

The guilt of it all nearly killed me. But when I told Harada, he patted my head.

"You're controlling your powers very well these days," he told me. And he had the butlers take me out for funnel cake.

But the guilt never went away. It shrieked at me, told me I was a monster. That, one day, people would die because of my powers. That I was a freak.

Harada told me differently. If not for that, I would have learned from what happened to John. If not for that, I wouldn't have created Livewire.

Livewire, a mean-spirited social media page designed to bring humiliation and ruin to people I don't like. Maybe it still exists in the future. Maybe the Eggbreaker who kidnapped Harada saw it in the internet archives and got inspired.

"Amanda? Are you . . . crying?"

I am. The tears are streaming down my face, my head hanging low so Sho can't see them. We were talking about rain, so I figured I'd give a demonstration. No big.

I'm a terrible person. No big.

I ruin humanity's future just like I ruined John's. No big.

I swallow my tears, surprised to feel Sho's hand around the

back of my head. It hesitates there for a moment before pulling me in. He lays my forehead against his cheek.

"The trick to using the BioSuit is easy," he whispers. "Let your mind do what it wants and accept whatever you find there. Fear. Anxiety. It's all just energy. Once you realize it can't hurt you, you've got your control back. Learning that is the only reason I'm alive today."

Is this a piece of advice given from monster to monster? Human to human? I don't think we're either at this point. But in this moment, it's enough.

"You need to overcome your fears. And you do that by allowing yourself to feel it," Sho continues. "So? What are you scared of the most?"

A heavy question. I take my time answering it. So many faces, human or otherwise, flash across my mind's eye. Only one sticks around.

"Amanda McKee," I answer.

Sho doesn't respond. The drama goes to commercial.

14

Running, jumping, squatting, meditating. This must have been how Rocky won that match. Over the next few days, Sho has me using the school facilities to the fullest.

"You're going to need to build up your stamina," he tells me on the track field, while somewhere the girls' soccer team is doing drills. I just know I'll be doing drills by the end of the day. I run miles. I sweat more than I have in years. Whenever I complain, he laughs. Not mockingly. It's a bright, boyish kind of laughter. His eyes twinkle a little too. He's having fun watching me flail around. Well, I don't blame him; I *am* adorable. But this is *not* fun.

Sho even becomes a member of a sports club—wrestling—so he can borrow Gym 3-A after practice and use the thirty-eight-by-thirty-eight-inch mats while on "cleanup duty."

"I've been trained in most of the fighting styles that were around in the twenty-first century," he says in black shorts and a white T-shirt with the school's logo on it. I'm glad he opted out of the silly bodysuit singlets, but I think those are reserved for official team matches.

"Just a quick question—and humor me for a second." I tug my orange-red shorts. "How long did it take you to learn all these styles of combat?"

"Eleven years," Sho taps his feet on the blue mat.

"Right." I fold my arms. "And you expect me to master all of them in—wait, how much time do we have before we dive back into the Digital World?"

"I'm not expecting you to be a master in anything," Sho says with a little smile. "You need to get used to moving. Maneuvering in the BioSuit is going to take strength, endurance, and stamina. You need to build what little you can before we go back in."

Right. And we did have time after all. In the Digital World, it took months to travel to the Inner Sanctum. We could spare a couple of weeks for training.

And Sho's training is brutal.

"Ow!" I scream when he flips me over on the wrestling mat. He forces me to memorize judo moves. He takes me through each sweep of the feet, grabbing my hands, my arms, holding me close to his chest. I can feel every sinew of his muscle. On the second day, after flipping me over again, I sweep my foot underneath his, and he falls on top of me. I smirk, looking up at his surprised expression. Then my cheeks feel hot. His heavy body is on top of mine, our faces close. Sweat drops from Sho's hairline down his flushing skin as he loses himself in the moment—but just for a moment. Boosting himself off me, he gives me his hand and gently lifts me to my feet.

It's like that day after day. Hot bodies touching. The more I notice how strong his arms are, the more grateful I am to Lily, who brings me a steady supply of ice packs from home. I need to cool down.

"You really are out of shape," Sho laughs after school one

day on the field as he watches me twitching on the grass. I was right about those soccer drills. Lily rushes in with another set of ice packs.

"Being a beauty influencer does not involve this level of physical activity," I say, rolling onto my back while Lily hands me a pack.

Sho leans next to me. "A beauty influencer?" His knee is close to my left arm. His hair dangles in the air as he hovers over me. "What's that?"

For a half second, I'm distracted by how pretty his face looks, shaded from the sun. Then, catching myself, I stare at the stands on the other side of the tracks.

"Her job," Lily tells him instead of me. "She goes online and tells people how to be pretty."

Explaining it like that makes me feel incredibly shallow and ridiculous. But Sho only laughs, grabs my chin, and shifts my head back and forth. It makes my heart flutter. Lily watches us both, suspicious.

"Sounds like a fun job," he says casually before standing. "Come on, get up. We're going for a run. A mile."

My legs weep in advance.

"Wait a minute!" Lily, who seems a little too excited to be a bystander to all this, rocks on her heels. "You guys are LYNKed, right? Which means you need to be mentally in sync to get the most out of your BioSuits?"

"That's right," says Sho.

Lily's eyes flash with mischief. "Okay, so how about this? While Amanda's resting up, why don't you tell each other one of your deepest, darkest secrets."

"This is not a slumber party," I whine, flailing on the grass.

Sho especially looks taken aback. His forehead immediately turns beet red.

"Oh, come on." Lily sidles up to us, hands behind her back. "You guys have to get close. Your closeness is key to defeating the bad guys, right?"

She's enjoying this. I snarl at her from the ground.

"Fine," I say as the lactic acid colonizes my body. "One time, in New York, I played a tree in the school production of *Sleeping Beauty* and peed my pants laughing because one of the dwarfs kept getting his lines wrong." I glare at her. "How's that?"

While Lily deflates and makes a disgusted face, Sho scratches the back of his head and turns around. Looks like he's laughing a little himself. Once he's out of earshot, Lily sits down next to me.

"You know, I was trying to give you guys a moment to get closer," she scolds me while lifting me up into a sitting position. "Like, actually closer. You think a story about peeing your pants is going to do the trick, Andy? Really?"

We've been in full-body contact since training started. He's touched me more in the last few days than I've ever been touched by a boy. How much closer do we need to be?

"What should I have said?" I ask, squirming a little. I blush, thinking of him on top of me on the wrestling mat. Then again, when I think of his hands on mine, that night we sat on my bed. I still haven't told Lily about that one.

"Something like this." She leans in close and whispers in my ear, "Yesterday Sho told me a secret. When he first saw your picture in that training facility he was kept in, he thought you were really pretty."

My mouth opens and closes, but no sound comes out. Then I shake my head.

"You busybody," I tell Lily, pushing her away before my heart could beat too fast.

Busybody doesn't even begin to cover it. By the end of the day, Lily reveals her evil plan to "get us close."

"A date?" I spit out my banana milk as the three of us sit on the ledge of the stone fountain in the quad. Lily grins evilly as the camellias and azaleas sway in the breeze.

"You know, when two people go out together and have fun." Lily explains it with her hands as if I need a diagram. I give her a push. "Come on, you two. Go out into town on Saturday. Alone. Have fun! I won't follow you with my camera, I promise!"

She looks like she really wants to.

A beat of awkward silence follows as Sho and I clearly think it over. And when I realize that we're both actually considering it, I spit out a wild "no way" at the same moment Sho says, "Why not." The two of us look at each other, both rigid, both awkward, until we look away.

Maybe it's because I'm staring at my feet that I don't react fast enough to avoid Lily. She puts me in a headlock and squeezes.

"You two are going on a date. You're *going*."

I suddenly am not surprised at all that Lily is as vicious a fangirl as she is online.

"Okay, okay!" Sho puts his hands up as if to stay a wild beast, which, well, a Jon and Sansa fangirl kind of is. Once she lets me breathe again, Sho and I shift uncomfortably, avoiding each other's gazes while Lily pumps her fist in the air, triumphant.

Saturday comes with much anticipation, but not because of the date alone. Sho has us break into the school gym that chilly morning. The locks are automated, so it's easy enough for me to mentally pick. I shut off the CCTV too. Yoshi meets us with a bunch of tablets and inconspicuous medical equipment to measure my process. Lily comes for moral support, with snacks from her family's restaurant and her camera at the ready.

The gym is big enough to hold two BioSuit Soldiers. Can it handle our hand-to-hand combat? Well, we'll see soon enough.

"All right, Amanda," Yoshi says from the bleachers at a safe distance. "We have your real-time biometrics locked in." He waves the tablet I've given access to my brain waves through a bit of technopathic parlor magic. "We'll be monitoring you from here."

He's set up a trolley by the side of the bleachers with every heart medication I've ever been prescribed. I've heightened his tablet with my abilities, hyper fine-tuning it to be able to monitor the electrical activity of my heart from a distance. Lily's face is obscured by her camera lens; though every once and a while, she peaks over, nervous.

I pull my eyes away and concentrate on Sho.

"Remember your breathing," he says, standing several meters away from me. "Close your eyes. Are you ready?"

"Yeah." I stomp, biting the skin off my lip, waggle my arms, and relax.

The others are quiet. Only Sho's voice echoes across the high ceiling of the gymnasium. "Exhale first and count to four," he tells me. "Hold it. Keep your lungs empty for another four count. Then inhale on a count of four. Hold it. Repeat the cycle three times."

I do. Thoughts chase me in the darkness. Harada, lost in the Digital World. Is he safe? Is he even still alive? Is he thinking about me at all?

That question leads me to a memory of my childhood. The kids in my expensive, extra-exclusive preschool who made fun of my kinky hair. And when I cried and told Harada, he had no interest, no empathy. "Who cares about your hair?" he'd told me with a disgusted look on his face and ordered some maids to take care of it.

"You can't control your thoughts," Sho tells me. "Just observe them. Listen to the prattle, but don't get sucked into it."

That's right. I watch each image without judgment behind a looking glass. I keep my breathing steady.

"Are you ready?"

I nod without looking at him. "On three."

The nanotechnology in my body stirs.

"One," Sho says.

"Two." My heartbeat is steady because somehow I know his is too. Sho is a psiot like me. No matter what horrors he's been through, he's survived it all. And if he survived . . .

"Three!"

I can survive.

Law's armor rips out of my flesh like an alien lifeform and wraps itself around me until I am sheathed head to toe in the gray-blue-streaked BioSuit armor. I hear the clattering of Yoshi's tablet as it falls upon the bleacher bench. The clamor is so sharp. Lily's breathing sounds heavy, even though she probably can't hear it herself.

I feel Sho. Feel the blood pumping through his veins. Feel his utter calm. I can't read his thoughts, but I can tell they're undulating, like he's on the tiniest boat, river rafting in the middle of nowhere. I can feel his sincerity. His dedication. His hope for humanity.

His growing care for me.

Maybe this makes me blush and maybe it doesn't. I can't really tell while inside this thing. My body is one with the machine, and the machine is beating blood and frigid cold at the very same time. It's okay. I'm starting to get used to contradictions.

By the bleachers, Yoshi is laughing through tears. "This is like . . . my dream come true . . ."

"I want you to retrieve a map of the school." I hear Sho's voice in my ears. I'm not sure if he's talking or just thinking it. "Ask your suit. Work with it."

I've had enough practice asking machines for things. And now that Law's suit and I are getting along swimmingly, it quickly obeys my command. The visual of the school's schematics through my helmet is all light blue streaks. It obscures my visual of the real world, so I move the map to the right and pull up CCTV footage of Harada Entertainment, perching it to my left. It's getting crowded here inside my helmet. But with the hand-eye-coordination techniques Sho's been teaching me, my reaction time isn't as slow as I thought it'd be.

"Your heartrate is steady," I hear Yoshi say by the bleachers. "But, at times, unstable. Make sure you don't push yourself too hard."

Doesn't seem like Sho is on the same page, though. Because the very next second, Sho says, "I want you to hit me with an energy blast." And he means it.

"What?" My mind starts wavering again, but the LYNK with Sho keeps it from becoming unstable.

"I'll block it with the Totsuka." He pulls the long, broadsword out of his back, and this time, I can actually feel his armor shifting to accommodate the removal of his weapon as if it were my own. "It's a sword, as well as a shield."

How did I do it before? Right. Law's suit reminds me. Concentrate. Feel the kinetic energy that exists all around you. I do. I absorb it into my hands and the exothermic energy warms my forearms. It's almost too much for my cells to handle. The extra electromagnetic charge sparks around my skin, creating a blue-like cloud.

"Are you ready, Sho?" I ask him.

Sho flips over his sword, getting into a guarding stance. "Yes."

We don't need to think.

"Now!"

With Sho's yell, a growl escapes my lips, and the blue energy tears through my arms, out of my hands, and toward Sho. It's a strong blast, but Sho doesn't use much effort to block it with his sword. I can hear Lily screaming and Yoshi cheering. Sho whips the Totsuka around to dissipate the last of the energy.

"Amanda," Yoshi warns, "your heart rhythm is wavering. So are your brain waves."

I can tell. But I don't stop. Sho doesn't want to either.

"She's fine," Sho says and concentrates on me. His voice becomes so much softer when he's talking to me. "I need you to stay in Law's suit for as long as you can. Get used to the way your own heartbeat feels. And your breaths. Nobody can tell you that but you."

"Okay." It's easier for me to listen to him when we're LYNKed. Walls exist between human beings that don't quite intrude in this connection we have while we're suited up. He's stubborn. Obstinate. Goal-oriented. He had to be in order to survive that brutal training. And at night, he'd cry and comfort himself. I'm not trying to pry into his memories. I can just see them. He can see mine too. My tests and evaluations. My loneliness. My fear when machines first began to whisper to me . . .

"Amanda!" Yoshi yells. "It's been an hour. Your vitals are starting to get out of control!"

An hour? I had no idea. I don't think Sho did either. He's as surprised as I am.

"Let's de-armor," he says quickly. Concern. Care. He cares for me.

"Okay. Together."

It's like we reach out for each other. Like we hold hands. And as we do, we become children again. Two little lonely psiot children, both poked and prodded, surrounded by strangers and yet completely alone. We grab each other's little hands and hold on for dear life.

"Thank you." Little Sho smiles at me.

"For what?" says little Amanda McKee.

But little Sho doesn't answer. He blushes innocently, his shy smile wavering, tears prickling the corner of his eyes. "This is the first time I've ever had a . . ." He trails off.

We clutch each other as our suits recede back into our bodies.

"Andy!" Lily cries, jumping down from the bleachers as I collapse to my knees onto the hard gym floor. "Andy, are you okay?"

Sho has barely caught his breath, too, before he runs up to me. Between the two of them, they get me back on my feet. My body is still hot.

"I'm fine." I use the back of my hand to wipe the sweat off my forehead. "I think I can go again in a few hours."

"That might be all well and good," says Yoshi, who walks up to me with a bottle of heart medication. "But we need to make sure you can stay healthy during a real-time combat situation. Right now, you're barely holding on in what can't even be called a sparring session. Slow and steady, Amanda." Yoshi pats me on the back. "And as for the real-time combat situation? I'll set everything up. I'll make sure you're ready for the Digital World."

"What do you have in mind?" Sho asks.

Yoshi grins his wicked nerd grin. "Just leave that to me. For now? Practice."

"For now, break," Lily says as Yoshi hands me the medication. "For now, date! You're partners now, after all." She winks.

Sho and I glance at each other with nervous expressions as we both utter the word: "Partners?" Sho's ears turn beet red.

This Saturday is about to get weirder.

15

Well, Lily wanted this, so I have no choice but to go along with it. Don't get me wrong—I love shopping in Shibuya. But Sho isn't used to this thing called fun. He stares wide-eyed and frightened at the huge crowds walking across the broad street intersections. The flashing lights. The music stores, the plazas, the jewelry in the windows, the restaurants. When he isn't gazing at the skyscrapers and other symbols of capitalism in disdain, he's squinting at posters of male idols in confusion.

"Their hair . . . sparkles," he says a little too loudly, and a few girls from another school walk by giggling.

"Yes, that's their whole point." I grab him and drag him away from the shop's brick wall.

I never expected Sho would be a picky eater. Maybe that's my own arrogance, expecting someone from a dystopian future to gobble down anything we give him, but he actually has quite snobbish taste buds. He loves the takoyaki and the onigiri. But at the height of his arrogance, when I offer him my beloved rainbow cotton candy, he tosses the half-eaten stick behind him in disdain. I gape as the wondrous, priceless sugar fluff sticks to the ground.

"This is the kind of unhealthy garbage that'll kill someone." Sho folds his arms, ignoring the shocked and irritated looks a couple of old ladies throw at him.

"Uh, yeah. That's the point!" I snap. "We like unhealthy garbage in the twenty-first century."

Sigh. This isn't going well.

"What's wrong with you, anyway? You're in a mood." I slurp my sugar crap with pride.

Sho just deflates. Maybe being in a crowd this big is just too overwhelming for him.

"Here, try this!" I hand him the ice cream I grabbed earlier.

Sho stares at the chocolate and rainbow sprinkles. "I guess I just don't understand it, Amanda. Aren't you all in the twenty-first century supposed to be . . ." He looks around at the crowds chatting, riding bikes, strolling hand in hand. "Healthy? Better off? All I see is the hubris of modernity. You have this beautiful earth, and it's still filled with pollution." He looks at the trash on the sidewalk. "It's warmer than it should be. In my time, states don't exist. Nations are underwater. All of you are so oblivious."

Talk about oblivious. As we're walking toward a cosmetic store, I bump into a group of rather unruly-looking male students. I recognize the uniform. They're from a high school around here. The biggest, thickest guy out of the group now has chocolate and rainbow sprinkles all over his white T-shirt. I doubt he was planning on springing for dry cleaning today.

"Hey, hey!" The guy's got this very heavy chin that looks big enough to swallow the two of us whole.

"Sorry!" I start to say, but Sho steps in front of me and bows on my behalf.

"We're terribly sorry," he says and, grabbing my hand, continues on, only to be dragged back by the student.

"You think that's enough?" He runs his ringed fingers along his dyed-blond hair. "That girl spilled crap all over me!" They all smell like cigarette smoke. Ugh, how cliché.

"That girl already apologized." And Sho's expression turns menacing. "Walk away."

The high school boys bristle at Sho's bravery. My heart flutters a little too. He turns his body into a wall between me and the delinquents. There are a lot of people around. They size Sho up, obviously wondering if they can take him. They can't.

"Come on," I whisper to Sho, pulling him away before something happens.

We find a convenience store to waste some time in. I show him around, pushing food and manga into his hands, before dragging him to the magazine rack. There, I see a familiar face.

"Ryoichi's on this cover!" After excitedly pointing out one magazine on the stand, I grab it and show him. I practically swoon before pursing my lips. Not cool to do on a "date." Not that this is a "date." We're training.

Sho gives me a sideways look. "Who is he?"

"He's an actor," I answer. "He's *the* actor. The hottest teen actor in the country, no, in the continent. He was voted 'Perfect Face' five times on Girl's Channel."

Yes, yes, he was. And I'm supposed to go out on an actual date with him tomorrow. The complicated lives we weave.

My eyes wander over to Sho. After sizing up Ryoichi, he gives me another strange look. "Are you . . . attracted to him?"

He asks in this weird way like he's trying to keep his voice stable and his expression neutral, but cracks of insecurity show. Insecurity? About what? I ignore my drying throat and shrug. "Isn't everyone? Aren't *you*?"

He blushes, taken aback. "What? No," he replies.

"Then you're missing out, bud."

He rolls his eyes and walks out of the store. Great. Looks like we're not as in sync as Lily had hoped. But there's a park on the other side of the street. I drag him there.

To my surprise, his expression softens once we reach the grassy field. It isn't anything he's used to, not in his destroyed world. I sit down next to a tree and gesture for him to park his butt next to me.

"What do you think?" I ask him, motioning at the nature all around us.

Sho takes in the air and nods. "It's beautiful. Peaceful. I wish—" He pauses. "I wish my mother could have seen something like this."

I look up at the birds flying through the sky. "You're not wrong, you know, Sho. There's a lot of stuff we take for granted. Seeing your memories makes that clear." I rub my hands along my picnic dress. "You deserve to be here. To appreciate what we don't. I'm glad you're here."

Sho really is so awkward. Sour he can handle. It's the sweet he's not so good with. "I didn't mean to snap at you," Sho says quietly, surprising me. He plucks a blade of grass from the ground. "Wonders like this are impossible where I'm from. That's why I'm so desperate to—"

"To stop my father." I smile at him, my grin widening when I see his features twist into a guilty expression.

"I didn't mean to—"

"To what, hurt my feelings? When you first got here, you were ready to kill me."

Sho falls silent for a moment. "I was wrong. I didn't know."

"Know what?"

"That we're so similar. And that you're . . . a good person."

I notice how full Sho's lips are when he purses them together. It makes me want to touch them lightly with my finger and see how he'd react. Something tells me he'd freak out and have some kind of meltdown. It's kind of cute to think about, but I stow those naughty thoughts away for now.

"We are similar. Orphan psiots." I smirk, sadly, because the sight of Livewire tearing him from his mother is one that could dash any smile. "My real parents—I mean, my biological parents—were from Jacksonville, Florida. I never knew them. They died when I was a baby. I was adopted by Harada before I turned two. Right now, he's the only family I have."

Sho stays silent. But I appreciate him listening.

"We have the same mission. To find my father and change the future. We're on the same side," I tell him. "I guess I have a little bit more faith in him than you do."

Sho lifts his knee and slings an arm over it. The clouds shift overhead, casting shade over his handsome face. "I have no faith in him," he admits. "But I do have faith in you."

I'm at a loss for words as he sits there unable to look at me.

"Amanda . . ." Sho trails off. His hands twitch. To still them, he places them on his lap. He waits for a moment before speaking again. "Amanda, the truth is, I—"

"There he is!"

I look up and see that same high school student I bumped into and his friends. I sigh.

"Hey, bastard," said the dude with a few rainbow sparkles still on his shirt. "I've got a problem with you." He runs his fingers through his blond hair like it's a strange compulsion. The other boys are puffing out their chests, trying to look intimidating. Sho doesn't even budge.

"And? What's your problem?" I ask, instead of Sho, placing my hands on my hips.

"This has got nothing to do with you, foreigner."

"Wait! Whoa, she speaks Japanese," says one of the kids.

"That's so weird. Where's she from?"

"She looks American . . ."

"Whatever," interrupts their blond leader, causing them all to go silent. "I want a *real* apology."

"And what would that entail?" Sho continues to sit.

The blond dude takes off his shirt and throws it over Sho's head. "Getting that cleaned for starters."

Something tells me he just wanted to show off his two-pack.

"No." As Sho slides the shirt off his head with an impatient jerk, I wedge myself between him and the gang. "He's off-limits, and this is a park, so if you don't want any trouble, just turn around and walk away."

"Back the hell off, bitch." Blondie takes a menacing step toward me, but he's such a joke I stand my ground. I can read his secret texts to his mother begging her to make his favorite sweet potato dish because he can't go to sleep without it. For good measure, I snatch the phone out of his pants pocket and manifest the texts for everyone to see.

"'Mommy, don't disappoint me, love your little sweetie, Eikichi!'" I read it in a sickeningly sweet voice, then toss the phone to one of his underlings, just in case they don't believe me.

They all stare at him in horror.

"Your little sweetie?" says one of the boys.

And as his so-called friends begin to laugh cruelly, blondie winds up, drawing back his arm. Sho is in front of me in a flash. He catches the boy's fist.

"Big mistake," is all he says before punching little sweetie Eikichi in the stomach.

And I'm not one to be left out. Although the blond attempts a sucker punch, he doesn't even finish his swing before my swift jab to the face sends him stumbling back. I'm a quick learner. I duck a punch and kick the back of one boy's calf, causing his knees to buckle. With an extra hit, I send him crashing to the ground.

"This is really easy!" I say. It helps, of course, that before I strike, I send their phones into a ringing frenzy—causing a moment of distraction helps me take them down.

I'm pretty good, but Sho is downright scary. His movements are small but precise and nearly perfect. On top of that, his strength is devastating. Sho dodges simultaneous punches from two boys simply by leaning back and, in the blink of an eye, places one hand on each of their chests. With just one push, he sends them both flying. It's clear that he's been trained beyond his limits, watching him fight. For better or for worse.

When Eikichi lunges to backhand me in the face, Sho grabs his arm and flips Eikichi onto his back before twisting it.

"You really don't learn, do you?" Sho hisses, his glare murderous. "Don't. Touch. Her."

It's only after I hear people whispering and calling their phones that I tear my eyes away. And I can hear what number they're dialing.

110. The police.

Damn, they're fast. I see blaring lights off in the distance. I grab Sho, pull him away from the boy he's about to grind into dust, and run out of the park.

"Fun date, huh?" I say as we flee through the streets.

Sho's breath hitches. "Date . . ."

At least, I think so with a little smile.

16

One date over. Now that it's Sunday, it's time for the next. New day, new boy. I really am wild these days.

I actually feel a weird pinch in my stomach as I think of Sho, but I brush it away. That date wasn't serious. It was training. This one is. Right?

I shouldn't have let Lily convince me to cover my head in a golden mom-scarf and wear these red shades that cover the top half of my face. The white face mask covers the bottom half. I'm trying *not* to look like a suspicious stalker.

This is the same place that one actor got caught dating his actress costar. It was all over the news. Hopefully, I'll be luckier. I don't need any attention on me right now.

Everyone stares at me as I walk into the smoky little restaurant. I, at least, have an amazing outfit on: a cropped wraparound blazer, a pleated miniskirt, and some derby shoes, all gray, all brand spanking new, just for today. The smell of grilled meat somehow pierces through my mask and enters my nostrils, sending me to heaven.

I call the headwaiter over. "My name is Aman—uh, Andy. I mean, my name is Andrea."

There are so many names rattling in my tiny brain; I just pluck one from the sky until it sounds right. The waiter seems to understand, though. He takes me up the stairs to the second floor, the walls lined with the shut doors of private rooms. He lightly knocks on the one in the furthest corner of the hallway.

"Come in." Ryoichi's voice sends shock waves through me. The headwaiter looks at me, nods, and opens the door, letting me through first.

There he is, buried in his menu, sitting on a red bench against a lit orange brick wall. And sitting on the other side of the wooden table, poking the ribs on the barbecue grill with a pair of tongs is—

"Carmen?"

At the sound of my voice, Ryoichi looks up, shocked. The moment I swipe off my scarf, mask, and glasses, the menu slips from his hands. "A-Andy!"

Carmen drops her tongs on the table with a loud clank and turns, grimacing at the sight of me. "What is *she* doing here?"

"What am *I* doing here? Ryoichi asked me to meet him. What are *you* doing here?"

Carmen looks between the two of us. "Are you two dating?" And then she covers her mouth in horror. "No way. No *way*!"

She looks like she's about to throw up. Okay, *now* I'm offended. "Is that so hard to believe?"

Carmen looks me up and down and makes a face. "Well, I've heard all about Ryoichi's exotic tastes—"

"Carmen!" Ryoichi spits, his cheeks bright red.

"Exotic?" Whatever. I'm not here for this crap. I swivel around on my heels.

"Wait, don't go!" Ryoichi stands up. "This isn't what it looks like. Carmen crashed. She knows I come here every other Sunday, and she just turned up."

"Just turned up?" Carmen slammed the table with her tiny fists. "Do you know what I've been through these past several days? I asked you for help!"

She does seem to need help. Her eyes are sunken and red. She definitely hasn't had a good night's sleep since—

"The rooftop," I whisper, and Carmen stands so quickly her chair tumbles over and clatters against the wooden floor.

"That's right. You were there too." Carmen scuffles up to me, her eyes wild. "You saw those monsters. I've been trying to tell people Harada's not on vacation. He was kidnapped."

"And I've been trying to tell you that's not true." With a sigh, Ryoichi slaps his menu down on the table. "There was so much commotion. We can't be sure what happened."

"Oh, please!" Carmen whips around. "One of my friends told me you tried contacting reporters about what happened, but your story was so crazy that they ignored you. Stop trying to act cool just to save your reputation!"

"I'm not trying to act cool; I'm just trying to act rational." He slips his fingers through his hair. "There's no point in dwelling on something we can't make sense of."

As Ryoichi trails off into contemplative silence, Carmen grabs my arms. "I'm not going crazy, am I? You saw them too, didn't you?"

Carmen looks like she's been through hell while being trapped in her own thoughts. I know what that feels like. Maybe if I hadn't exposed her on Livewire, she wouldn't have been here tonight.

"I'm sorry," I say, and I'm not sure exactly what I'm apologizing for. Everything, I guess. "I think you should go home. Get some rest. That's what I'm going to do."

Carmen lets her hands slide off me. She stands in the middle of the private room, the chandelier hanging overhead, illuminating the dark bags underneath her eyes. She looks lost.

"Sorry, Andy," Ryoichi says. "I've been trying to send her away."

"Yeah, right!" Carmen growls. "You kept me here! You're the one who said we should eat together."

"Th-that's not true!" Ryoichi rounds the table and zips up to us. He gets close, but not too close. His eyes dart between both of us. "Don't believe her, Andrea."

Unlike me, Carmen isn't intimidated by his proximity. "Please. The whole industry knows how you treat women."

"Quiet!" Ryoichi snaps.

Both Carmen and I are shocked, but we're too rigid to even exchange glances. I've only ever heard Ryoichi sound nasty in that drama where he played the bad boy with a heart of gold. But in real life? His social media is basically either him posing for photoshoots or hugging puppies and fans.

In a heartbeat, he calms himself. "Carmen," he says, giving her a warning glare that seems antithetical to his innocent prince looks. "Maybe the stress of being put on hiatus from your group is making you say things you don't mean." As Carmen bristles, he continues, "Maybe you *should* get some rest. I'll bet you've been hysterical for days. Some rest will do you good."

I wince at the word *hysterical.* I don't know what to say, but Carmen does.

"Nice try. I know all your tea." She turns to me. "You really want to know the truth about your prince charming? What he did to those girls in France? The drugs he did with Erica in Spain while she was on probation?"

Her words are starting to sound like some kind of alien language. Like, the words are becoming mush in my ears. Drugs? Ryoichi's hands ball into fists. He's shaking.

"How he threatened to use his Yakuza ties to beat up his

own friend out of jealousy because Ryoichi here thought the poor guy was dating Chiho, who, if I remember, Ryo, was one of *seven* girls you were dating at the same time. Not to talk of what you've done to girls who reject you. Sick *pig.* Watch out, Andy-P. He's probably just interested in you because he thinks you're easy—"

"I said quiet!"

Ryoichi raises his hand, and for one terrible second, I think he's going to slap Carmen. Another hand grabs his wrist. It isn't mine. My hands are gripping my high-waist jeans.

It's Sho.

I didn't even hear him come through the open door behind me. Carmen scoots out of the way. Sho grips Ryoichi's wrist so hard it almost snaps. Ryoichi swears underneath his breath before Sho pushes him back.

"Who the hell are *you*?" Ryoichi spits, holding his own wrist in pain.

Sho glares at him, then lifts his chin. "You're shorter in real life."

Ryoichi's actually a little taken aback by it. My jaw drops. Without waiting for Ryoichi's answer, Sho turns to me and places a hand on my forearm. "Are you okay? Lily told me you were here."

That busybody. "Y-yeah," I stutter with a nod. I'm still not sure what's happening.

"Good. Then we can get the hell out of here."

Carmen is way ahead of us. With a huff, she stomps back toward the table, grabs the bottle of merlot next to the grill, and takes it with her out of the room. The slam of the door sends a shudder down my spine.

Sho takes my hand, but Ryoichi isn't done.

"How dare you!" He's bristling. "D-do you know who I am?"

"Shorter in real life." Sho doesn't let go of my hand as he glares at the other boy.

Ryoichi's had enough. He strides up to Sho, his fist in the air, but the punch he throws misses. Sho sidesteps him with ease, catches his arm, then cracks him in the face. Ryoichi slams against the table.

Wow. Sho just beat up the recipient of the Valiant Pop Awards' Number One Perfect Face Award. I'm not mad at it either. Ryoichi flounders on the floor, knocking a glass of water over that tips over and smacks the top of his head on its way to the floor.

Sho grabs me and begins leading me out of the room. "Oh!" I add. "And your last movie sucked! Stop playing the live-action version of my favorite childhood comic book characters! You ruin them!"

The actor's face pales. Before I can squeak out another insult, Sho drags me out the door, leaving Ryoichi to sizzle with the grill.

"That's the guy you're all so crazy about?" Sho frowns as he tugs me down the hallway.

"Yes. No! I don't know! Wait." I slip my hand out of his grip. "Why did you come?"

Sho stops so suddenly on the staircase, I almost trip over myself. "It had nothing to do with him," he says quickly and turns his head away quickly. But not quickly enough. I can see the flush in his cheeks. "I came to get you. Yoshi's got a mission for us, and we can only get it done tonight."

"A mission?"

"A real-time combat situation." At the foot of the staircase, Sho looks up at me. "We're going to stop a robbery in process."

I cannot believe this is what Yoshi had in mind. Through Harbinger Foundation connections, a long chunk of Sotobori-dori Avenue has been shut down. I've been here a few times, especially in the autumn, to see the foliage in Korakuen Gardens. Once with Lily. But usually by myself. Seeing the red fluttering leaves helps calm me down. Now I'll be playing cop.

In the dark of night, Sho and I stand on top of a white, high-rise company building. We don't need inner-ear coms. Sho's been fitted with inner-ear coms that fit like earbuds. I don't need any. Scanning the telecommunication lines, I can hear Yoshi just fine.

"In about three minutes, a black van should be taking a detour down Sotobori-dori," Yoshi tells us. "They'll have guns—and some tech that's worse."

"I'm glad you had our safety in mind when you planned this little event," I grumble underneath my breath. "They're not real robbers, at least?" I say loudly so he can hear me through Sho's coms.

"Oh no, they're Harbinger Foundation employees. But they've been briefed and instructed not to go easy on you."

Sho presses a finger against his right comm. "And our mission?"

"Is to disable their weapons and round them up without killing them. Of course, you'll be doing this all in your fancy BioSuits." Yoshi sounds practically giddy. And also, strangely, like his mouth is full of food. "Thanks to Amanda, we've commandeered all the CCTVs in the area. We're watching you from our screens at headquarters right now."

I scrunch my nose. "Headquarters?"

"Yeah." Yoshi chews very sloppily. I hear plates and glasses clattering in the background. "We're at Lily's aunt's restaurant. The egusi soup is particularly delicious."

"Ah. So you get to snack while you watch me fight for my life."

"It's all part of the plan." Yoshi honors me with a very lengthy *slurp*. "It's so I can evaluate you, Amanda."

I roll my eyes. "From a safe distance."

"Well, yeah! Like I'd want to get caught up in that mess!"

I sense the main CCTV camera by the stop sign and give Yoshi the middle finger.

"H-hey!" Yoshi stutters. "I saw that!"

"I know."

Sho cuts us off. "Let's prepare."

Right. Meditation. I breathe in and out. But I'm bad at this. Carmen and Ryoichi's nasty scowls revolve in my mind, taking turns sneering at me. I wonder how long Harada has been in the Digital World. What he's seen. How it's changed him.

My heart skips a beat when Sho takes my hand again. It's softer than when he pulled me out of Ryoichi's private room. I'm getting used to this touch. Its intimacy.

"Thirty seconds!" Yoshi warns us.

"Are you ready?" Sho looks at me, and he blushes a little, taken aback when I give his hand a squeeze and smile at him.

"I'm absolutely ready, Matsuoka Sho," I answer. "Let's do it."

His lips part for a moment. Then he grins and nods.

"Fifteen-seconds!"

We suit up. The Izanagi. Law's BioSuit. The symbiotic nanotech swirls around us, entrapping us in deadly full-body armor. My heart is pounding. It's like I can feel every cell in my body in the dark of this claustrophobic suit.

"They're coming around the corner!" Yoshi cries. His voice reverberates into my armor.

Indeed they are. The black van swivels around a corner, takes a left, and starts down Sotobori-dori Avenue.

"Are you ready, Amanda?" I can hear Sho's voice echoing inside my helmet. "Amanda?"

My body is buzzing. These aren't the usual nerves that come from excitement. This isn't about the thrill. Those black vans. I've seen them before. And now that I'm inside this suit, now that my senses are heightened to superhuman, superpsiot levels, the sight of those vans drags a memory out of me, out from the deepest recesses of my mind.

I'm back in Jacksonville, Florida. A mere child. Black-suited men with guns in hand and their faces completely covered storm into my bedroom. My parents are screaming.

What is this? What's happening?

Black van, I think, my head spinning as the van continues to speed down the street. *Black van*. Law's suit is ravaging my mind. The memory is now vivid. I know something's wrong. These exact vans. I've seen them before. I've seen them before . . . !

My father is keeping something from me. Information. This is the information I retrieve from the BioSuit of Harada's future soldier.

It takes nanoseconds for my mind to infiltrate the Harbinger Foundation's computer files of me—their secret files. The ones I'm never supposed to touch, by Harada's decree. I ignore Sho calling my name while I break through every firewall and pick every lock.

Then, I see it: the security camera from that night. The men take a limp child out of a house and into a black van, like these ones, stomping on toys lying across the lawn on the way.

"Amanda!" Sho calls me again, but I've already found footage from the six o'clock news that aired the next day. The headline in big red letters against a white strip freezes me:

PARENTS MURDERED IN JACKSONVILLE, FLORIDA.
2-year-old DAUGHTER MISSING . . .

"What did I just see? What was that?" My metal knees are knocking. My thoughts swirl around, racing along the hot blood rushing through my veins, pounding against my ears. "Jacksonville, Florida. Was that me? Was that my—"

PARENTS MURDERED IN JACKSONVILLE, FLORIDA.
2-year-old DAUGHTER MISSING . . .

My stomach heaves. I almost throw up in my helmet. Too many questions batter my skull. Why would this be in the Harbinger Foundation's secret files? What the hell is my father keeping from me?

It can't be.

It can't be!

"Were you the ones who did it?"

My voice is so hoarse; it sounds inhumane, even to my own ears.

"Amanda!" Sho reaches for me, but I've already jumped off the building and throttled myself toward the van.

My suit can fly. Clumsily, though. I'm swiveling everywhere, knocking over streetlamps, but I don't care. My visors home in on the truck, the digital locking-system inside my helmet placing a target on the license plate. Good. Law and I are on the same page.

I catch up in a moment and land on the top of the van with a heavy slam. Then I start tearing the metal roof open.

"Was it you?" I scream, because the worst accusation I can ever launch at my adopted father is now racing through my brain and the only way I can quiet it is by learning the truth.

Inside the van, the Harbinger employees look menacing. They've got military-grade uniforms on, their faces covered in black masks.

And guns. They point their guns at me.

But I have my own. "Was it you?" I scream, pointing my hands at them, but as they begin to spark, Sho grips me around the waist and carries me off just as a hail of bullets fire in my direction. Sho launches me up into the air.

"What are you doing Amanda?" He chides me, his silver-armored arms squeezing my stomach. "You don't just jump in—"

"I need to know if they killed my parents!"

"What?"

Yoshi and Sho say it at the same time. While Sho's distracted, I push him off me and launch back toward them. This time, I park down on the street with such force my metal feet break through the asphalt. Then I slam my hands into the truck. It lifts off its wheels for a second before gravity takes over and drags it back down on the street.

Two of the Foundation men have weapons that look like canons, just small enough for them to carry. They zip and crackle with energy before opening fire. One blast to the sky, where Sho still is. Another blast at me. I dodge it, gliding above the street, then flying up the side of the building. Empty. Probably Yoshi's doing. His preparations for my big tests.

Tests. Always tests. I've been tested since I was a child because Harada just happened to discover that the child he adopted was the only psiot on earth.

Did he plan it? Did he plan it all?

Sho shoots past me and, with his sword, cuts their cannons in half. I use hand to hand combat to snap their guns in half. But I'm not here to disable. I'm here for answers.

"Toyo Harada!" I grab one man and lift him into the air. "Did he order you to kill my parents?"

"Wh-what?" The man's voice is high and whining. He

sounds absolutely terrified. "I have no idea what you're talking about! Please! I'm only following orders!"

"Amanda!" Sho grabs my arm so quickly, I release the little man. He cries in his military garb and runs off down the street. "Enough! You're out of control."

Am I? The truth is, I've been a good, obedient little adopted girl all my life. If I've gone feral now, it's long overdue.

Harada. Who are you?

I push Sho away from me.

What did you do to my parents?

The men drop what's left of their weapons and take off running down the street, following their friend.

Why did you adopt me?

I raise my arms. Blue energy swirls around my hands.

Is Sho right? Is everyone right?

I open fire. Sho is in front of me in a flash. He blocks my blast with his sword, but I'm not finished. If Sho's going to stand in my way, then I have no choice. I'll beat him to a pulp until someone, anyone, tells me what the hell is going on with my life.

I'm fighting hand-to-hand combat, but he's blocking each of my kicks and punches with his sword. "Stop, Amanda!" he cries. "I don't want to fight you."

"Then tell me! Who am I?" I grab Sho's sharp shoulder plates and lift him up into the sky. I blast him, but this time, I don't take off an arm. I take out a building window.

"Stop, Amanda!" I hear Yoshi's groveling voice inside my helmet. "Oh damn, it wasn't supposed to get this heated. What do we do?"

"Just tell me the truth!" I scream, and I growl, furious, when Sho sheathes his sword. So he won't fight me. He won't tell me. Then what are we even doing here?

I raise my arms to blast him again, but Law's suit won't

cooperate. It's starting to rebel, the joints stiff, the armor shutting down.

"We're LYNKed," Sho reminds me, his arms out, pleading with me. "We have to be on the same page, Amanda. You need to calm down!"

But I can't calm down. Harada was never much of a father, but he was a father, yet he abandoned me at the drop of a hat to follow Livewire. It can't be true.

Did my father kill my parents? Does he then go on to destroy humanity?

I can't take it anymore. I won't wait anymore.

I need the truth. Now!

There's a shop nearby selling LED televisions, tablets, and every other manner of gadget. I see them in the display window. Sho seems to know what I'm up to. He tries to stop me, but I give him the hardest uppercut I can manage, catching him off guard, putting every bit of power I have into that one hit. It knocks him out. The sight of him on the ground frightens me. But my vicious emotions won't let me rest. Without wasting another second, I crash through the glass and digitize into the television.

I enter the Digital World.

17

"Amanda, there's a proverb I learned from my parents," Harada once told me. We were in New York, inside one of his sterile labs. I was ten years old. We'd just finished a test. "I rather like it. Tell me if you know what it means."

Another test. Ten-year-old me wasn't happy about it, but, obedient as always, I waited.

"Sometimes to make an omelet you have to break a few eggs."

I burst out laughing. "That's a proverb?"

"What does it mean?"

I stopped laughing when I realized I didn't know.

Harada sighed and sat down on my white bed, pushing away the IV drip. "The greatest developments in human history have never come without a cost. Civilizations don't rise without sacrifices. As new technologies, new economies, new ways of living emerge, there will always be those left behind. But that's how it's supposed to be." He said it without empathy. "It's just how the world works. But it's beautiful."

The look in his eyes that day. The glitter. He truly believed it.

"I don't think the eggs would agree," ten-year-old me replied.

And he just smiled.

Digitizing in such a state shocks my system and knocks me out cold. But I didn't expect to wake up in a forest. The cries of an owl fill the dark of night. And as I peer up through the tops of the trees, the moonlight filtering between the evergreen leaves, I see the tail end of a train heading off into the sky and disappearing.

Harada. Where is Harada? As I lie here on the dew-wet grass, my memories of Jacksonville blur together with my years in New York and then Tokyo, mocking me. Nothing's making sense. But I know I need answers. I need to confront my father.

I rest my forehead against the forest soil, trying to catch my breath. The chirping of crickets can't overtake that annoying little owl. It continues to hoot incessantly.

"Hoot, hoot," says the owl, in a tree somewhere close. "Ryoichi is so beautiful. Hoot. He's so dreamy. Hoot. How can anyone look like that? He was born handsome."

Um . . . what? Is the talking owl on drugs? Am *I* on drugs? I thought I heard someone say Ryoichi's name . . .

I try to crawl off my stomach, but a metal foot crashes into my back, nearly breaking my spine in half. Maybe it would have if not for the nanotech fortifying my cells. I let out a gasp of pain, a spurt of blood splashing from my mouth.

"Let me guess—you're here for Daddy," says the sassy metallic grunt above my head. "Livewire's stashed him somewhere in this Digital Castle." He sweeps his arms around the forest. "Surprised you found us. I guess you're pretty good."

Wincing, I technopathically invade his suit. Just like on the rooftop, BioSuit armor are tough cookies, not easily breakable, but I do get a name.

"Stronghold," I spit on the prickly grass. Big beast of a thing. "You owe Harada Entertainment a new grill."

"Harada Entertainment. I heard Harada ran an entertainment company in the twenty-first century to hide his dirty dealings." His laughter's as cold as fusion. "Kinda funny. We don't exactly need real-life entertainment anymore, unless you count torturing norms as a leisure activity." He thinks about it. "Which for me, it is."

"Take me to my dad!" I struggle to get off my stomach, but his foot is firm on my back.

"Sorry, you can't see him. Livewire's orders." Taking his foot off my back, he turns me around and pulls me up by the collar of my gray cropped blazer. I can see him now, in his bulky copper and gray BioSuit, his eyes flashing gold. "But lucky you. I'm just aching to play."

With his other hand, he snaps a thick branch off a nearby tree. It disassembles in his hand just like the grill did on the rooftop. But that matter begins to transform. Dismantled wood into destructive energy that glows red like a flame. It's hot. Radioactive hot. My eyes follow the flickering yellow tips.

"Say, Amanda McKee from the twenty-first century . . ." He leans in so his helmet is so close to my face I can almost hallucinate him breathing. "Is torturing a leisure activity? Or a sport? Because if it's the latter, I'd say I'm pretty good at it."

"I'll bet you are." I call out Law's suit, but only enough nanotech to cover my forehead. That way I don't shatter my skull when I crack him with the headbutt of a lifetime.

Yelling, he lets me go and stumbles back. I run forward, hiding behind a tree. The pitch-black night is a perfect cover. But when I try to suit up, I can't. Law's engine stalls.

"Sho," I whisper, biting my lip. "I can't do it without him . . ."

A beam of radioactive red energy disintegrates a tree to my left. Covering my gasp with both my hands, I try to stay perfectly still.

"That hurt, Amanda," Stronghold groans. "God, you're such a little *snot* in this century."

Is this really the Digital World? The moth that flutters past my hands, still clamped over my mouth, feels so real. I shiver at its touch, then immediately scold my body. I have to stay perfectly still, or he'll find me.

There has to be something I can do. Of course, there's something I could do. I'm a psiot. A technopath. This whole place should be *my* playground!

I'm not powerful enough to bend this place to my will, not yet. But there are some moves I can make.

I shut my eyes. Sho's meditation training wasn't a complete waste of time. I poke around into Stronghold's suit again, this time quieting my mind, focusing on specific weak points in the armor, trying to find a clearer way in. I needed more than just a name.

"I can feel you digging around in there." Stronghold's voice sounds further away, but not far enough. "Ugh, get the hell out!" Growling, he blasts a beam of fiery energy into the sky, lighting up the whole forest, but I keep my body rigid against the scratchy bark.

This Eggbreaker's impatient. Arrogant. He has a temper. And when he lets loose, his circuitry weakens, just a little. That's all I need. My mind slips inside the wires.

A self-defense system? Stronghold's suit didn't need to talk to me willingly. From behind my eyelids, I can see the nanotechnology quivering and whirling like clockwork. Words written in blue Fira Code typed across black space: Warning Energy Reaction Blast. Cell-Protection Barrier Activated.

Energy reaction blast . . . cell-protection barrier . . . ?

Of course! He deconstructs matter and converts it into energy, but what if there's some kind of bodily cost? He can fire as many blasts as he wants, but if his cells need protecting from his own internal weapon . . .

"Hey." Stronghold sounds almost sleazy on the other side of my tree. My muscles seize. "You there, Amanda?"

I make a break for it, trying to head through a crooked path of evergreen trees, but my human legs are nothing against a Bio-Suit Soldier. Stronghold powers toward me, wraps his clunky arms around me, and launches me up into the sky.

I can't breathe, because he's crushing me so hard. My vision blurs, but I can still see the moon, round, full, silhouetting my sure demise in the quiet of the night.

"I could just decompose you right here and turn you into cold fusion. How about that, darling?"

He can't. Amanda McKee must survive. Livewire said so herself on the rooftop that night. This big idiot is bluffing. But two can play that game.

"Go ahead and do it. I'd love to see your boss kick your loser butt afterward," I snarl.

"Huh?" Stronghold gives me another violent squeeze, forcing a painful gasp from my mouth. "What did you say, brat?"

"Please! You're not going to do crap to me. You're just a henchman! You follow orders. Harada's. Livewire's. I bet as far as Eggbreakers go, you're on the bottom of the goon totem pole. How does it feel . . . ?" I pause for a second before my lips break into a crooked smile. "Eddy? Your name is Eddy? Little Eddy the Eggbreaker?"

My suit never worked when my mind was in a shambles. I figure it's the same for the others. And I'm right. A split second is all I need. As Stronghold yells, "Enough," as he begins to growl, as he gets ready to dismantle one of my arms, I use every bit of mental power I have to shut off his Cell-Protection Barrier.

Stronghold must know something is wrong. His grip on me relaxes, and that's when I slip out of it. With one powerful kick, I push him away and begin tumbling toward the earth. The rushing wind batters my weightless body, sucking out any oxygen I have left in me. I panic, watching Stronghold flail in the sky above me, waiting for the cold, hard ground to break my fall—and my spine.

"Amanda!"

Before the inevitable thud, a pair of metal arms swoop in under me and catch me instead. My body drops against the Bio-Suit soldier, bruised, but unbroken. And when I look up and see all the silver, tears nearly well up in my eyes.

"Sho!" I cry, looking at his familiar sleek helmet. "You found me! Um—" I pause. "Sorry about knocking you out!"

"Transform, Amanda!" Sho tells me, heading toward the ground.

"I won't give you the chance!" Stronghold tugs a tree out from its roots with a monstrous roar and turns it to dust. Soon his arms, no, his whole body begins to pulsate with that same red energy, except something's wrong. It's like he walked into a nuclear power plant and absorbed all the waste. I don't have to imagine how painful it is. I can hear his guttural shrieking.

The red heat covers his entire suit, but no matter how many times he tries to aim, it won't release. With his Cell-Protection Barrier broken, all that power, heat, energy, and *rage* remain trapped inside his cells, pulsating until it swallows him whole, screaming.

Stronghold disintegrates before my very eyes.

As pieces of what is left of Stronghold drop from the sky, Sho finds a safe spot to put me down and de-armors.

"Are you okay?" He grabs my shoulders, his eyes wild with worry.

My little toothy grin is, I think, half relieved, half crazed. "I really am sorry for that uppercut, you know. Adrenaline and trauma, and all that."

Sho's hands slip off my shoulders. "It's fine. I'm just glad I was able to find you."

"You can track me?"

"Sure." His smile's a little shy. "We're LYNKed, remember?"

A wave of emotion flows through me. Anger at my father. Confusion. But this smile in front of me. Somehow, as I concentrate on it, all the knotted ropes binding me just loosen and flutter to the ground like they're supposed to. I can't help it. I clasp his cheeks with both my hands, not caring at all that his face is now beet red.

"Thank you," I say, and the tears really are falling this time. After hesitating, Sho places a shaky hand on my waist, his lips fluttering nervously.

I'm not interrupting anything, am I?

Terminal. Interrupting. With an irritated sigh, I lower my arms. "I could have used you back there when I was trying not to die, you know."

Hey, you were the one who jumped into the Digital World half-cocked. *I was the one who guided you here. This Digital Castle that you're in right now? It belongs to someone who's been particularly chatty about Toyo Harada in secret social media spaces. Oh, he's been trying to tell everyone from his bodyguards to his manager to his mafia buddies what happened. And that's what's made this castle the perfect one for Livewire to stash your father in.*

My father. Toyo Harada. My fingers curl into fists. "He's here."

Yes. And just so you know, this is one of the Digital Castles I had mapped out for you.

"None of that matters anymore if I can get to Dad before he goes to the Inner Sanctum."

And I'm going to get to him. I'm going to get to the bottom of all of this.

If you want to leave a Digital Castle, you need to reach the exit in the dungeon, where all the memories are; a golden door should appear in front of you.

A golden door, just like in Sho's dungeon. Well, Sho, having only been in the twenty-first century for a day or two, didn't have a complete castle at the time. In comparison, this Digital Castle looked pretty advanced.

Just be careful, Amanda. Like I said, this'll be a different experience than before. A finished Digital Castle is . . . strange. The one you're in right now is no different. People's digital domains are a manifestation of their digital footprints. They reveal who people really are underneath all the barriers and all the facade. All the artifice.

"Sometimes artifice is needed to hide what truly lies beneath," I whisper. Dad's words. I won't let them become mine.

Just like before, a yellow path lights up the ground underneath us, weaving around the trees and fallen branches.

Okay. Let's do this. I crack my knuckles. "Follow the yellow brick road, I guess."

Sho furrows his eyebrows. "What?"

"Just come," I order with a little laugh, pulling him along with me.

18

A castle within a castle. Or is this Gothic structure I see before me more like an evil lair?

Sho and I have come to the edge of the forest. And this is where the yellow brick road leads: a twisted Gothic palace that looks pulled straight out of *Dracula*. Bats hover around its flying buttresses and pointed, spiraling towers. Every arch, every spiral, and every turret point up toward the full moon. And resting atop of the central clock tower above the cast-iron double doors is a single gargoyle, howling in the night as if turned to stone in the midst of battle.

"A castle within a castle," Sho mutters under his breath.

"Right?" I shake my head before heading off toward the double doors. A pair of guards in clunky, ill-fitting medieval armor stand watch in front of the doors, but their faces—oh my *god*—they are the faces of dogs.

"Who goes there?" The faces of dogs and the voices of old men. They sound like they chain-smoke. One of them lets out a series of disgusting hacks and spits on the ground next to him. "Who dares come here to bother Lord Ryoichi, our king, our god, our divine star who shines the brightest in all the world?"

The other guard just continues to hack.

"Ryoichi?" I narrow my eyes, and as if on cue, that same owl flutters past the turrets.

"Hoot, hoot," it cries. "Ryoichi is the most beautiful man in existence. Hoot!"

"Oh, this is going to be very strange," I say as the owl flies behind the turrets.

Sho takes a menacing step forward. He looks more irritated than when he caught Ryoichi's wrist in the yakiniku place. "We're here to see Ryoichi."

Pulling him back by his shirt, I scuttle forward. "We're here to worship Ryoichi," I correct him. "To bask in his glory. To be blessed by his presence."

A nudge in the ribs is not enough to get Sho to say the same, but he, at least, with a slump of his shoulders, gives them a curt nod of agreement.

"We're . . ." Sho's expression sours as he looks away. "Fans."

That, apparently, is the magic word. The guards bark happily, step aside, and push open the cast-iron doors. Before long, I wish they hadn't. The only sources of light inside the palace are the flickering torches perched upon darkened red-bricked walls. Crossed-arched ribs of the same color comprise the vaulted ceiling that stretches far above our heads. The stained-glass windows remind me of an old Gothic church. But if this is a church, the subject of worship is clear. Every painted window displays the splendor of exactly one person.

"Ryoichi?" I really can't believe what I'm seeing here. As we walk down the narrow halls upon the checkered black and white tiles, it's Ryoichi in each painting, healing the sick as if he's Jesus, conquering armies as if he's Alexander the Great.

Sho snorts in disgust. "*This* is the guy you like?"

I suddenly feel my body flushing with embarrassment, "No,

not him. I mean, Ryoichi isn't like that . . . at least, he never seemed like—"

A complete jackass. That's what we see when another pair of guards opens the door to the central throne room. A rush of giggling hits us like a powerful smack in the face.

"My goodness," I say, clutching my chest.

The throne room itself is breathtaking. Like the inside of a garden. Dark, thin tree branches crawl around the walls and vaulted ceiling. In between the bark buzz more colorful fireflies, shining red, yellow, and orange. They move across the ceiling with choreographed precision, producing an ever-shifting sunset. And they sing the praises of the man sitting on the throne at the far end of the room.

Ryoichi. In his underwear. Well, at least he's wearing boxers. He has one leg dangling over the golden arm, and another resting on the top rail. His head dangles, but not quite enough for the twisted golden crown to slip off it.

Girls clad only in leaves and flowers sit at his feet on the floor, sipping cocktails, feeding him grapes, and braiding each other's hair. It's hard to watch. The way they're fawning over him, rubbing his smooth, bare chest, intertwining their fingers in his wild black hair, caressing his face—

My body went lax. His face. His face is beautiful, even more beautiful here than it is in real life. There's something dangerous about it, about his alert brown eyes that summons me to them, inviting me to melt into them. Something thrilling about their earnest gleam that promises me like a whisper in my ear, that even when he strips me of my will and imprisons me, he'll still give me the purest of happiness if only I worship him.

"Amanda!" Sho grabs my arm and pulls me back. I gasp, my heart skipping a beat. I didn't even realize I was walking toward him.

Ryoichi does. He finds me with those scheming, deadly eyes. And he grins.

The hair on my arm stands on end. That isn't Ryoichi's usual sweet, friendly boy-next-door grin he's perfected over the years. It's sleazy, twisted, and arrogant. It gives me goose bumps. Am I supposed to be feeling this cold inside?

It's not really him. I have to remind myself. The real Ryoichi is somewhere in the real world, maybe still in that stupid restaurant. As a regular human, he's not coming inside the Digital World any time soon. No, *this* Ryoichi is a mirage. Just like the paintings and the gargoyle, the man before me is a manifestation of his digital footprint. He's data taking the shape of Ryoichi's secret digital exploits. A metaphorical aggregate of who Ryoichi is.

I grab my head with both hands and force it down to break away from his eyes. That's when the incessant giggling begins again. I recognize some of the girls draping themselves all over Ryoichi. Some of them are actresses. Some of them are idols. A few fans are probably thrown in too. A digital metaphor. A digital confession. So this is how Ryoichi sees women. Like handmaidens obsessed with him. I guess if you're treated like some kind of god because of your good looks, eventually you fool yourself into thinking you're one. Carmen was right about him.

Tilting his head, he watches me with a bemused expression that makes my heart jolt. He opens his mouth, wet with wine. "I'm entirely convinced that you've already heard of me, so I won't bother introducing myself," he announces with a wide grin.

My jaw drops. "Come again?"

He doesn't repeat himself. He does, however, lean over and squint. "Wait," he says and strokes his head. "Is that you, Andy? Andy-P? The *P* stands for Princess?"

When he laughs, so too do the women. I bristle in anger, my fists shaking.

"So you've finally come. I knew it was only a matter of time. I can't help but be almost as excited to see you as you surely are to see me. Welcome, my lovely, to my castle. Ryoichi promises to take good care of you."

My *lovely*? God, you give a guy a few magazine covers and he really does turn into a cartoon villain. I stomp forward, but Sho grabs my wrist, holding me back.

"Oh, and you brought your bodyguard." His expression darkens. Looks like Ryoichi can't handle competition. His distorted "beauty" is nothing compared to Sho's earnestness. The little "Prince" scowls as Sho tugs me back.

"We're here for Toyo Harada," he says. "Tell us where he is. Now."

Elegantly raising a hand, Ryoichi takes one of the peacock feathers in the hair of one of his adoring fans and brushes it across his nose, enjoying the sensation before addressing us again. "You don't give the orders around here, little boy. Guards!"

The doors burst open, and four guards with spears in hand run inside the throne room, their long terrier noses sniffing out danger while their tongues wag, ready.

"These two have displeased me," Ryoichi says, and the girls begin screaming in agony.

"How dare they do that," one says, scraping her nails across her face.

Another girl is tearing out her hair. "Do they know who Ryoichi is? He's the most handsome actor ever on Earth! He was voted 'Perfect Face' *five times* on Girl's Channel!"

Is this what we sound like to him? Us fangirls? I cringe, my muscles rigid as I see blood pouring down the scratch marks on the first girl's cheeks.

"Managers! Agents! Hairdressers!" His claps ring loud and clear. "Take them to the torture room and lock them up! I'll see to them later." After giving his orders, Ryoichi gives me a disgusting wink. "I think I'll spend the most time with you, though, Andy. Don't be scared. You look like you'd enjoy it."

"Oh *hell* no." I don't even bother suiting up to take these goons down. They're barely even a match for the two of us as we crack them in the face with our fists. Sho finishes the last guard with a swift kick to the head, grabs my hand, and makes a run for it back through the doors.

"After them!" Ryoichi screams behind us, not that he's going to move his royal butt to come after us himself. I'm sure he thinks his royal butt's too precious for that.

I can't *believe* there was a time I wanted to see that butt.

"Where do you think Harada is?" I say, trying to keep up with Sho as he pulls me through the gloomy corridors.

"If anyone can find him, you can."

But this place is saturated in Harada's presence. Terminal and Yoshi were right. The best place for Livewire to hide him is wherever his name is plastered all over someone's digital footprint. It's like trying to find a needle in a stack of needles. But Sho is right. If anyone can find him, I can. Especially now that Toyo Harada, the man, is presently less flesh and bone, and more data and algorithms.

What did Harada always tell me when I was a kid and he had me parked in front of a room of monitors, hoping I'd be able to spy on his enemies? Right. Stretch out your mind as far as it'll go. Blanket every piece of technology and dig until you find what you're looking for.

Precision. That's what took down Stronghold. Finding the tiniest crack in his armor that allowed my mind to wiggle its way inside.

"Halt! Haters discovered!" Several more guards round the corner, their spears primed.

"Concentrate on finding him." Sho gives my hand a squeeze before reluctantly letting it go. "I'll take care of this!"

He flies off in the guards' direction, taking one doggy knight down after another. As I see them fight, a strange, hollow lull comes over me, along with the dull chill of an epiphany: Terminal is right. Digital Castles really are freaking weird. Like, really, *really* freaking weird. Twisted, even. As twisted as people are, I suppose, in their heart of hearts.

Shaking my head, I press my hands against my cheeks, squishing my face, and concentrate. I blanket Ryoichi's entire Digital Castle under the oppressive iron will of my technopathic mind. There are more women of every race and creed lounging around in the rooms upstairs. The torture rooms have reporters in them.

Focus, I tell myself, squeezing my head harder. *Focus. On Harada. Not the reporters on the Rack. Oh, there's a Judas cradle. No! Focus!*

"I got it! The dungeon!" The strongest aggregate of Harada's data is there hiding Ryoichi's real memories. "Oh, but not the dungeon of this castle. The dungeon of Ryoichi's Digital Castle." I make a big waving motion with my hand so he gets me.

Sho takes one of the guards, steps over the unconscious bodies—or rather, the bodies he made unconscious—and slams him against the brick wall. "Where's the dungeon of this Digital Castle? Is it in this building?"

The dog sniffs his pug nose and forces his face to the side so he can answer. "How am I supposed to know? I just clean Ryoichi's laundry and keep track of his schedules!"

Sho punches the wall next to his face, making the guard yelp. "Tell me. Don't make this more painful than it needs to be."

I run up to the guard before Sho can do anything he might regret. "Hey, Ryoichi's a dickhead, isn't he?" I carefully tap the guard's armor, which is slipping off his shoulder. It wasn't properly on in the first place. "I mean, it's clear how he views women. It's clear how he views his own team. Just give up the ghost. I promise we won't tell anyone."

The guard turns around and flattens his back against the wall, his eyes darting around. "It's in the garden outside. Go out the front door and around to the back. You'll find a gazebo with a trapdoor inside." The guard pauses to catch his breath. "Oh gosh, don't tell anyone I told you. Don't tell Ryoichi."

"As far as anyone's concerned, we beat it out of you." I pat him on the shoulder. "You fought bravely until the end."

A little tear trickles down his furry cheek. Then he jumps onto the pile of unconscious guards and plays dead.

"This place is just so weird," I sigh, my fingers in my hair.

"Come on." Sho's all business as he pulls me out of Ryoichi's palace.

The gazebo is actually where the guard told us it'd be. Ryoichi must be a nature guy. The cedar gazebo blends beautifully in the midst of the flowers and trees behind the palace. The trapdoor is right in the center of the wooden floor. Sho opens it, revealing a staircase descending into darkness. After exchanging a worried look, we both steal ourselves and begin climbing down.

Both our minds are calm, Sho and I. So when we land in the middle of Ryoichi's favorite childhood cottage, the one by the lake he always talks about in interviews, there's no rushing wind battering us, tossing us about like we're in the middle of a tornado. Just a light breeze as a seven-year-old Ryoichi stands around on the front steps of the cottage, surrounded by woods, flowers, and nature—and a crowd of people flocking around him.

"Oh my!" The men and women look like they're locals from the area, invited over by Ryoichi's parents, who sit on the front steps next to their son. "Your child is so beautiful!"

"He's so young, but his face is already perfect. Oh my, how can anyone look like that?"

"He was born handsome."

I've heard all this before. Ryoichi looks somewhat confused, but he smiles at the flattery. His mom and dad soak in the praise too, rubbing their pretty son's hair, proudly telling the local women how many entertainment agencies have already hounded her to let Ryoichi join.

The locals nod. "He'll be in commercials soon! Oh, I can't wait!"

"Enough of this freak show." Sho's face twists in disgust. "Is Harada here? If not, can we go now?"

"No. He's not here." I turn and walk toward the crystal clear lake, fireflies buzzing around me and disappearing behind some trees. As the locals continue to coo, I latch my mind on the dungeon. *Take me to him*, I demand.

Light static shocks me from the inside of my body. I shut my eyes from the slight pain, and the next time I open them again, I'm at the bleachers beside the track and field of a middle school. Ryoichi must be a preteen here. None of the students here need anyone to point out how perfect he still looks as he plays a forward in soccer. As they watch him play, the crowd's already squealing about it.

"Chiba Ryoichi is so beautiful!"

"He's so dreamy."

"I'm so jealous."

"How can anyone look like that? He's, like, the most beautiful man in existence!"

They'd make good bosom buddies with that owl. Middle schooler Ryoichi hears them too. That much is clear. It doesn't matter if the ball he kicks is stopped by the goalie. By now he's been in commercials and dramas. His head is already so swollen from the constant praise, he grins as if he made a hundred goals.

But this isn't where Harada is.

I feel like Samantha from *Bewitched*, twitching my nose when I need some of that old magic to work. But when the scene shorts out with a static shock and we reappear in a dank nightclub, I don't feel nearly as iconic. I recoil in horror.

The dance music assaults my eardrums. I can feel the base pounding against my chest as if each beat is from my own heart. The bar is busy. The dance floor is crowded with people. But I'm looking at the words on the specially made napkin: "Club Zodiac."

Club Zodiac? I've heard of it from the whispers of music fans on social media. It's that nightclub in Thailand a whole bunch of celebrities from the continent go to. I see Shim Hyun here, drenching alcohol all over himself and smoking one cigarette after another, scarfing peanuts. And he's palling around with Carmen's boss, the CEO of the biggest K-POP entertainment label in existence. With his big belly, he can barely wedge himself between the red leather seat and his table, but he certainly has no problem fitting his little arms around girls young enough to be his daughters. Filthy *pigs*.

I see Ryoichi too, standing next to another actor by the pillar by the bar. They're watching the girls dancing without a care in the world. Assessing. Appraising.

Choosing.

Ryoichi nods to his friend, who walks onto the dance floor.

Ryoichi then nods to some goon at the bar. With a slippery grin on his disgusting face, the goon slips some powder into a tall glass of vodka and hands it to Ryoichi—right around the same time his actor friend brings him a girl fresh off the dance floor.

I can't believe what I'm watching. My blood is boiling. My stomach is hot. I ball my hands into fists. I have to save that girl. Even if I have to break every one of Ryoichi's teeth just to do it. No, maybe I'll just break his teeth for the fun of it.

Before I can take more than two steps forward, Sho grabs my elbow.

"This is a memory," he reminds me. "Whatever he's about to do to that girl, he's already done it. We can't save her. I'm sure he's been getting away with it for years."

The fact that I was so excited when he asked me out . . . all those years I spent staring at his face on magazines, saving his pictures on my phone. And now here he is, dragging an unconscious woman up a private stairwell, his sick friends rubbing their hands and following behind. Tears burn my eyes. I'm shaking, but there's nothing I can do. Not a thing because this is a memory. This is something that happened in Ryoichi's past. Something he did before he dared to fix his mouth to ask me out to some grilled meat restaurant. Harada was right about something. The world is filled with artifice. And the entertainment world is sick.

"Amanda." Sho nudges me in the ribs and flicks his head toward a man in a suit too clean for a sordid nightclub like this. He's walking toward us. But isn't this a memory?

"Amanda McKee?" the man says and bows. "Please come with me to one of our private VIP rooms. There's someone here waiting for you."

Someone. Harada?

I swallow the lump in my throat and follow the man through

the first floor of the club. Just when the pounding of my own heart begins to overtake the frantic beat of the music, Sho softly grabs my hand as if to remind me that I'm not alone.

"Stay close to me," he whispers, his voice melting my nerves.

In a quieter hallway away from the music and the dancing, the man opens a tall black door that leads to the VIP room.

His back is to me as he faces a window so expensive it seems to take over the entire wall. He's still in the same clothes he was in when he swept off the roof. His arms are placed behind his back as he stands upon an expensive bloodred rug, the chandelier overhead glittering, catching the moonlight. Toyo Harada.

He's not alone. Two Eggbreakers flank him, standing watch on each side of the room. One of them is Livewire. The other is in an ice-blue suit. I remember his name from the rooftop battle: Ion. His eyes spark with electricity.

"Amanda."

My bones chill as I hear my father say my name, so casually, so simply it's as if he's really been on vacation in Hawaii, instead of a captive in a parallel universe made of technological data.

No. He was never a "captive" to begin with. This much is made clear when he turns to me slowly and smiles at me.

"You finally made it here," he says. And that's what's confusing about him—terrifying. Because despite everything I know about this man, everything I've learned, this still sounds like my father—the only father I've ever known. Father, mentor, drill sergeant. At his word, I'm used to jumping at attention. It's almost a habit. My fingers clench and unclench as he takes in the sight of me and nods, proudly. "I knew you would. There's much we need to discuss."

I'm so caught up in my thoughts, I don't notice Sho, letting go of my hand, struggling and failing to control his breaths at the sight of the man who rules over his ruined world.

Not until it's too late.

"The only thing I want to hear you say," Sho says, "is your prayers."

"Sho!" I say as he transforms into his silver BioSuit Armor, but it's too late. Sho pulls out the Totsuka and stabs Harada through the chest.

Sho kills my father.

19

My father dies in slow motion.

The giant sword pierces his stomach, cutting through his spine and cracking the window glass behind him. Blood drips from his lips, his nose, his eyes.

I stumble back, clasping my hands, pressing them against my chest. This can't be happening. I don't know what to think. I feel like I'm going to throw up.

"Dad . . ." I bury my face in my hands, panting, crying. "Dad, I . . ."

Silence. It takes a few eerie moments to realize that I don't actually hear anything. Not Sho removing his sword from my father's flesh. Not the Eggbreakers rushing to attack him. Not my father slumping over to hit the ground. Everything that should have happened after Sho's brutal attack.

Still on my knees, I lower my hands and look up. The VIP room has somehow turned black and white. And nobody is moving. Not Sho in his armor, whose sword is still in my father's gut. Not Livewire or Ion standing on opposite sides of the room, completely still. The scene before me has frozen solid. And now, so have I, unable to move from my spot on the red carpet.

"Amanda," says a voice behind me, "so this is what you wish, deep down, would happen to your own father?"

With my heart in my throat, I jump to my feet as if I've been electrocuted and whip around. Toyo Harada stands before me, his hands behind his back, wearing the same suit with the same smile. Have I gone crazy? I turn back around. The scene hasn't changed. Sho is still in the process of murdering my father as the Eggbreakers stand and watch.

None of them are moving.

"What's . . . what's happening?" I peer at my father's wrinkled face, my throat dry, taking hurried steps from him as I grip my gray skirt. "What's going on?"

"You're a technopath, Amanda." Harada peers down at me underneath the dangling chandelier. "There are many things your mind can do, but I promise—there's no mind on Earth more powerful than mine."

I roll his words around on my tongue. I let them echo in my mind. I take in the sight of this frozen murder scene. I shudder when my father begins taking steps toward me, closing the gap between us. I take another step back as I realize.

"This is an illusion," I whisper. "You did this. But how can you do this unless you're—"

I don't want to say it. There've been too many lies already. But I will no longer look away from the truth. And the truth is the man standing before me is indeed the man who will one day destroy humanity. Toyo Harada.

A psiot.

"Why." I grit my teeth, my entire body trembling. "Why did you lie to me and tell me I was the only one?"

"I wanted you to channel that loneliness," he tells me. "Let it become your power. Let it make you feel like a god, like my power did mine. There are many human beings who have the latent ability within them to do the impossible." His steps are steady and sure. "I discovered my own power after my family turned to ashes decades ago. In my anger and despair, I unlocked the power within me. I learned about the special things I can do with my mind."

"Telepathy?" I guess, still gripping the hem of my skirt.

"Among other abilities." He looks at his own death and tilts his head. "This is the first time I've used them in quite a while. I was far more . . . experimental in my younger days."

I can't look at his shining dark eyes. Instead, I stare down at the carpet, my vision blurring with fury as I ask the question dripping on my lips.

"Have you ever used them on me?"

"On occasion," he answers simply. "Though you'd never remember."

"You bastard!" I growl, striding toward him, my fists clenched. We're now face-to-face and a breath apart. Father and daughter. Mentor and mentee.

Kidnapper and kidnapped.

"You had my real parents in Jacksonville killed," I whisper, tears budding in my eyes. "You sought me out and killed them so you could take me with you and experiment on me."

Harada looks a little taken aback, but that mild look of surprise dissipates as quickly as it appeared. "So you've figured out that much. I knew, eventually, that you would."

I am so close to fainting. But I will my body to stay strong. I order my tears to stop falling. I can't show weakness in front of this monster. He doesn't deserve it.

I lift my chin with defiance. "If you knew I'd find out eventually, how did you figure I wouldn't just kill you once I did?"

Harada smirks. "You don't have the power to. And even if you did, how could a daughter ever kill her father?"

Now my mind is swimming. This annoying, persistent "care" I have always had for Harada, growing up under his roof as both his ward and lab experiment. Was that a result of some kind of . . . mind control? Did he force me to love him? Maybe I'll never know the answer.

"No, Amanda," he says, snapping me violently back to reality. "I've never manipulated your feelings for me."

"Get out of my head!" I slam my hands against my head so hard I get dizzy and almost sway off balance. "Get out! How dare you!"

"I've always known that forcing your love was unnecessary. You were always such a happy baby. Always so grateful to be adopted. Always so hungry for any shred of affection I gave you. That's what loneliness does. It makes you obedient. It makes you see the truth." He places a hand on my shoulder. It makes me want to die. "And I know that you'll overcome this painful moment. You'll overcome your anger and see the greatest truth of all. That my plan to save humanity works. According to the Eggbreakers, according to Livewire, you and I do it together. We can't let that future change. We must work hand in hand to complete the construction and mass production of the BioSuits. We must tame the Digital World and turn it into humanity's Garden of Eden if human beings are ever to have a chance to escape this awful world riddled with aggression and war." His hand slides to my chin, and he lifts it up, tapping it affectionately. "I know you'll understand one day, Amanda. And you'll join me."

"Oh, I will, will I?" If looks could kill, I would glare a hole right through his head. "You sound confident. How the hell can you know that?"

"Because I've seen it," Harada says simply. "Here in the Digital World, I've seen the future. And in the future, you and I win."

"No!"

"Come with me, Amanda." If eyes are the window into the soul, it's his eyes that expose his madness most clearly. He grips my chin so hard that he almost shatters the bone. "Come with me to the Inner Sanctum. The Seed that created all digital life. The beating heart of this digital parallel universe. Once you and I seize its power, we can control the Digital World. Then there's no stopping my dream for humanity."

"There's no 'you and I' anymore!"

I slap his hand away and lunge for his neck. He steps quickly out of the way and, with one look, sends the chandelier crashing down in front of us. I jump back and fall to the ground as everyone unfreezes. The Harada who Sho skewered disappears like bad data deleting itself. Confused, Sho looks around the room, his grip still tight on the hilt of his sword. Livewire and Ion take a menacing step forward, then turn toward the door to see the true Harada standing safe, pompous, and proud of his little trick as the broken chandelier keeps me from trying to choke him again.

Harada gives a meaningful glance to Livewire, who returns it with an obedient nod.

"You will always be my daughter, Amanda," he says, and his fatherly smile has never looked so malicious. "Always. To the end of time."

In a flash, Livewire flies forward, grabs Harada, and bursts out of the VIP room, taking the door and a bit of the wall down with her. I stumble to my feet, shaken, but ready to follow suit. A zap of white electricity shoots across the room, blocking my path.

"I'm sorry," says Ion in a voice that sounds lifeless and

robotic. "But if your goal is to kill Toyo Harada, I cannot let that happen. Your deletion is now necessary and imminent."

Whoever he was in the past, his humanity is fully gone. So be it. This is all-out war.

I suit up. Law's armor grips my skin like a warm hug. Sho and I are on the same page.

"Let's get rid of this asshole," we say at the same time, and the battle begins.

Ion lets loose a branch of electricity that I can't completely dodge, but I know this armor can take the buzz, even as my head rocks in the helmet. Sho launches up into the ceiling to avoid the hit, then rams into Ion, pushing him through the wall out into the hallway.

This is a memory. Nobody cares when I pursue Ion, blasting him with blue energy. Nobody feels it when Sho and I chase him through the narrow hallways into the main nightclub. The electrical charge bursting out from Ion's body goes through Hyun, the K-POP CEO, and the underage girls they're with as if they're all just a mirage. Well, they are. It blasts across the bar, but none of the glasses hanging upside down on the mirror behind the bartender shatters.

Still, it's like Ryoichi's sick memories know that I'm somehow in the building. The nightclub DJ changes the music to an oldie but a goodie: Utada Hikaru's "Movin' on Without You." And I'm ready to dance.

Ion meets each one of my kicks with his own, our fists clashing as we move across the dance floor like incorporeal ghosts, the force of our punches canceling each other out. But I'm not alone. The moment I retreat, Sho drops down from the ceiling, slicing down with the Totsuka sword. He hits Ion's chest. The high-pitched whine of metal torn in two gives me the confidence to go for Ion's right arm, grabbing it with both my hands, charging up, and then blasting it off before he can recover from Sho's strike. But even armless, even with a gash down his torso, Ion isn't finished. Rising up in the air, he stretches out his one remaining arm and releases a torrent of electrical energy that ensnares the entire energy and us with it.

I can feel Sho's pain. It's as palpable as my own as we're caught in this electrical web, our eyes flashing, our brains rattling.

I can hear him thinking, panicked: *I can survive this. But can she? I have to do something quick! I have to save her!*

Is it because we're LYNKed that I can hear his thoughts as the same pain thunders through us? Is it because we're LYNKed that I can feel his desperation, his desire to rescue me from this violence at all costs?

Maybe it goes both ways.

I'll disable his weapon. But I don't think I can do it for more than a second. It's in that second that you've gotta strike the final blow!

I don't have time to check to see if he heard me. In the midst of this crushing pain, all I can do is train my technopathic mind on Ion's suit. The blows Sho and I landed have weakened it, which means it can't take much more of his electrical dam breaking. I'm not going to wait and see how it cracks under the pressure first. I stretch out my technopathic mind, searching the weapon's system in his suit. It appears in my mind: a single pipe running throughout his suit like a pulsating blood vessel. It's carrying the current. So what happens when you grab a gushing hose by the hand? We're about to see.

You're not the only one who can do crazy crap with your mind, Dad.

Screaming in anguish, unable to take anymore, I wrap my mind around the pipe and crush it. The electrical current fizzes out, only zapping out in spurts. But turning off the hose works. Sho doesn't waste another second. He flips his sword around and swipes off Ion's head with a clean stroke. The BioSuit's body crashes to the ground, lifeless.

I crash to the ground too, landing on my knees. Doubling over, I place my hands on the dance floor so I can catch my breath, but the aching still shudders up my flesh and down my bones. Sho wraps his arms around me.

"Are you okay? Suits are regenerative when given enough time. Keep yours on now."

I nod, too tired to answer with my voice. My mind's too weak to de-armor anyway.

Right in the center of the dance floor, a golden door appears.

"Harada and Livewire have probably already left this Digital Castle," Sho says. "We've got to catch up to them. And I think where they're headed—"

"The Inner Sanctum." That's all I can cough out with my ruined throat. He's going to the Inner Sanctum. He wants me to meet him there, where the Seed is. To show me. To recruit me.

I'm going to stop him instead.

Sho doesn't seem to need any more words to understand. Lifting me to my feet, he helps me walk toward the golden door. I take one last look at Ryoichi's memories, at the ugly heart of the boy who has it all, and go through the door.

20

I've already punched your ticket, so you don't have to come to my information desk, Terminal tells us once we land back in the train station. Little golden pieces of paper appear in our hands. *Follow my route and you might even beat your dad to the Inner Sanctum. Needless to say, I feel queasy thinking about what he's planning to do there.*

The golden tickets Terminal gives us takes us through the automated gates just fine.

I don't think my body has ever been so battered and bruised. Sho helps me to the platform. It's just like waiting at a real train station, except there's nobody else here, so I don't feel self-conscious when I collapse on the floor, my tired legs unable to keep me standing.

Sho sits next to me with one arm around my waist, keeping me from falling over until our train arrives: Train 98.102.71.114. He lifts me up and ushers me in.

This time, we sit together on the red-cushioned seat. The train rushes off to the next Digital Castle. Sho was right. The suit is regenerative. I can feel my body begin to cool off and heal as I stare through the windows on the opposite side of the train. An array of metallic colors blasts by us in the darkness. They're just as awe-inspiring as the first time I saw them.

"It might take a while to get there," Sho says. "You should rest."

I don't need telling twice. Right there in my BioSuit, I lie back, relax my whole body, and fall asleep. Nightmares of my father haunt me. And now I don't know whether they're really nightmares, or if they're messages he's transmitting to me from wherever he is now. A mental transfer from one secret psiot to another.

But in my dreams, Harada and I stand together in space, among the stars, surrounded by a dark void, looking at the planet Earth beneath us. Such a beautiful planet. Such a shining star. Why does it look so small?

"You must understand how I feel, Amanda," he tells me. "My family was a victim of the very worst humanity has to offer. And from the day my eyes were opened as to what humanity is capable of, I knew that I had to use my gifts to do what few ever could."

He stretches his arms toward the planet as if to embrace it. "I want to help people, Amanda. And to do that, I have to rule over them. It's a great burden, but someone must bear it. And with my gifts, I will make a better world, one where tragedies like the one my family suffered never happen again."

"But did you know, Dad?" I watch the clouds shift across the blue planet. "Victims of one perpetrator can go on to become perpetrators themselves, creating more victims with their own hands. Violence begets more violence. It's the same song and dance. You're not changing that. You're perpetuating it." I look up at him, a shooting star blazing past us, illuminating the determination in our stone-cold expressions. "*You* are what you hate in humanity," I tell him. "*You* are the never-ending aggression.

The never-ending contradiction. The never-ending war. You killed my parents. How many more victims will you create to *help* humanity?"

"I did kill your parents." Harada closes his eyes, and for a time, he doesn't speak. The galaxy seems to be moving on its own around us. The earth continues its slow spin, unaware of the danger we two psiots pose it. Unaware of the Sword of Damocles dangling over its head.

Slowly, deliberately, Harada opens his eyes. He looks at me.

And he smiles.

"But sometimes to make an omelet, my dear daughter, you have to break a few eggs."

"Dad!"

I jolt awake. My languid vision slides from the empty red bench on the opposite side of the train to my arms resting on my lap. The hairs on my right forearm are standing on end. I move to rub it before realizing—I've de-armored. I'm sitting here in my cropped blazer and my miniskirt. The burns on my skin have healed. The sore sensation is gone. How long had I been sleeping in that suit? My head is still spinning a little, dizzy from the abrupt start. But a steady arm around my waist keeps me rooted and calm. I look up to my right.

And I meet Sho's gaze.

That's when I realize I was sleeping on his shoulder.

My mouth goes dry, and my heart begins to pound, but I don't scooch away from him. Somehow it feels more comforting to stay right here in his arms.

"You're awake." His voice is creamy and gentle. It melts my panic and somehow intensifies it at the same time. "Are you all right?"

His arms are dangling between his lap, his long legs spread out as he sits rigidly on the bench. I see the fingers on his left hand twitching a little. Like he wants to do something but doesn't quite know how to initiate it.

It's awkward. But somehow that awkwardness is comforting. Because it's real.

"Nothing was real," I whisper before I can stop myself. "Between my father and me. He killed my parents. He stole me. He used me. He still wants to use me. You were right, Sho. I believe now that Toyo Harada and Amanda McKee destroy humanity. My blindness . . . my inability to accept the truth right in front of me is what causes the downfall of us all."

Sho shakes his head. "He's the only family you had. The only one you knew." His arm squeezes me around the waist. It's soft and compassionate. "Adults tell us so many lies. I wonder how they can live with themselves. I was trained to believe you were a monster, but it wasn't true. You're just another psiot kid who wants a family. Like me."

I let my head fall onto his shoulder, listening to the pace of his breathing quicken. "It's not fair," I say. "All I ever wanted was to belong somewhere." I giggle a bit as I remember my past self in California, standing in a long line, waiting to audition for yet another commercial. "You know, I thought being this beloved star with tons of fans would do it. That was my dream when I was a kid. But I heard those casting agents talking behind my back about how I was too dark and too short and too fat, etc., etc. Instead of recognizing them for the body-shaming trash they were, I started to believe them. I wanted people to like me . . ."

I stare at my own hands. At the unique lines tracing paths on my palms. "I wonder what would have happened to me if I had a father who told me I was beautiful just the way I was. If I had a community that supported me."

"The past is past. It's gone. You can't—"

"Change it?" I give him a teasing smile.

Sho's ears turn red. "Well," he changes course after clearing his throat. "If you can't use decades worth of humanity's latest technological resources to punch a hole through space and time, a suicide mission you take on because your world is on the brink of collapse, a mission only you can survive because of your special psiot healing powers—"

"I mean, if I could do that, I never would have done that stupid music video." I groan, covering my face with my hands.

Sho pries them away from my head and lowers them. "If you can't physically go back in time, well, then, you can only live with the past and deal with the present."

"Is there anything else you wish you could change?" I ask Sho. "I mean, aside from the obvious?"

Sho raises his head and looks up at the ceiling. "I wish I could have met my mother."

His words linger in the air as I wonder what my mother looked like. Was she short like me? The reality is, when I try to imagine my mother's face, I see a blank, featureless slab of nothing. Frustration builds up inside me. So do the tears.

"I wish I was a bit nicer to you when we first met too," Sho adds under his breath.

His awkward confession makes me laugh. Wiping my face, I look up at him. "Now that, I agree with. You were a real pill when we first—"

Sho grabs my hand and pulls me in for a kiss. It's unsure at first. I can tell he's never done this, and to be perfectly honest, neither have I. But soon I can feel him growing in confidence. As my heart thumps against my chest, he grabs the back of my head and crushes me against him. The kiss is long and deep, his full lips enveloping mine with little restraint. It's soft but passionate. My whole body begins to shake as I melt into him.

And then, a silly, adorable jingle signals the train's arrival.

Sho lets go of me quickly, his eyes wide as if he'd been possessed. His mouth still open, he tries to speak, then scoots away from me, his body stone petrified.

What, did he not like it? Am I a bad kisser? Was it a mistake? One made in a fit of passion between two lost souls fighting for their lives?

But my heart is still thrashing. My cheeks are still hot. And my body still longs for him. It longs so naturally, like it's used to wanting to be near him. Maybe it has for a long time, and I've just been ignoring it. But who would Amanda McKee be if she wasn't ignoring what was right in front of her? I clasp my hands together.

I guess "ignoring" is just what we're both going to do, then. Sho says nothing, so I turn away too, biting my wet bottom lip, listening to the music jingle and jingle until it practically screams at us to get off the train.

We both stand at the same time. I suck in a deep breath and straighten my skirt. "N-next Digital Castle?" I stutter, gripping its hem.

Sho nods. "Next Castle. Let's go."

The gold tickets Terminal gave us were apt if not foreboding. The train had deposited us into what I can only describe as Charlie's Chocolate Factory. And that damn locomotive must know how messed up this place is because it takes off and disappears before I can get back on it.

"So first it was *Dracula* and now it's—whatever this is?" I take in the sight before me. Sho and I are standing in a massive, explosively colored production plant. Conveyer belts bring huge gingerbread cookies round and round under a bloodred ceiling covered with white light bulbs the size of basketballs. But this production plant is living and breathing. Chocolate birds fly over our heads, making a strange warbling sound. Lollipops grow out of the green carpet like flowers, though some are as big as trees. And the *sprinkles*. Colorful sugar sprinkles pepper the air, buzzing around the ceiling lights like fireflies. I'd be in heaven if I were a kid again.

"Wait a second," Sho says as he walks up to the conveyor belt. "Do these cookies remind you of anyone?"

I tear my eyes away from the purple vat of melting chocolate and run up to where Sho is standing. The gingerbread cookies make my mouth water. Strange—I didn't think I could feel hungry in the Digital World. I don't feel hungry, not physically. Maybe it's just a Pavlovian response. I look at sugar; I salivate.

But this time, the sugar's looking back at me.

They're not gingerbread men. They're gingerbread *Carmens.* Oh my god. I cover my mouth in shock. The other members of BAD CUPID are here, too, in cookie format: Minju, Kelly, and Arin, but Carmen is by far the most represented on this conveyor belt.

And she's moving. They're all moving. Wiggling around their little cookie arms.

"Hello, my name is Carmen!"

"My name is Minju!"

"Hi, I'm Kelly."

"I'm Arin!"

"And we are BAD CUPID!" They say together with their little sprinkled-covered mouths.

"Oh, this is weird." I shake my head and stumble back, gripping Sho's sleeve. "This is really, really weird."

I look around me and suddenly realize BAD CUPID's arrow-struck heart logo is on all the candy. It's on the lollipops growing out of the ground. On the vat of boiling chocolate. The chocolate birds aren't shrieking but humming "Smart My Baby," one of their earliest singles. "My sugar, sugar—*chirp*!"

"Sho," I back away. "I'm serious. I'm gonna run."

"Wait!" Sho grabs my hand and pulls me into his chest just as one of the sugar sprinkle fireflies drops down from the ceiling and explodes next to me. For a moment, Sho and I stare into each other's eyes as he grips me with his strong arms, holding me firm.

Then, before we can both get carried away, we break eye contact and simultaneously turn to look at the explosion. The sugar sprinkle has ballooned into a life-size Carmen doll.

It's as if Carmen were a float in a Thanksgiving parade. Yeah, that's what this is like. Except she's made completely out of cotton candy.

"I love my fans," her sugar mouth repeats over and over again with an empty, robotic smile.

"I love you too, my sweet!"

The voice comes from behind the chocolate vat. He pokes his head out, and I see his dyed white, gold, and green hair first. I'm about to recognize his face when he drops to the ground and begins scurrying along the green carpet like a rat.

"T-Taylor?" I remember him now. "Taylor Ronaldo?" The crazed BAD CUPID fan from Ohio I once had to have security haul out of Harada Entertainment for stalking.

Obviously, he's more crazed than I'd realized. He's scurrying, sniffing the ground, and quivering his body like a dog trying to shake fleas off its fur. He launches himself onto the conveyer belt. Then, after breathing heavily, he grabs one cookie and looks at it in awe and religious adoration.

"So sexy." His sigh is more of a swoon. "It's just what I'd expect of a group of the most beautiful visuals the idol world has ever seen. And they're all mine."

Then he begins scarfing them down. One after another. The cookies are screaming. But he's screaming louder. "You're mine! Mine! And you better not be dating anyone, or I swear—"

"Stop it, you weirdo stalker fanboy!" I run forward, grab his arm, and pull him away from the conveyor belt. I can't stand to hear the girls scream in pain, even if they are just cookie versions of themselves. "What the hell kind of Digital Castle is this?" I demand, throwing him into a bunch of lollipops. "Is this what you think a girl group is? A treat for you to *consume*?"

Rubbing his ass, Taylor wipes the crumbs from his mouth and begins kicking his feet up and down. "But they're mine!" He really throws a tantrum like a greedy little child. Where's an Oompa Loompa to drag him away when you need one? "They're mine, and you can't have them. They were made for me."

"They're not products on a shelf, you freak!" I scream. Oh no, wait. They are. There's a wooden shelf right there at the east end of the room, and row after row lined with edible chocolate BAD CUPID dolls.

"This is getting us nowhere," Sho says as he peers around this house of horrors. "Is Harada here or not?"

I close my eyes and spread my mind out until it blankets the entire Digital Castle. "No." My shoulders relax. I'm not sure I should be this relieved to know our fated showdown has been deferred by now.

Sho walks up to me. "If he and Livewire are on their way to the Inner Sanctum, we need to get to the dungeon of this Digital Castle and find the exit." He places a hand on my shoulder, but in a second, he withdraws it, his cheeks burning red. What had become so natural has returned to being unnatural again. His touch. His intimacy.

We look at each other, neither of us knowing what to say,

but both of us, surely, thinking of the same thing. The moisture of each other's lips. The heat of our embrace.

We're lost for just long enough for Taylor to scuttle his way toward the end of a conveyor belt, where he grips a lever I haven't noticed until this second.

Well, it's too late now.

"I hate people who ruin my fun. It's just entertainment, you know," he snarls. "Nobody's getting hurt."

My memories drift to Ryoichi dragging that unconscious girl up the stairs, but it doesn't linger long. Taylor pulls down the lever, and suddenly I don't feel the carpet underneath my feet.

"Oh hell—" I begin to curse, but gravity soon does its work, pulling Sho and I into the darkness below.

21

Terminal was right. Nothing about the Digital World makes sense. I awake on the ground in the middle of some dark woods. But unlike in Ryoichi's Castle, there's something almost cartoonish about the tall, crooked trees, their leaves glimmering with dew. The colors are oversaturated, so much so these so-called dark woods don't feel very dark at all. I feel like I'm stuck in a comic book with incorrect coloring. Blue branches sway in the wind. Silver fog veils red stumps and metallic-purple grass, shadows shimmering under the bright hanging moon. This is another one of Taylor's playgrounds.

"Antis detected," a mysterious voice screeches above us. "Enacting security measures."

As a haunting moan sounded in the distance, Sho balls his hands into fists. "What is this?" He lifted them, ready to fight. "Where are we?"

And what's that shadow slipping fast behind the trees?

"You're just a hater!" I hear quiet, angry echoes from deep inside the forests.

"Don't judge what you don't understand!"

"Don't you dare come for our girls!"

Okay, if I wasn't earlier, I'm officially freaked out now. I hear twigs snap in the distance and growling. Growling? It can't be Taylor, can it? Though I wouldn't put it past him, this sounds like the kind of snarling that can only be made by real animals. And whatever animals they are, they're getting closer.

"Someone compile a list of hate comments and send them to the CEO!"

"The company isn't *abusing* them! This is just how the industry works!"

"Don't translate anything that'll make the company look bad!"

The voices are growing louder. Getting closer. I grip Sho's sleeve, tugging on it frantically. "Um, should we run? Hello? Sho?"

But the boy is too busy tracking the shadow's movement through the fog.

"Get ready," he says. Not the words I wanted to hear.

A shadowy figure leaps out at us from behind the trees, running at us so fast, I barely have time to react before its teeth chomp down on Sho's arm. The blood drains from my face as he screams in pain.

"Sho!" I wrap my body around the beast and drag it off him. It flips around and lands on its hind legs. Long and lanky, the beast stands as tall as I am, its ribs sticking out uncomfortably through its pitch-black fur.

A black dog. The wild bloodlust in its red eyes screams for more flesh. I've heard of black dogs in myth. They're monsters, harbingers of death. The saliva dripping down its jaw tells me it dreams day in and day out of nothing but tearing its prey apart.

"BAD CUPID is better than your faves, loser!" it says.

As I blink, confused, Sho uses his nanotechnology to manifest the Totsuka sword alone. Even without suiting up, he can wield it just fine. With a fierce yell, Sho swings the beast off him, only for it to lunge at him again.

"Watch out!" Diving, I push him out of the way, only to find myself pinned down against the ground by another black dog. With its paws on my back pushing me into the mud, I can't breathe, can't even turn around to see its menacing face. But I can hear it snapping, feel its breath against my neck. I always knew stans would be the death of me.

The black dog shrieks in pain, its screams echoing into the skies. I flip onto my back the moment the dog's feet are off me, just in time to watch Sho pull his bloody sword out of the dog's side. The second black dog dodges his next swing and, using its hind legs, kicks him back. I barely have time to spit the mud out of my mouth before Sho jumps back to his feet, grabs my hand, and pulls me to my feet.

"Come on!" Sho drags me with him as we make for the woods. We jump over pink stones and brush past yellow trees, snapping twigs. It's a multi-metallic-colored nightmare. All the while I can hear more howling following us.

"We can't shake them!" I say in between desperate attempts to catch my breath. My foot almost snags a root and sends me flying.

"It's tracking us by scent." Sho's hand is rough against my arm, keeping me steady. "We need a way to the dungeon. We need a plan."

"Terminal!" I send out a mental SOS, and Terminal is quick to respond.

Over the river and through the woods, you'll find the elevator that'll take you to the dungeon, kiddies. But don't tarry! Pop music fans are vicious.

I grit my teeth. "You're enjoying this, aren't you?"

The dogs howled in the distance as a yellow path sparks beneath our feet.

"Fine, chase us," I say defiantly through gritted teeth. I want to sound tough, but my back is still crackling with pain.

We run anyway, following the yellow path until it takes us to a bubbling bog on the other side of a thicket of tall sickly looking trees.

"River, my butt," I grumble. Sho and I stand in front of the thick, mosquito-filled waters.

"Come on in; the water's fine!" I say with a little nervous chuckle, but my feet aren't moving. This blazer and miniskirt are brand new, and the water looks like someone died in it. "Wait," I say when Sho reaches out for me. "Let me just catch my breath."

"Are you okay?" Sho hesitantly squeezes my shoulder. I tremble a little at his touch.

"I've been better," I whisper. My head's starting to throb. What took it so long?

"I don't know how long we've been in the Digital World, but we can't stay here forever. It'll harm us in the end. We have to get a move on."

Harada's probably spent weeks in here. Is it because he's this all-powerful psiot that he's held together so well? I think of his pompous grin and shudder.

Sho goes quiet for a while before parting his soft lips to speak again. "Thank you," he says, his other hand still gripping the Totsuka so tightly his knuckles paled.

"What?"

"You really saved me back there."

Ah, before with the black dog. "When do I not save you?"

"Th-then," Sho stutters. "Take this as a thank-you for all those other times too."

Sho doesn't look at me as he speaks. His eyes scan the periphery of the trees on the other side of the bog, but even in the dark, I can see his cheeks flushing. I don't imagine Sho ever had much experience with girls while undergoing brutal training in the C.A.R.D facility. He's clearly not this suave king who's going to sweep me off my feet with the right words. But I've already learned my lesson with those types. It's clear now—the sound of someone's voice when they're truly genuine. I far prefer it.

Maybe we should have found another time to have our little moment. The leaves shake. The trees sway. And then out of the darkness prowls three black dogs, each of their steps slow and deliberate, their murderous gazes trained on us.

"I'll hold them back," says Sho, wielding his sword. "You go ahead."

"Are you sure?" I say that, but my feet are moving on their own, stepping back farther and farther until I can feel the bog water around my ankles. "Okay! Be careful!" I shout as he launches at them, taking them all on.

I turn toward the muddy water. "Okay, on three," I breathe, my heart thundering against my chest. "One—"

A pair of hands grab my legs and pull me down into the bog. Who is it? What is it? I can hear Sho screaming for me above the surface of the water. Struggling to hold my breath, I swivel around to see a pair of blank white eyes belonging to none other than Carmen. Even in the black waters, I can make out the details of her face—her straight nose, her gorgeously crafted lips. But it's her dead eyes that arrest me as she holds me in a vise grip.

"You did this to me," she whispers, her voice clear, but distant. Her indictment surrounds me. "You exposed me. Do you know how stressful this job is? How much I have to go through every day to avoid the freaks and criminals and supervillains who work in my industry just so I can get a bit of the fame and fortune I deserve? It's not fair!"

I struggle and fight for my life, kicking my legs hard against the waves, but her slowly withering hands are more than strong enough to drag me down.

You bullied Rachel! With my mouth shut against the waters, I think it angrily, but here in the Digital World, anything goes. Carmen hears me. And her response?

"Rachel deserved it! She stepped on my foot once!"

Unbelievable. I peer up through the black waters, trying to reach for the moonlight reflected on the surface. What I didn't expect was the bodies of two black dogs crashing right through the water. I almost gasped. The heavy dogs sink fast. And the moment Carmen catches sight of them, the target of her fury switches. Needless to say, Carmen doesn't much like her obsessive fans. She has no problem gripping both of their paws and drowning them.

While she's distracted, I swim wildly, trying to get to the surface before my air runs out. But Carmen is greedy. She manages to catch my ankle with a long, spindly finger. She won't rest until she's taken me with her into the depths of despair.

Sho makes the difference, diving into the waters, his black hair floating up with the waves. Grabbing my hand, he yanks me out of Carmen's grip, and with our combined strength, we burst back out into the open air, greedily gulping in as much oxygen as we can.

"Come on." With no time to waste, Sho takes me and swims across the bog as I catch my breath, depositing me onto the ground once we reach the other side.

We practically have to drag ourselves limping through the rest of the woods, following the yellow path until it takes us to an old-timey elevator, the kind with mesh and steel doors.

As Sho's wounds heal from the fight, he helps me pry the elevator doors apart with whatever strength is left in our bodies.

And we crash together into the far-end walls, the doors shutting behind us. For a moment, I stay cushioned in his thick arms, feeling his haggard breath, my head pressed against the rise and fall of his chest. He looks down at me, at the exact moment I look up at him. Our eyes lock. My body warms with an almost painful ache as his hands slip up my back, but as if snapping out of a trance, he sucks in a quick breath and untangles himself from me, slipping across the elevator wall. With a hand on my chest, I turn—not too fast, because my head is spinning—and scope out the elevator buttons.

😈 B MF 1 2 3 4

"Click the smiling demon face," I tell him after collapsing to the floor. And as the elevator rumbles and begins to fly up into the sky, I shake my head. "Harada, I swear, you'll pay for all of this." I curse underneath my breath before lying flat on my back against the cold floor.

The elevator deposits us into a musty bedroom. Clothes litter the beige synthetic carpet. Dirty socks, T-shirts, baseball caps. BAD CUPID posters line the walls. The bedding is BAD CUPID. The bookshelf is filled with BAD CUPID albums and photo books. And in the littlest corner of the room, underneath the window, through which only a little bit of light could peek through the shut blinds, is a boy in a stained sweatshirt at a desk typing furiously on his laptop.

"This is his dungeon," says Sho. "Where's the door? It must be around here somewhere." He begins searching the room.

But I don't move. I can see Taylor's on social media, but

I'm too far to see where he's typing. But after making a technopathic connection to his laptop, I can hear the furious insults loud and clear:

> Did you just fix your mouth to tell me that group of tone-deaf bitches is more popular than BAD CUPID? What the **** are you talking about? You're literally speaking like a coked-out mess rn. Take a look at their album sales. Take a look at their sold-out dome tour and say that trash to me again. You literal walking piece of **** turds spending your days and nights worshipping old hags who can't even dance in sync anymore let alone snag anything close to Minju's brand ambassadorships. *****ing trash stains. Your mother should have ended you when you were still in the womb—

And he's still going. Bile rises up in my throat at the irresponsible hatefulness of his words. I shudder so hard; I feel it in my soul. The responses he's getting are just as horrific. These anonymous usernames are going back and forth, doxing each other, giving each other panic attacks, telling each other to die . . . all because of *pop music*?

Old boarding passes to different parts of the world scatter the floor near the garbage can. Stalker receipts. Tickets to his favorite toys. The action figures on his chestnut wardrobe don't count. The products he really wants to play with are those living, breathing girls.

Don't you think it's ugly?

"Terminal?" I whisper, looking at the popcorn-plastered ceiling. It sounds like Terminal. But there's something frightening about the hateful lilt of his voice.

There are people in this world so lost they create unhealthy relationships with strangers, celebrities, and even companies through the internet. They distort their whole personalities to fixate on their concocted fantasies, doing the unthinkable just to keep their false dreams alive. Even if it means hurting others.

The clacking upon Taylor's keyboard echoes louder and louder.

But then, you're no different, are you? Livewire.

Terminal's voice suddenly sounds different. It loses any pretense of familiarity. Then it lowers several decibels as the man pretending to be Terminal begins to laugh, louder and louder. I watch Sho place his hands on the wall by the door. He can't hear it. What's going on?

Just like this, you hid behind the safety of anonymity to destroy people's lives. You even sent one of your old classmates to an early grave.

My heart drops as memories begin to flood my thoughts. *I was wrong*, I think frantically, trying to push them back out. *I know I was wrong. It wakes me up at night.*

The man chuckles. He sounds like a snake, high-pitched and hissing. *Haven't you ever wondered why Toyo Harada is so certain you'll follow him?* He lets the question corrode my insides before slithering again. *He's seen the evil within you, Amanda McKee. He's seen with his own eyes your potential to do wicked things.*

No . . . I clasp my ears. Taylor's keyboard typing is getting too frenzied. *No!*

A psiot who abuses her power to destroy her enemies. Like father like daughter . . .

"Stop!" I scream, drawing Sho's attention. He lowers his arms and turns to me.

"Amanda?" He takes a quick step toward me. "Amanda, what's going on?"

Once he's close enough, he grabs my wrists and tries to lower my hands, but I won't let them budge. The incessant clacking. It's like there's a rattling in my skull, and it won't stop.

It's already been foretold. You'll betray him. You'll betray Lily.

I shake my head. "No!"

Yes, Amanda! Hand in hand with Harada, you'll destroy humanity.

"I said stop it!" I scream and burst out of Taylor's room, ignoring Sho's frantic calls. Everything's a blur as I run around this dusty basement. The Snake Man's voice is following me. His laughter is my shadow.

What do you think will happen once you get to the Inner Sanctum? he taunts. *Once you find Harada. What are you envisioning? A triumphant victory over Daddy Dearest?*

My heart is thrashing against my chest; my jaw is stiff as I run past the couch, almost knocking over the television.

But what if that doesn't happen? Snake Man continues. *What if a different kind of victory awaits? One where the father finally reaches the evil seed he's always recognized within his precious daughter and finally brings her over to the dark side.*

I find a broom closet next to the wooden staircase and hide myself inside. But Snake Man's voice gets through. He's in my head. He's in my very cells. He's in the tiniest crack in my heart. And now, his voice sounds like Toyo Harada's. Now, I can see that man who kidnapped me from my parents hovering over me, his hands outstretched as if to embrace his prodigal daughter.

You're no hero, Amanda McKee, he says. *Your destiny is to be the* right-hand *woman of a supervillain. Your destiny is to tear children away from their mothers and stomp out humanity wherever you see it. That's who you are. That's who you are, Amanda McKee!*

"P-please!" I stutter, stepping backward inside the broom closet until my shoulder blades hit the wall and I slide down, my whole body buzzing as if I'd been electrocuted by ion. Snake Man is laughing in my father's voice, and I keep begging him to stop, until my voice devolves into an incoherent string of non-words and sobs. My eyes are starting to sting and blur, but I still see Toyo Harada standing in front of me, right at my feet. I feel like I'm going to faint.

"Amanda!" Sho yells. He tears open the door and tackles Harada, pulling him out of the closet. "Amanda, don't be fooled! Trust yourself! What do you really see?"

Harada elbows Sho in the stomach before he can say anymore. But Sho doesn't give up.

"Not all Eggbreakers fight with physical strength." Sho ducks Harada's swipe. "You've got to calm down, Amanda! Remember, fear is—"

Harada cracks him across the face, sending him over the tweed couch. He lands on the floor with a heavy thud. It's my fault. Sho can't transform, because I can't transform. And I can't transform, because my brain is a scrambled egg. I need to snap out of it!

Remember, fear is what? Remember, fear is what? Sho . . . is Sho okay? Is he dead? Did I get him killed? Will I kill him in the future?

I bring my knees up to my chest and rock back and forth, wrapping my arms around my legs. And then, gradually, I remember. I see a glimpse of the couch through the open door and remember Sho and I sitting on my dorm-room bed. Holding hands. Breathing together.

Sho . . . what was it he said to me that day? Yes. Yes! It was the same thing he said to himself as a child as he struggled to survive in that dystopian training facility. My thoughts travel back to the memories I saw in his dungeon. That little boy, alone and afraid in his little iron room.

It's all just energy, little Sho said. *Feel the wave and let it wash over you . . .*

"Fear is just energy," I whisper to myself. I don't fight it. The more I fight, the more arrogant it becomes, colonizing my entire body. Instead, I make room for it. I observe it but refuse to let it win. I don't let it cloud my eyes or trick my ears, not anymore. Even as this anxiety continues to thunder inside me, I fumble back onto my feet and look at the figure of Toyo Harada. I gaze at him without judgment, breathing in and out the way Sho taught me.

And then I see the truth: That isn't Toyo Harada at all.

It's an Eggbreaker, his BioSuit, pitch black as he stomps on Sho's spine relentlessly, keeping him pinned to the ground. He leans over and whispers something in Sho's ear, making him shudder and gasp.

I know who this is. I've seen him before. That night on the rooftop.

I know who this robot jerk is!

"Panic!"

At the sound of his name, the BioSuit Soldier spins around. How dare he. My whole body quakes with rage. Screaming out all the frantic energy built up inside of me, I suit up and, without even wasting a moment, blast a blue cannonball of energy at him. Panic can't get away in time. Before he can even slither around, it blows him to pieces.

Immediately, returning to my normal self, I run to help Sho sit up. "Sho! Sho! Are you okay?" I grab his cheeks, forcing his head back and forth. Then check his back and his arms for bruises. All the while, he gazes down at me, saying nothing.

"Oh no, your eye!" His left eye is half closed. I touch the bump, wincing at the feel of the puffy, bumpy flesh.

"It's all right, Amanda," he whispers.

"It's not all right." I'm such a crybaby. How can I cry this many times in a day? This must be a record. But the tears are building up again, threatening to fall. I can still remember Panic's laughter. It's like he plucked every irrational fear I've been holding in my heart and showed them to me one by one. "I listened to that creep. I listened to him, and I forgot what you said. I forgot what—what you taught me—"

Sho cuts me off with a kiss. It's quick but fulsome. In just that fleeting moment, he managed to part my lips and wet them just enough that the taste of him remains.

"But you remembered, in the end."

As my arms fall to my sides, his rise. He grips my face and looks into my eyes earnestly. "I don't know what he said, but I can guess. And I can tell you right now, he's wrong. I know you now, Amanda. I know your heart. You're not the girl who'll destroy the world. You're the girl who'll save it. I know that now. I trust it more than I've ever trusted anything." His eyes are smiling even more brightly than his grin. "If there's one thing I've learned being in this century with you, it's that we are in charge of our own choices. We make our own destin—"

It's my turn to cut him off. The golden door at the top of the staircase glows, but both of us ignore it. As I bury myself in his chest, I let myself breathe again, in and out, returning each of his kisses with the same shy vigor. The door will have to wait a little while longer.

22

What do you do after you make out with a boy, but then have to take the same train as him right after? Especially if that boy is a kinda anti-dad terrorist from the future who came back to the past originally to kill you? Whether you're going to the next town or the inner beating heart of a parallel universe, it's going to be pretty awkward. But nice. Awkward and nice.

That's how I feel as we take the train to the next Digital Castle on Terminal's list. I'm a little giddy, resting against Sho's shoulder for the next stop while he shyly but confidently wraps his arm around my waist. Neither of us speak, despite being wholly aware of each other's presence down to the molecular level. Despite my being able to sense when a hair on his arm twitches, despite feeling his soft breath caressing the top of my head. This is the kind of sensation I always wanted to feel, ever since I was a little kid watching romcoms in between Harada's technopath experiments. It's nice to know joy doesn't disappear even in the middle of a hellish ordeal. Maybe it's a little harder to find, but once it pokes its head out of the muddy ground, if you can catch it, you sure as hell better not let it go. Because soon—

Amanda! Sho! Terminal calls us over the intercom.

"Wh-what's up?" says Sho, straightening up in his seat, sliding his arm quickly out from under my back. Darn it.

Who taught your friends to commandeer my communication line? That's impressive, though a little annoying. Apparently, they want to talk to you and—

There's a bit of scuffle and static. Then a panicked voice takes over for Terminal.

"Andy!" It's Lily! I shoot to my feet, having to grab on to the ceiling straps to keep steady. "Andy, are you there? Are you really in the Digital World?"

Lily's voice is my mana from heaven. The presence of my best friend envelopes me like a warm embrace. It's like I have a connection to the real world again.

"Yes!" I just blurt it out, hoping she can hear me on the other side. Thankfully, she does.

"Thank God! Oh, Andy!" Lily then begins to ramble so furiously that I have to strain my ears to pick up every word. "Are you okay?"

"I found my dad," I tell them, stopping Lily in her tracks.

"What?" When he's that surprised, Yoshi's voice is even higher pitched than Lily's, if it's possible. "You actually found Harada?"

I calmly explain everything. Lily starts rambling "oh my god" over and over, while Yoshi starts digging through every memory he's ever had of Harada now that he knows his boss really is a supervillain. We've both been tricked.

"Your dad . . . a psiot." Yoshi exhales, unable to believe it. "That must have been how your father's been able to survive inside the Digital World. And how he survives into the twenty-seventh century wearing a BioSuit, which only psiots can wear. Amanda McKee isn't the first known psiot. Toyo Harada is. I can't believe we missed this."

"Well, my dad's a telepath," I offer, though saying those words still doesn't make it feel real to me. "Maybe he did something to hide the truth from everyone."

"I don't care about the details," says Sho from the bench. "Our task is clear." Sho's expression turns deadly. "We have to stop Harada."

"And then what?" Yoshi says so suddenly it makes Sho and I exchange glances. "I've been meaning to ask, Sho, but what happens to you if we manage to change the future?"

I'm glued to Sho for a response, but he doesn't move. His hands slowly stiffen upon his lap as his lips stay resolutely pursed.

"I've read multiple theories about time travel. And I've read a lot of science fiction. I mean there's the Novikov self-consistency principle, which basically states that even if someone travels back in time, it's already been factored into the past, so the timeline won't change. Then again, I think one Dr. Emmett Brown taught all of us that changing the past will result in another timeline being created. Which means, should you succeed, Sho's dystopia will still exist in some format. Just not for us."

Yoshi is saying all of this too quickly for me to grasp. I'm trying to put the pieces together, but I've never been a particularly good student. This time-travel stuff is beyond me. All the while, when I look to Sho, his gaze is to the floor. He's not saying a word.

"But there are paradoxes. And loops. And—well, I wanted to have this conversation with you before you went after Harada, but now that you're already on your way—"

"It's a little too late for the talk." Sho's tone has become quiet as a grave. "Prescott and C.A.R.D have already told me what they felt I needed to know before I started this mission."

He won't look at me. Why won't he look at me? I turn to face him. "And that is?"

Sho didn't speak for a long time. The technicolor of space-time zips past us outside the window, casting pulses of shadow across the inside of the train car. The train bustles along, the straps rattling against the ceiling as silence continues to stretch between us.

"They told me," he whispers as he clasps his hands together, "that if I go back in time and change the past, I'll erase the future. Our births will never have occurred. I cease to exist. Once we stop Harada, I'll disappear."

My arms are heavy and weightless at the same time. They feel as if they're going to fall off. My throat closes as I take a seat next to him, dropping onto the bench with a heavy plop.

"When were you going to tell me?"

Guilt slips into his voice as he squeezes his hands together. "I didn't think it mattered."

"You didn't think it mattered?"

"We weren't exactly friends when we first met."

"But aren't we friends now?" The painful tingling in my skin won't stop. "Aren't we—"

I stop. Not because I don't know what we are, but because I know I don't have to explain it to him. It's clear as day by the way he refuses to look at me.

"Well," Yoshi says. "The future would have more information on the intricacies of time travel than we do, I suppose."

"Sho . . ." Lily's whimpering voice comes through the coms. I know she's crying. Typically, despite what the past few hours have suggested, she's the crybaby out of the two of us. The honest and sweet one. Her heart is breaking. Mine is already shattered.

"Maybe they were lying to you!" Lily tries, and the possibility gives me hope.

"She's right!" I grab Sho's sleeve. "You know how cruel those jerks were. The way they trained you? You don't know if everything they said was true."

"They had no reason to lie," Sho replies. Short and sweet.

"There's also the possibility that they could be wrong," Yoshi says. "Even in the future, this was your organization's first rodeo with shattering the space-time continuum. And they were desperate. Maybe they didn't have all the pieces in place before they sent you here."

"Regardless," Sho says, steadier this time. "I came here prepared to die."

The curtness of it sent me into a spiral. My heart beating in my ears, I searched for another clue, another theory that might open up a new possibility and stall the inevitable.

"That's not . . ." I shake my head, wrapping my arms around myself. "That's not fair. That can't be how this ends. We just met. We just—"

Seeing my despair shatters Sho's "tough guy" act. His eyes soft, he reaches for me, but right now, I can't bear his touch. I scooch away from him and lean against a metal pole jutting up from the floor to the ceiling, my stomach churning.

"Amanda . . ." he whispers.

"Why does this always happen?" I whisper, the metal cold and hard against my skull. "Is this my destiny too? Am I meant to be alone?"

Or is Harada right? Is this all part of the grand design of the story of Amanda McKee? A psiot with no one to rely on, so she turns to her villainous father . . .

"No!" The word bursts out of me as I clamp my hands down on my ears.

"Andy?" Lily is tentative over the comm. Her voice shakes. "Andy, don't be upset. We'll figure something out, I promise! No matter what happens, we're here for you!"

"Wait." Yoshi cuts her off. "I'm picking up a disturbance in the Digital World. The IP closest to you is shorting out . . ."

Maybe they have bad Wi-Fi. I don't care. Revelation after tragic revelation. I can't stand it anymore. My life has become unbearable. I just want to disappear . . .

Sho jumps to his feet, his fists clenched. "Amanda. They're coming!"

"What?" My sluggish mind struggles to keep up but doesn't have the time. Two crashes landing on the roof of the train cause the train to swerve and go off course. I hold on to the metal pole, to keep myself from flying onto the ground.

Before I can get steady on my feet, bullets tear through the roof and begin showering down on us.

"Suit up!" Sho says, his armor already encasing him in protection.

I don't need telling twice. I'm not dying here. We're completely on the same page on that. Law's suit grips me just in time, just before a bullet can lodge itself into my brain.

One pound. Another. One final powerful kick breaks a hole into the train that two Eggbreakers jump through. The gold and brown BioSuit Soldier remains still just long enough for me to see her long black ponytail swaying from out the back of her helmet. Then she moves so fast, she melts into a blur, ramming Sho through a window. Mak. As the glass shatters and she begins her battle against Sho, another hail of bullets flies toward me. I dodge quickly, my metal feet barely touching the ground as I glide down the train compartment.

A gush of wind envelops Saturn's red and blue suit, but that's not the power she chooses to use to try to take me down. Those two huge military-grade machine guns she's got in each hand, however, are. An Eggbreaker packing heat. Great. I have to leap out the window, crashing through the glass just to avoid the next hail of bullets, but Saturn follows me.

I fly up to the top of the train and plant my feet into the roof so the locomotive won't get away from me. Here in the expanse of the Digital World, where light mixes with dark, where infinity blazes with fiery color, then dies like stars exploding in space, I turn to face my enemy.

If I'm going to beat her, I'll need to pull new tricks out of my hat. Within nanoseconds, I mine Law's suit for information while Saturn readies her next rounds and points her guns at me.

Oh, really? I think as Law's suit whispers back some little moves Law herself used to do when she was still alive and kicking for Team Evil. *Okay. Let's try it.*

Saturn aims and opens fire, but I'm ready. I wave my hands so fast, the blue energy swirling around my metal arms forms a shield that absorbs and melts the bullets before they can reach the armor. But the attack won't stop. Saturn steps toward me, each foot denting the train roof, her guns rattling.

"Livewire said we should keep you alive, but she didn't specify in what condition," Saturn says as she forces me to my knees. "You've taken out too many of us already. As far as Mak and I are concerned, you're too dangerous to stay in one piece."

The pressure against my arms is insane. The blue shield I'm holding up is about to shatter. So I do it myself. Winding up, I punch the energy shield. It explodes into little shards that cut through her guns, tearing them to pieces.

Saturn screams in fury as her weapons fly off into space, but she's not done. As the train speeds on, she lunges for me. I meet her, clashing my hands against hers, both of us pushing so hard our armor begins to crack. Out of the corner of my eye, I see Sho slashing off Mak's ponytail with the Totsuka sword, the two zipping alongside us as they battle.

Regardless, Sho taunts me in my memories, *I came here prepared to die.*

My heart wavers. *Sho . . .*

I shouldn't have lost focus. In that one moment, Saturn manages to shatter both my hands. I let out a bloodcurdling scream and stumble back. Somewhere, in this wild digital space, Sho is screaming my name as Saturn takes my helmet and knees me in the head. Blood spurts from my nose. The schematics inside my helmet start going crazy. But I don't give up. I have more than one way to fight.

Amanda McKee. A human miracle.

I remember Harada back in the lab. The way he looked at me like his most prized possession. An emotion of pride I mistook for fatherly love.

I never knew until after I adopted you that human beings could exist that are capable of what you're capable of. You represent an evolution in humanity. There's no other like you . . .

I scrape my throat for every breath as Saturn grabs me by the neck and lifts me onto my feet. Harada. He's been wrong about so many things. But he's right about one.

There's no other like me.

I dig my broken metal fingers into Saturn's suit and cause her armor to malfunction and heat up, so fast and so hot, Saturn has no choice but to eject herself from the suit before it explodes. She screams as the technology protecting her erupts into flames, leaving her with nothing but a weak, twisted, melted corpse of a body that lifelessly floats off into space. In a flash, it becomes a speck in the distance as the train continues its relentless trek.

"Saturn!" For the first time, I hear Mak's robotic voice. She drops everything to fly toward her comrade, but Sho won't let her escape. As she flees, powering up his Totsuka sword with energy, he throws it with such herculean force the sword rams straight through her body. Mak lets out a bloodcurdling scream as Sho flies to grab the hilt and pull the sword out of her body. Two Eggbreakers down. But the train is still rattling, flying off to parts unknown.

We can catch up to your father, Terminal says as Sho lands on the train next to me. *We can get to the Inner Sanctum. But we'll have to take a major detour first.*

"Which Digital Castle?" I say, my voice surprisingly rough and torturesome, as if I haven't spoken in years.

Yours, Amanda.

Still inside the Izanagi, Sho holds my broken armored body in his arms. "Amanda?" He places a metal hand on my armor.

A beat of silence passes.

"So be it. Let's go," I say. "To my Digital Castle."

23

I stay inside my armor as long as I can, so I can heal up for the final spurt. It works. But when the train drops Sho and I, newly de-armored, off at my Digital Castle, my body spasms in surprise. I didn't expect to be standing inside Harada Entertainment. Though the concierge desk is empty, this place looks just like the building in Shinjuku. The fake plants. The music videos of agency idol groups flashing on the television nailed to the wall. The map of Earth stretching upon marble floor. Only this time on the map, I see weird lines stretching from place to place: network hubs and IP addresses. I could barely see the continents.

The Digital World. A parallel universe to ours . . .

The blue paint of the oceans arrests my attention despite the network connections crossing over them. Voices from inside the Atlantic Ocean call to me.

Sho grips my shoulder. "Are you okay?"

I snap out of it. "Yeah," I say, though I'm not sure how much of that is true. Because I didn't only hear them calling to me. I heard them giggling. Jeering . . .

The room begins to short out like an old TV screen losing

its satellite connection. Indeed, there is suddenly something wrong with the round white lights in the ceiling, now blinking uncontrollably. The entire room begins fizzling out.

Once the lights turn off for good, Sho and I find ourselves standing in a den of cobwebs. A kind of ghostly, spiritual light coming from nowhere and everywhere all at once allows us to see, but only just. The pillars, the marble floor, the map of the world, the walls. Strings of silver webs overrun it all.

In the front wall directly ahead of us appears three silver elevators, evenly spaced. Each of them beckons to me, demanding that I choose one. I stare at them with a shiver.

The zippy girl group song blaring from the television has long ended. A new music video begins to play on the television screen. One I remember all too well.

I'm not the same girl that you used to know.

You'd probably crap your pants if you knew just how much I've grown.

I'm a pretty young thing, I swear you'll regret it.

"Oh, just kill me," I mutter as I turn away from the television quickly, just before my fourteen-year-old self starts dancing on that damn abandoned island. And it's because I turn that I now notice that the concierge desk is no longer empty.

"Is that what you really want, Amanda McKee? Because that can always be arranged."

It's a sneering, high-pitched voice with just enough cockiness to it that it would have irritated me if the man now sitting at the front desk was actually a man. Sure, he's wearing a blue vest and tie, the same uniform as the Harada Entertainment staff. He leans over the front desk, his chin balanced on his left hand, his other fingers lightly wrapping the surface. There's a mischievous spark about him, but it's hard to tell much from looking at his face alone.

Since he's a skeleton.

"Okay," I say, my legs weakening underneath me. I grip Sho's arm. "You know what? I've changed my mind. Let's go back. We can save the world another time!"

"Oh, oh, *sure*! *Run away*, little Amanda, just like you always do," the skeleton cries rather dramatically. "Tell Daddy Warbucks to fire up his private jet and send you off to another part of the world with a brand-new identity. That'll solve everything, right?"

Now tapping his skeleton fingers against his jawbone, the concierge straightens his back and leans in, peering at the two of us. I think. He has no eyes.

"What a privileged, spoiled little girl you are," he says. "*Some* of us don't even have homes to go back to. Right?" Then he makes a throat-clearing noise. "I'm a sexy psiot from the future, waging a dangerous angsty war against the past." My blood chills. The voice that comes from the skeleton sounds exactly like Sho's. "But my life's been so hard, and I'm so torn up inside; I don't even care if I die. The angst of it all. Please, somebody love me!"

Sho's face pales as the skeleton burst out laughing, pushing his head back so far it nearly falls straight off his neck.

"How was that?" Clearing his throat, the skeleton claps his hands together. A finger bone breaks off. "Pretty great impression of the twerp, right? I nailed the 'tortured soul' aspect of it, didn't I? Impressions are kind of my thing, you know."

It was a good impression, and it had its intended effect. Sho stands there stiff, burning with quiet anger.

"What are you?" Sho asks through gritted teeth, controlling himself.

"I'm the concierge. Can't you *read*?" He picks up a little golden plaque with the word written in English. "I'm an old hat here. One of the first ever employees in Amanda McKee's Digital Castle. Gosh, I must have been working here since"—he looks at his bone hands—"well, since *forever*."

He laughs like a hyena, his jaws split apart to cackle into the darkness.

"Needless to say, the health benefits suck," he finishes, wiping a nonexistent tear from his eye.

"Whatever," I say and slam my hands against the desk. "Just end the freak show and tell me how to get to my dungeon."

"You sure you want that, little Amanda?" The skeleton scratches his chin. "Some memories are hard to relive. And some truths are hard to face. The past, the present, the future. What does it all mean for a girl plucked from her family before she was even old enough to learn what the word meant?"

I swallow the lump in my throat, withdrawing my hands from the desk and hiding them behind my back so neither the concierge nor Sho could see them tremble. The truth is, I've already seen parts of my dungeon. In those early days, when Sho had just crash-landed to the past and I was digitizing into the Digital World without realizing it. I saw myself on the operating table. Harada's irritated and somewhat sickened expression as he waited for the doctors to be done . . .

I hesitate. And my hesitation seems to make the skeleton elated. As he laughs his hyena laugh, Sho grabs my wrist and pulls me behind him as if to shield me from the concierge's cruelty.

"Which elevator do we take to get to the dungeon?" Sho demands again. "Tell us."

"Geez, this guy's not fun at all. Hey, Matsuoka Sho! Hello! This is Amanda's Digital Castle. You want to know where to go? Ask her." The skeleton points a bony finger at me. "Just don't complain when you find what you're looking for." Even though the concierge has no eyes, his sockets do the work in peering through my soul. "What is it that you're looking for, though, Amanda McKee? What is it that you're hoping to find? Oblivion? Release?"

He pauses.

"Death?"

"Enough!" Sho cuts him off, grabbing me. "He won't tell us anything." And as the skeleton chuckles, Sho drags me to the three elevators. "Amanda, you choose. I'll follow you."

I needed to hear it. To feel his support, but it still didn't bring me any confidence. The concierge's taunts followed me as I stepped toward the center elevator. It's always the middle door, right? Its gold glitters tantalizingly.

"It's not too late, Amanda." The skeleton's whisper feels as if it's coming from inside me. "Harada is still your father. A well-intentioned extremist is still well-intentioned. Maybe you can reach that goodness still inside him. Maybe you can still get your father back . . ."

Is that what I want?

The elevator door opened. And without looking at the skeleton's mocking face, I follow Sho inside.

A wohkoh, mu mohne; kambei ya le; li leei tohmbe.
A wohkoh, mu mohne; kambei ya le; li leei ka.

In the center of a field of tall grass, women glittering like coal sing a spiritual hymn. Their voices reach across space and time, past the coast of the Carolinas and the plains of Georgia, but nowhere is it more vibrant, more sorrowful, more hopeful than here, in the north of Florida. Rows of women in tweed dresses.

In trees, they swing their legs, their bare brown feet catching the wind. Obscured by the grass, they sit and braid each other's hair. Mothers and daughters, grandmothers and great-grandmothers. Young and old. Some dancing in the shrubs. Some chopping wood by the shed. They all look like me.

Under a vast blue sky, the children say a rhyme I don't know:

Two women came to Solomon
Both had given birth
I'm troubled, though, dear kindly king
Please help me set the birth
One night while I lay sleeping
This woman's baby died
She laid its body on my bosom
Trading it for mine . . .

I don't know it. That's the whole problem. I don't know any of this. They're speaking English in a dialect I don't understand. They're in a region I never had a chance to live in. None of this is familiar to me, and that cuts deep, more than any knife ever could.

"Are you okay?" Sho asks, seeing me back away from the women.

"I grew up not knowing how I got here. Or where I came from. Or why I was born." The hymn of the women floats overhead. It should have given me peace, but I feel strangled. I see beyond the grass, beyond the trees that disperse into the swamp. Beyond the swamp is the Atlantic Ocean. I've never crossed it. Maybe they have.

"I don't know where I belong," I whisper, gripping my skirt. "I don't belong with them. I don't belong with Harada. Maybe I don't belong anywhere."

The women stand up, and suddenly their faces disappear.

Each one blank. Even with no expressions, I know they're looking at me, sizing me up from head to toe. But without their expressions, I can't tell what they're thinking. Do they approve of Amanda McKee? Or are they disgusted?

I'll never have a chance to ask them. One by one, they sprout the wings of a bird and fly off toward the sky. They're not going to heaven. They're going back home.

"Wait!" I say, chasing after them, trying to catch up, but my feet get tangled up in each other, and I collapse upon the ground. "Wait, don't leave me!"

This is the wrong elevator. It was a trick. The skeleton set me up. Harada set me up.

Yes, Harada did set me up. He tore me away from them. From my family. From my roots. From the life I could have had.

I think back to the skeleton's words and laugh as coldly and cruelly as he did. "I'm just like you, Sho. It doesn't matter where I go on this earth. I don't have a home to go back to."

"Amanda!" Sho calls after me as I run off toward the shed, my eyes burning.

The Florida air is hot and heavy. I need to escape it. I burst through the shed before Sho can reach me. I collapse onto the wood, burying my face in the dirt, pounding my fist into the ground. The hymn has faded away, gone with the women. It haunts me regardless.

I can still see the women's blank faces behind my shut eyelids. The beating of my heart sounds like a drumbeat in my ears. It pounds louder and louder, calling me to my feet.

There's a knock on the door.

"Sho?" I say, lifting my head and wiping my face. "Sho, is that you?"

I turn around, and the shed is gone. I'm not in Florida anymore.

I'm . . .

Wait, where the hell is this?

"Welcome to the Game's Room! Welcome to Reversal of Fortune!" cries some invisible announcer's smarmy voice, followed by a round of applause that abruptly goes dead.

Applause from an audience that didn't exist.

I'm outside again. A maze sprawls out in front of me, and I'm in the thick of it. Standing, I swipe my hands across the prickly green hedges of a labyrinth. The hedges are high, but not enough to block the night sky. I can see the moon.

More terrifyingly, I can see the moon's smile.

A grinning moon.

"Sho?" I can't see him anywhere. "Sho, can you hear me?"

No response. But inside I know: If I'm to make my way back to him and reach my dungeon, I have to brave this labyrinth.

Where's a ball of yarn when you need it? I begin through the path lined out by the high wall of green hedges. But I wasn't hallucinating before when I heard that invisible audience. As if they're on one of those wild game shows I used to be obsessed with as a kid; every time I turn a corner, they gasp together in awe.

"Our heroine is so *courageous*!" the announcer says. Her voice makes the hair on my arms stand on end. "Even though she was torn from her family and has no place in the world, she soldiers on. She can't let her father destroy humanity. But no matter how it happened, her father is the only family she has. If he were to die. If she were to kill him . . ."

My heart stops at the thought.

"Would she really be okay with that?"

I think about the fake Harada dead against the nightclub window from Sho's sword in his stomach and shudder. Enough. I'm tired of the mind tricks. I glare up at the moon, but the moon isn't the announcer. It's not the culprit behind those cruel words. Its mouth simply stays stretched—a frozen, friendly, creepy as hell smile.

"Would I be okay if my father died?" I searched within myself for the answer. "No. I don't think so. But I've made my peace with it."

At this, the invisible audience booed loudly in bitter disappointment. Disappointment at what? Me trying to be at least somewhat well-adjusted?

I raise an eyebrow. "What the hell is this? Why is my Digital Castle so *weird*?"

The announcer ignores me. "Well, well, it seems our heroine indeed has a good and noble heart!" she decides. "Then again, she's been so bitterly lonely all her life. Separated from humanity just by the off chance of being born a psiot. An evolution. A mistake." Her voice turns wicked. "Psiots aren't human, so they can't be capable of normal human feelings."

"That's not true," I mutter, trying to focus my concentration on not getting lost.

"Isn't it, though? Otherwise, how could you make the website Livewire, stealing secrets from strangers and exposing them for the public to see? Even after doing this to your classmate is exactly what gave him the push he needed to finally end it all."

I freeze. That boy in Manhattan. John. I remember the looks on the rest of my classroom's faces when his death was announced. They'd all just been making fun of him the day before. And before that, making fun of me.

I grip the ridge of the grassy hedge with both hands.

"You killed that boy, and you liked it," the announcer proclaims.

The sting in her words sinks deep into my skin. "No," I deny it, my body frozen a few steps away from turning a corner. "No! Shut up. Just shut up!"

This answer delights the audience, and the audience's delight makes my flesh crawl.

For good reason.

"Reversal of Fortune!" they all cry in unison and begin whooping.

"What?" I let go of the hedge and turn around in a circle. The laughter and hollering are coming from everywhere. "What's going on?"

And then, I look up at the moon.

Slowly, it spins around until its amicable face can no longer be seen. In its place, once it finally stops turning, is a vicious, bloodthirsty scowl.

The moon is *furious* at me.

"Here in the Game's Room, lying is very much frowned upon," explains the announcer.

The growling behind me is so quiet that I almost don't hear it until I spin around.

"Good to know," I squeak at the announcer while staring at hungry wolves, all sleek and robot silver as if clad in their own BioSuit armor. Everything's metallic but their sharp teeth. They foam at the mouth at the other end of the green hedges.

I run, and the wolves give chase.

"You mustn't tell lies, Amanda McKee," says the announcer in a singsong voice. "But you've told so many. Andrea Porter. Andy-P."

I trip, hitting the ground hard. But I flip onto my back just in time for one of the wolves to step on my stomach, saliva dripping off its sharp teeth.

"Admit it!" snarls the announcer.

"It felt good to hurt him," I say, laying my head back against the floor. John. He had brown hair and red freckles and always wore this stupid black baseball cap. He always talked about how his dream was to be a star quarterback . . . "I couldn't handle it. I couldn't handle how he made fun of me. Every day, even before the video came out. Called me names. Short. Fat. He said sick, sexist things to me when nobody was looking. So when I had a chance to hurt him—" I took it. But when the weight of a life lost hit me, it was more than I could stand. I couldn't be in Manhattan anymore. Harada helped me run. Gave me a new life.

But I just kept repeating the same old mistakes.

"Sometimes the power I have makes me feel like a freak. And sometimes it makes me feel so arrogant, like I'm better than other people. Better than humans. Like I have a right to—"

Hurt them.

"I'm sorry." I barely see the wolf snarling over me as tears blur my vision. "I'm sorry for the past. I'm sorry for the future."

"Maybe your place is with Harada after all. You have no home. Nowhere to belong. No family." The announcer laughs. "Where else should a devil go but hell?"

I shut my eyes, and despite how hard I fight it, the tiniest part of me gives up. As the invisible audience cheers, anticipating blood, the wolves bark, ready to tear off my flesh. But a bright, flashing light from above blinds them.

My eyes snap open.

An elevator door appears, carved out of the skies just above the top of the green hedges. It spits out Sho, his body basked in light, his armored sword in his grip. As he falls, he swings the Totsuka down onto a wolf's robot head, cutting the metal in half.

"Amanda, what the hell are you doing?"

His scolding is just enough to breathe life back into my bones. I crack the other wolf's nose with an armored fist while Sho dispatches the other one. The last wolf squeals and flees in the other direction.

"My, my," says the announcer. "What a—"

"Reversal of Fortune!" The audience cries and whoops like drunkards in a bar.

Sho drops his sword and grabs both my arms, checking for wounds. "Amanda, are you okay? Are you hurt?"

I think of the past. The future. But the only thing that has ever existed before me is the present. Seeing me whimper, Sho envelopes me in a hug.

I don't belong anywhere. Is that really true? Right now, it doesn't feel true.

But if we succeed. If we win, Sho will die. He'll disappear from my life. He'll leave me like everyone else. Fear grips me so viciously; I push him away. He stares at me, confused, as I clutch my chest and gasp for air.

"Amanda, what's wrong?" he asks, narrowing his eyes. But I don't answer. I can't.

"This is certainly getting very interesting!" The announcer is clearly as enthralled as her audience. "So dramatic. Will the psiot from the future save the psiot from the past? Will he reach her in time, saving her life from the echoes of the future?"

Reach me in time? But Sho's already here? We exchange confused glances. But as the moon above us swivels around, its mouth stretches into a mischievous grin.

A little pocket mirror appears in my hand. It's just small enough to fit into my right palm, the golden ridge glittering in the moonlight. Before I can ask what it is, a tornado-like blast of wind separates me from Sho. He reaches for me, but it's too late. A square trapdoor opens beneath us, and down I go, into the void.

I awake in a room of mirrors.

Mirrors. Mirrors everywhere. The floor, the walls, the ceiling.

A thousand Amandas staring at me.

A thousand Amandas laughing at me.

"Goodbye, my lovely followers," says one above me. She's got the coolest sunglasses on, and it totally goes with her dress. She's clearly edited. The filter makes her eyes bigger and her face leaner. Still, she lies to her audience with a great big cheesy smile. "This is Andy-P signing off! And remember, the *P* stands for Princess!"

"The *P* stands for Princess!" the others repeat in mocking tones and then laugh.

"You really are the pits," another Amanda says inside the mirror to my right.

"How can anyone hate themselves so much they end up with, like, three different names?"

"And running to Japan? What, America wasn't good enough for you?"

"Self-hater."

"Race traitor."

"Ugly. *Stupid*. Weak!"

"Stop it!" I cover my ears against my own cruel laughter. "Stop it!"

"No!" I cry. "I'm not weak. I'm not—"

"Don't believe me? Take a look into that mirror in your hands and tell us what you see?"

I can't bear to look at it, but I can't stop myself. And what I see doesn't disappoint. My distorted face stares back at me blanketed in a putrid dark green, filthy as if swimming in a waste bucket. I drop the mirror before falling to my knees after it, the mirror floor sending a shock of pain through my bones. My chest clenches as the reflections laugh and laugh.

"Help me," I whisper, burying my face in my hands. "Someone, help me . . ."

"Only you can help yourself, Amanda," they all say. "But don't worry. Another you is coming to the rescue."

Another me? I pry my hands away from my face when I realize the compact mirror is beginning to stir on the mirror floor. Green smoke swallows up the mirror in a swirl, seeping out into the air. I scream and stumble back in horror as the BioSuit Soldier known as Livewire crawls out of the compact mirror. She stretches her neck first, then her shoulders. It's that same red and orange suit I saw on the rooftop. The gold streaks glitter in the mirrors. After seizing up the scene around her, her gaze finally falls upon me twitching in front of her.

"Livewire?" I whisper, my husky voice no match for the cacophonous laughing of the Amandas.

"You really haven't figured it out yet, have you?" Livewire taps her chin. "You always were the type to see only what you wanted to and ignore the rest. Ignore the truth."

Now that she was so close, I could hear more of her real voice behind that distorting helmet. Why did her off-putting chuckle feel so familiar?

Oh god.

The Amandas have gone dead silent. My mouth tastes like metal; my body goes cold as I stare up at the Eggbreaker I once hated for kidnapping my father. I break into a chilled sweat. Goose bumps rise on my arms as a slow, ugly realization dawns on me. And I don't want to believe it. It's unacceptable.

But I can't escape the truth any longer. This is where my future with Harada leads. This is the result of Amanda McKee taking her father's hand in obedient misery.

Livewire de-armors. She is a beautiful Black woman, long and lithe. She's wearing a bodysuit the same color of her BioSuit: red, orange, gold. Her thin waist, perfect curves, and strong abs look as if they were drawn by a comic book artist. She has the face of a woman in her late twenties.

She has my face.

Livewire smirks as she extends her hand to me. "It's nice to finally meet you, Amanda McKee. I'm Amanda McKee."

I'm already screaming by the time Livewire smashes the mirror floor beneath us and takes me with her into the unknown.

24

I don't know which memories are mine or hers. Then I realize they're both of ours. Me, standing alone in Bryant Park. Me, as a child in a room full of toys and butlers. Me, in a cold lab room, Harada patting me on the head as I break into other people's computers for the very first time. His wicked smile as he gives me a chocolate treat in return.

But then the memories turn from my past to my future past. Amanda McKee in her BioSuit. Livewire. Leading her Eggbreakers in a march across barren land. Stomping out hideouts for anti-Harada resisters. She's there in her red, orange, and gold suit, cracking the skulls of old men begging at the foot of the Harbinger Foundation tower for a scrap to eat. She's there in Haven, tearing a baby Sho away from his mother.

"How could you?" I whisper, standing rigid next to her.

"It's a living," she says with a shrug.

And it makes me livid. Livid enough that I transform, armoring up. "Not anymore."

As I power up the energy in my hands, my future self doesn't even suit up. She only looks down at me with an awful, pompous smirk, as if daring me to do something.

"You're a powerful technopath in the past, Amanda," Livewire says, lifting a hand. "But not as powerful as me."

Before I can get a shot off, she places a hand on my chest. That's all it takes. Law's suit bursts out of my cells. The separation is excruciating. The technology rips from my body and drops to the floor in pieces.

"How could you do this to us?" I'm still shivering in pain, but I can bear it. What I can't handle is the sight of my future self. "How could you let yourself become Harada's puppet?"

Livewire suits up and grabs my throat with a metal hand. "When have we ever not been his puppet? Might as well just accept it. Don't you think? *Amanda*!"

Yelling my name, she tears through the golden door of my memories and takes me through the vastness of the Digital World. But we're not alone.

I'm not alone.

"Amanda!"

Sho. As if connected to me by fate, he's following behind, keeping up as we race beyond the technicolor shooting stars.

"Good," Livewire says. "Chase me."

Amanda—er—Amandas! Terminal's voice echoes all around us. *You're approaching the Inner Sanctum. You need to be careful! If you die in here, that's it! You're gone forever!*

"Shut up," Livewire says, and with a technopathic slash I can feel in my bones, she cuts off our line to Terminal, shorting him out for good.

Without Law's BioSuit, I feel helpless as we approach a burning sun flaming in the distance, growing closer. I shut my eyes against the blinding light, the warmth of the sun swallowing us in fire. We melt through the wall of heat, coming out the other side.

Livewire drops me onto the floor. And that's when I finally open my eyes. Perhaps Harada has already found a way to distort the Digital World to his liking. Because I'm back on the rooftop of Harada Entertainment. The Shinjuku city lights sparkle at night. Toyo Harada stands at the edge of the roof, his hands behind his back, as always.

Yes, the rooftop to him has always been a place where he can get some air and do some thinking. I can only imagine what he's thinking now as he stares over the Tokyo skyline, a tiny seed of pure white light floating at the center of the roof between us. The Seed. The origin of the Digital World. I never knew it would be so small, like a speck of dust drifting with the wind.

"From here, I can see it," Harada says without turning around. "The future I'll create. The positive change I bring to humanity. It's all just within my grasp. And you will help me do it."

"I won't."

Livewire stomps on my back, flattening me against the roof, but with a wave of Harada's hand, she backs off like a good little soldier.

"Why don't *you* do it?" I tell my future self. "Now that you're here, you can help Daddy Dearest destroy the world. You don't need me."

Maybe I shouldn't have said that. If Livewire really can stay in this century, there's no real reason for Harada to keep me around. And maybe that's how it all happened in the first place. A time travel closed loop? This crap is way above my pay grade.

Harada turns and faces me. "It has to be you, Amanda. You're my daughter." A hint of fatherly compassion sparks in his dark eyes. "No matter how we were brought together. No matter how much you must hate me. We are family. It has to be you."

Tears of rage bud in my eyes as I drag myself up to my feet.

How dare he. How dare he pretend as if he loves me after he killed my family and manipulated me. Even if he really does love me, that's an evil greater than sin. Because nobody who truly loves his child can commit such crimes against them.

"You know what the worst thing you ever did to me was?" I blink away the tears, not allowing a single one to fall. "You disconnected me from my *self.* My mind from my body. My present from my past. You adopted me but had no actual desire to raise me. To affirm me. To help me remember where I came from. To teach me to accept and believe in who I am."

"Who you are is who and *what* I tell you to be." Harada lowers his head. "And what I'm telling you to be now is silent."

I can't speak. I grasp at my throat with shaking hands. The words are forming and dying on my frozen tongue. It's some kind of mental block. Harada's power.

"Toyo Harada!"

Sho's howl pierces my soul as he breaks through the fiery barrier. Clad from head to toe in his armor, he readies the Totsuka sword, flying overhead, past Livewire and me, past the fabled Seed. This time, he's determined not to miss. I can feel his rage. But no sooner does he lift the Totsuka sword over his head does Toyo Harada lift his own hand.

Sho freezes in place.

"From what I hear," Harada says as Sho struggles against the invisible pressure of my father's mind, "the Izanagi is originally supposed to be mine. The most powerful BioSuit. Of course, a child like you wouldn't know how to take advantage of its full abilities." Harada grins. "So, let me take it back."

It's not Harada who moves but Livewire. Blasting forward, she tears the Izanagi off Sho's body, gathering and contracting the silver until it's nothing more than a chip in her hands. With a crinkle of Harada's eyebrows, Sho plummets to the ground.

That doesn't stop him. He tries to go for Livewire again, aiming a flimsy, fleshy punch at the woman who stole him from his mother. She sidesteps him with an easy sway of her body, elbowing him in the neck. Blood gushes from his mouth as he goes down.

"Sho!" I scream, running up to him as the other me, the future mess of a "me," bows her head in deference to Harada.

"The chip," she says, offering it to him.

Harada takes it.

And eats it.

I stop in my tracks. I always thought a supervillain would laugh whenever he gets what he wants. But Harada is silent as the Izanagi suit envelopes him, granting him the same armor Sho once donned. But it looks somehow more vicious around Harada's body. Sharp spikes protrude from his elbows, from his knees. The ominous shine of the eyes of his helmet sends nightmares of blood and death shuddering through me.

Work, I beg my terrified legs, even though I'm arrested at the sight of my father finally transformed into the monster he truly is. *Work, damn you. Work! Work, or else he's going to—*

Kill Sho. He doesn't even use the Totsuka sword to do it. He simply grabs the back of Sho's shirt and tosses him over the building.

"No!" It feels like the world around me is collapsing as I run to the edge of the roof, shrieking, my mind whirling, my feet nearly fumbling over each other. Sho can't be gone. He can't be. This is a nightmare. This isn't happening!

"The Seed is the beginning," Harada says, ignoring me, stretching out his arms. "With you by my side, Amanda, I'll bend this place to my will. And with your help, my control over the Inner Sanctum, over the Seed, will serve as a deterrent to anyone who tries to get in the way of humanity's evolution."

"No! You won't do it!" I scream. "You won't kill anyone else!"

Livewire steps in front of me. The stars above illuminate her red and orange suit just as it did that night. Livewire is me. Of course, she is. The name of the site I used to make people's lives miserable. That misery stands before me now, and it sickens me. She is a reflection of everything I hate in myself. Everything I couldn't accept. The loss of hope.

But she's also proof of how powerful I can be. Me. Amanda McKee. The technopath. In a way, Harada was right when he chided me in the limo on the way from school. I've been wasting my powers. I'm capable of so much more.

Even without a BioSuit, my determination sustains me. My rage spreads through me like a beautiful sickness. I am Amanda McKee. A psiot. A technopath. I talk to machines.

I'm *in* a machine.

With one desperate scream, I stretch out my mind across the Inner Sanctum. I mustn't let this place fool me. This isn't real. This isn't the real Shinjuku. This isn't a rooftop. This is data, and I can feel all of it. Sho's body close to landing on the asphalt below. The Izanagi suit poorly adapting to Toyo Harada's twenty-first century cells. The crippling weakness of Future Amanda McKee's body, a sacrifice made when she donned the Livewire suit.

Livewire. Yes, I can feel the suit pulsating. Calling.

I bend and distort the Inner Sanctum, the Shinjuku buildings turning inside out, the moon, stars, and sky flipping and expanding. With a flicker of mind, I send Sho hurdling out of the Inner Sanctum. I can feel the connections of the digital networks. I search out the exit to where Lily's phone is. The Wi-Fi connection of the West African Snack Hut blips but holds. I throw him out of the Digital World, out of Lily's phone, into the restaurant. Lily must be freaked. But he's safe.

As Harada looks behind him, Livewire's eyes widen. "How did you do that?" she demands. "Tell me!"

I grin and crack my knuckles. "I'm a beauty influencer."

And grabbing her suit, I tear Livewire right out of her. The suit combines with me instead, and it's a much better fit than Law's. It's known my cells, my DNA, intimately for centuries now. I welcome it with a warm embrace, feeling it enhance my technopathic powers beyond what I ever thought possible.

I turn to the woman crumpled on the ground, but it's not me who gets rid of her. It's Harada. With one thrust of the Totsuka sword, he skewers her through the back, killing her. The woman who Amanda McKee becomes dies in front of me, the light disappearing from her eyes.

Suiting up, I fly away from him, my teeth chattering, my mind whirling. "You killed her," I say, my arms shaking inside my new armor. "You killed your own daughter."

"I still have you," Harada says, hidden behind the Izanagi. "And from what I hear, I have a whole host of you, clones grown in a lab, ready whenever I need one."

"You sick bastard!"

I'm off, flying out at full force. But I don't go for Harada. I go for the Seed. And that's what scares the hell out of him. He gives chase.

"Amanda! What are you doing?" he shouts behind me. "We must keep the Seed alive."

He takes the Totsuka sword in hand, ready to strike, but it's too late. My metal hand wraps around the Seed, ready to crush it with my technopathic will.

"Amanda." He lifts his free hand, as if staying a wild animal. Maybe that's all I am to him. "Amanda, if you destroy the Seed, the Digital World, the internet, everything goes with it. Nothing in the world will work. We'll be blasted back into the Stone Age."

"Isn't that what you want?" It's my turn to taunt him, and it feels so good. I'm just sad he can't see my smirk inside my helmet. "Isn't that what makes the Seed such a powerful deterrent to anyone who might dare oppose you?"

"Silence, you stupid girl!" Harada clenches his fist before catching himself. "This is a delicate moment, Amanda. Now that we know the Seed exists—and what it entails—we must keep its fires burning. Only then will the future I envision—"

"You know what, Dad?" I say, shaking my head, looking upon him with pity, because I can't believe I was ever afraid of this sad man in front of me. A man who could never overcome his past or his pain. A man who responded to every question he ever asked himself about the world with the worst answers imaginable.

The man who killed my parents. Who just killed *me*.

"I'm so tired of hearing about the future."

Harada might be a telepath, but here in the Digital World, technopaths reign. I beckon the Totsuka sword to come to me. It rips from his hand, and though he tries to call it back with his telekinetic powers, here in this wonderland of technology and data, my psiot skills overpower his. I grab the hilt of the sword, and I don't hesitate.

I drive it through his heart.

His armor cracks. Once. Twice. Then the Izanagi shatters to the ground, leaving him a man, just a man, as mortal as any other. He opens his mouth—whether to apologize or to cast a spell, I'll never know. I don't let him speak. I twist the sword in his chest, and he slumps over.

Dead.

I have killed my father.

My eyes are dry. Of all the times I've cried during my adventure, this isn't one of them. Ironic. And yet, time stops.

Every moment I've ever spent with him blends into this one blood-soaked moment. My father. I've killed Toyo Harada.

As I stare at his corpse, I can't separate the truth from the lies. And then, before the doubts begin to creep in, I shut my eyes and see their faces—the faces of my parents lying dead in their bedroom, where they were murdered while I was stolen from my crib.

It's not so easy as revenge. It's not so simple as hate. As long as I have been conscious and aware of life, this man has been my father. Maybe some fates are destined.

Amanda!

I forgot. With Livewire gone, Terminal's line of communication is no longer blocked. I hear his voice echoing in the Inner Sanctum.

Amanda! Little Amanda! Are you okay? I'll get you out of here!

A golden door appears on the roof to my right, but I don't walk through it. Instead, I pull the sword out of Harada's body. He falls backward almost in slow motion. And when his back hits the ground, he shatters into blocks of data that dissolve and disappear like a bad dream. Maybe all of this is a bad dream.

This isn't a triumphant moment. Like Oedipus, I've murdered my dad, but I won't freak out like he did. I'm done with being blind to the truth. As I stare at the roof where my father's dead body lay, I stop my pessimistic mind before it can spiral any further. I remember Sho. Lily and her family. I think of the life still ahead of me. The choices I have yet to make.

And I swear, I'll make better ones this time.

"I'm fine, Terminal," I whisper. And I get to work transforming the Inner Sanctum. It will no longer be a reflection of Harada. It will be a reflection of what I think it should be. With everything I've been through, I've earned that.

And so it becomes the grassy fields of northern Florida. It

becomes a place of memory, where my family once danced in the grass and played in the trees. It could have been a home for little Amanda. She would have been happy here. But that girl no longer exists. I accept that. I accept my past. And I welcome my future, because this time, it'll be one that I choose for myself. Without fear. Without judgment.

I let the Seed shine its blinding white before I turn and walk through the golden door.

EPILOGUE

"And here she is, everybody! It's model and teen philanthropist Amanda McKee! Please welcome her!"

Toward the tail end of the Tokyo Girls Collection fashion show, Utada Hikaru's "Passion" pounds through the overhead speakers. That's my cue to walk onto the runway. But behind the black curtains, I hesitate. I'm waiting for a few people. The crowd applauds and lights flash. But still, no Amanda.

Yoyogi National Gymnasium has been transformed for the event, all atmospheric smoke with blue laser lights. I peek out from around the curtains. The long, elevated black runway is surrounded by adoring fans, celebrities, and wealthy patrons.

My outfit is fabulous: a ruffled chiffon white dress with a black sash. Not to talk of the jewelry. I'm busy soaking in the glamour when some telephone typing catches my ears. Damn. The program manager's somewhere in the green room running around with headphones on. I can't see her, but I can hear the angry texts she sends to one of her lackies.

Where the hell is she? Her name
just got called. What is going on?

This is LIVE TV. Ryoichi's facing life in prison. And I have no more models left! I'm gonna lose it!

She's *already* losing it, so that ship has sailed. Well, I don't blame her. When I exposed what Ryoichi's been doing in nightclubs across the world, jail was really the next natural step for him. He was to be the star of the show. The crowning jewel. But oh well, it's fine. I'm here.

That's one thing my excursion through the Digital World taught me. All is not what it seems in this world. Too many use artifice to keep their dirty dealings in the dark. They thrive, waving to the public after committing wicked crimes, while the innocent suffer. I'll put all those monsters in jail. I'll expose the true sickos and demons in this world and keep them from hurting the rest of us. If there's anything I can do as Livewire, that's it.

WHERE IS THAT GIRL? I AM GOING TO LOSE IT.

I wince at the manager's text.

I'm right here.

In a flash, I mentally send the text to her phone.

Just waiting for a couple of people.

Oh, and here they come! All dolled up, pretty, and ready to strut.

"You ready?" Lily says, grabbing the crook of my right arm.

She looks beautiful in a sweet pink sheer short dress, ruffled to the hem. She wiggles her bare shoulders in excitement.

"Yep," I say. I can't believe I managed to swing this, but I did. The project manager's a pill, but bribe her with a few vintage luxury bags and she can be quite open to suggestions. I turn to my left. "What about you?"

Though he looks positively scrumptious, Sho looks very uncomfortable in a black blazer, white shirt, and tie. His pants are a little tight, not that I'm complaining. Well, he doesn't have a BioSuit anymore, so he's just going to have to get used to wearing a normal one.

"I don't think I've ever been, or will ever be, ready for the twenty-first century."

I kiss my boyfriend from the future, hook my arm in his, and together the three of us walk out onto the runway. The flashing lights swallow us whole as the crowd goes wild.

It has to be like this. I couldn't have come out here alone. Because after everything that's happened, I realize that I've never been alone. And I'll never be alone. I may not belong in one community or the other. Bloodlines have been cut. Families have been shattered. But I can make my own family. A family of my choosing in the place of my choosing.

A life on my own terms.

And that life will involve glamour and runways. It'll involve best friends and boyfriends. But as Amanda McKee, I've got more work to do.

For the sake of the future.

I'm dead tired after taking a private jet to Pittsburgh the minute Tokyo Girls Collection ended. The headquarters of Harada

Conglomerates. A brand-new morning faces me. With my coffee in hand and a pair of heart-shaped sunglasses on my face, I walk into the lifeless, gray boardroom with coffee in hand. I'll have to change that once I get some interior design folks in here. Harada was never one for color, but I am. Maybe some pink. I like pink.

The investors of Harada Conglomerates fidget uncomfortably in their custom leather seats as they see me take my seat at the front of the long oval table, right at the front, where the king sits on his throne—or in this case, the queen. My assistants, who followed me inside, were not hired by Harada. They were hired by me. They're good people with clean pasts. I should know—I hacked them and found out myself. It's my vetting process.

No schemers and villains in training are going to work for me. Nor will I let the new Harada Conglomerates remain the heartless corporation Toyo Harada had once used to fund the Harbinger Foundation.

I have ideas.

"Amanda McKee!" One investor with a scraggly white beard slams his pasty white hands against the table. "It's been three weeks, and you haven't even bothered to tell us what really happened to Toyo Harada. Where is he? We know he didn't die of a heart attack in Hawaii."

Well, that's my story, and I'm sticking to it. I left a data trail and faked enough records to make it an ironclad cover-up.

"I still don't believe for one second Harada would leave his entire fortune, his resources, his company, to some random teenage girl." Another investor, emboldened by his decrepit brethren, shook his head. "This has to be a joke."

"It's no joke," I take a sip of my coffee and plunk my feet on top of the table. "You all have a copy of his will. Hell, he published it in every major newspaper across the world."

"His body has never been found!"

Because his body is currently rotting in the Digital World. "He was cremated," I lie instead.

"This is outrageous! Who the hell are you in the first place? I refuse to believe you're Harada's adopted daughter!"

Harada had been a very distrustful man who kept his cards close to his chest. He never told anyone outside the Harbinger Foundation about me, my adoption, or his father-daughter relationship. Nobody but them knows I'm a psiot. These angry, irrational boomers don't know about my powers. That's what makes it easier to get rid of them.

The police rush in right on cue. I've already given the federal authorities every dirty detail from every filthy thing they've ever done. I've already published it online with a mental flick of my technopathic abilities. As Harada's former investors scream and resist arrest, as the feds handcuff them and drag them out of the boardroom, I smirk and adjust my shades. This is my building. My business. My rules.

Harada killed my parents, after all. I consider this reparations.

But taking the trash out today is just step one in a long process. It'll take a while to clean house, especially as big a house as Toyo Harada once owned. The Harbinger Foundation. His butlers. His scientists. I don't want any of his people near me. I want my own people. People loyal to me. People working for me. People who care about humanity, because I aim to transform Harada's toys into tools that can really help people. And not "help people" in that distorted supervillain "the road to hell is paved with good intentions" sort of way. Really help people.

And then there's that other point of business I aim to take care of while I'm the new leader of Harada Conglomerates and the Harbinger Foundation. But that'll take some time too.

One of my assistants bends over and shows me a map on her tablet. A red dot is blinking above Los Angeles.

Just seeing it flashing makes my heart skip a beat. "You sure there's one here?"

"Yes, ma'am," my assistant says, and I hide a little giddy grin. "According to our research, the girl's in high school. Faith Herbert. She edits her school paper. Oh, and she can fly."

One thing Sho's future made clear. One thing Harada's secrets made clear: There are other psiots out there. There are normal humans with the latent ability to one day be super.

I'm not like Harada. I don't want to use these people as my own personal army, nor do I want to control them and force them into my own utopian-dystopian hellscape.

But I don't want them to feel alone either.

For the rest of my life, I'll use Harada's tools to find, protect, and affirm others like me. Those who don't fit—those who may have powers that frighten them. Powers they fear.

Powers that, if used incorrectly, could turn them into the kind of monster my father became. I won't let that happen.

It's only a matter of time before more psiots come out into the open. I don't know what the world will look like when the general public learns who and what is really out there. But what I do know is that whatever happens, I'll be here to keep things moral and sane. To stand for peace and justice—whether I wear a symbiotic nanotech suit or a fabulous dress.

"Can you book me a flight to Los Angeles?" I ask my assistants.

Nodding quickly, they get busy clicking away at their tablets.

Good.

I've got work to do.

ACKNOWLEDGMENTS

Writing this book was such a fun, wild ride, and I want to thank so many people for giving me the opportunity to indulge in my Black girl nerdiness! First, thank you to Valiant and Blackstone for trusting me with this wonderful character, Amanda McKee, a Black superheroine. Trust me, we need so many more, and we should treasure the ones we have. Valiant gave me the opportunity to interpret Amanda however I like, and my approach was to bring a little bit of my own pop culture and geek interests to flesh out what Valiant Comics has already created in Livewire, the heroine who rules the technological world. In the comics, Amanda McKee is a young Black woman adopted by a powerful Japanese businessman who doubles as a dangerous psiot who brings about chaos for the greater good. It's such a fascinating premise, and I'm glad Valiant gave me room to interpret this character, her history, her subjectivity, emotions, and relationships.

I want to thank my agent, Natalie Lakosil, and my editor, Brendan Deneen! I'm also so grateful to my copyeditor, Windy Goodloe, who, being Black Seminole, was so excited to see nods to the Gullah community in the book! Seeing her excitement filled me with so much joy! I hope readers feel the exact same excitement when they see nods to the different cultures Amanda encompasses in the book.

I want to thank my academic overlords, Lakehead University, who encouraged me and gave me time and space to write this book. I want to thank my family, who always support me. Finally, I want to thank the fans of comic books everywhere, especially Black comic fans and especially all fans of Amanda McKee. Thank you for opening up your hearts to my interpretation of her story and for keeping Amanda McKee, aka Livewire, a character whose name should be on everyone's lips.